FIRE BORN

Book One Of The Guardian Series

RAYANNE HAINES

SOUL MATE PUBLISHING

New York

FIRE BORN

Copyright©2017

RAYANNE HAINES

Cover Design by Fiona Jayde

This book is a work of fiction. The names, characters, places, and incidents are the products of the author's imagination or are used fictitiously. Any resemblance to actual events, business establishments, locales, or persons, living or dead, is entirely coincidental.

Published in the United States of America by
Soul Mate Publishing
P.O. Box 24
Macedon, New York, 14502

ISBN: 978-1-68291-538-7

eBook ISBN: 978-1-68291-511-0

www.SoulMatePublishing.com

The publisher does not have any control over and does not assume any responsibility for author or third-party websites or their content.

This book is dedicated with much love to

Patty, Kelly, and Catherine.

Acknowledgements

I want to thank my sister, Kelly, for pushing me, for badgering me, for encouraging me to *"get writing."* She's been my biggest champion. Love you, sis.

Thanks also to my husband, my children, my mom, my village.

Thank you to my writing and editing community for all your support, especially Sandra, Kate, Janet, Cheryl, Astrid, and Laurel. You all helped bring this book to life.

Chapter 1

Alex hated her goddamn hair. She pushed the ratted, red nest off her face and out of her eyes as sweat and yesterday's curl definer spray blurred her vision. She'd run the track early today hoping to burn off some excess energy. Her new editor had given her an assignment about a corrupt city official taking bribes. There was a quick deadline and after flaking out last week, she had to prove she could handle it. Now, sitting in the sauna she looked at the three ladies sharing the space and begged her subconscious to stay awake.

Sweat dripped like lava against her flesh, and she could feel her freckles melting down her cheeks. She tried to stretch out in her little corner of the sauna. It was getting harder to stay awake and she was terrified of passing out again. Last week, she'd had an episode while trail running. When she'd come to an hour later, she'd found herself lying in a circle of blackened and burnt earth, and her mouth tasted like she'd been chewing on cotton balls for a week. She hadn't been able to leave the house for two days after. Aunt Quinn had covered for her, but they couldn't keep doing that.

She leaned back against the wall, discreetly listening in to the conversations around her. Sauna talk was always good for a few laughs. She bent over and began massaging her foot and legs. They were extra tight after this morning's run and her muscles had been aching for days already. She wondered if she was coming down with something.

Almost on cue, her stomach rumbled loud enough to attract the attention of the other women. A few odd looks had her ready to start telling them off. But as she opened her mouth to give them a piece of her mind, a sharp pain racked her gut, doubling her over. Her lower legs cramped and she almost fell off the back ledge she was sitting on.

"Damn." She groaned and began kneading her calves and digging her thumbs into the bottom of her feet. "Runners cramps," she explained as the other women in the sauna turned to stare at her.

Nodding with sympathy, they returned to their conversation.

One woman though, stared a bit longer. She looked puzzled and after a few seconds hopped up and leaned in to whisper, "Are you sure you're all right? If it's almost your time, you shouldn't be out right now."

Alex hadn't noticed her until then, which was strange since she was wearing a leopard print two-piece bikini and had short blue hair. I mean who wore that to a public sauna? With a strained laugh, she said, "Okay, That's the first time someone's asked me about my time of the month in the sauna. I gotta say, you're a little creepy, lady."

Alex sat back to regain some of her personal space hoping the woman would get the message, but no such luck. The woman kept staring. So, she did what she knew how to do—Alex stared back just as hard, before asking, "Are you new?"

Blue hair ignored the question and leaned in to whisper conspiratorially, "You know you can't be with humans right now. Let me take you home. Where do you live?"

Convinced she was leading her on, Alex winked at the ladies who were not-so-subtly eavesdropping from the bottom bench, and replied, "Yeah right-those humans are sooo tiresome," before turning away from her.

"You don't know?" the crazy lady marveled.

Alex had had about enough of the game and didn't need to deal with any more weird today. Her body was saying it was definitely past time to leave. She was feeling faint and could swear the woman's eyes flashed silver. She stood on shaky feet, bumping against the blonde Barbie below her in her haste to get away.

"Sorry about that. I just need to get by." Hands from above and below reached out to steady her.

"Are you okay? You don't look so good," Barbie said.

As Alex weaved, the other ladies' voices chimed in until they were a chorus of concern.

She tried to hold on. She truly did. Tried to reassure them that everything would be fine, only the words wouldn't come out. Fire flashed in front of her eyes and pain seared her hands and feet. The last conscious thought she had before passing out was, *please God, don't let it out!*

~ ~ ~

The concrete floor was cold to the touch and Alex winced. Her head pounded and there were at least five hundred people yelling at her. Or maybe it was five thousand?

"Not so loud . . ." The cotton balls were back. Alex tried to lick her lips. "I need water."

"Get her some water."

"Are you okay?"

"Beth, get her some water. Did the staff say they were on their way?"

"They're sending an ambulance."

"No, No, I don't need an ambulance," she managed to croak out, before pushing herself up to a sitting position. "I'm fine. I just over did it you know."

"You sure? You took a nasty fall trying to climb over us."

Alex's gaze shot frantically around the room before turning back to their concerned faces. "Did anything else happen?"

"What?"

"Like, did I do anything else?"

"I don't know what else you could have done mid-faint."

Alex considered the young woman in front of her. Up close, Barbie wasn't so perfect after all, and she had kind eyes. They were probably around the same age. Alex had seen her around the marketing department. The majority of the staff at the paper used the connected YMCA facilities to save money on gym memberships; at least the ones her age did since most were paying off student loans. The weirdo from earlier was gone.

"Can you get me a towel please?"

"Hey, Beth, get her a towel too. I'm Denise. Just sit still and put your head on your knees. I took a first-aid course last month and in cases like this, we need to keep you calm and talking."

Alex closed her eyes and did as asked. She felt fine now, but also utterly exhausted. She could sleep for a week.

Beth rushed back with the water and draped the towel over Alex's shoulders. "Here, take a drink."

"Thank you. I'm sure it wasn't part of your morning plans to babysit a fainter."

Beth laughed. "Hey, gets me out of work a little longer. Cool tattoo by the way. I like how little it is. I think if I ever get one I want something small like that."

"What are you talking about?"

Beth pointed to her foot. "Your tattoo."

Alex looked over her knees to her feet. Gazing back at her from the base of her big toe was the tattoo of an orange flame, licking up her toe onto the top of her foot. As she studied it, trying to make sense of what she was looking at, she realized Beth and Barbi . . . ah . . . Denise, were giving her strange looks.

She stammered out, "Oh, that's a Henna. Sorry, I'm

spaced out. Maybe I did bump my head when I fell." She shook her head a little and pushed the knotted mass of red curls off her back. Sweat covered every inch of her body. She looked at her foot again and managed to reply, "You know, I don't need an ambulance."

"I really think you need to get checked out. Especially if you bumped your head."

She knew they meant well, but Alex had had enough with the helping twins. "I didn't eat this morning, and I've been feeling run down this week. I shouldn't have had the steam. That's all."

"Are you sure?"

"Very sure. I'm a big girl. I just need some protein and rest." Pushing herself up, Alex towered over the other women. At 5'10" she took full advantage of her height. She'd learned that lesson early on in high school.

Beth was already nodding and ready to move on to the next thing. Denise was a bit more reluctant, but she agreed quickly once Alex put on her don't-fuck-with-me-face. Another skill left over from high school.

As soon as the two women moved on, Alex rushed to her locker to get dressed. She refused to look down. It was the only way to keep from having a panic attack. She didn't bother trying to dry her hair; just shoved the mess in an elastic band and threw her gym sweats back on. As she raced out to the parking lot, she could swear she felt a thousand eyes drilling into her back and a fluttering against her foot.

Just ignore it, ignore everything.

~ ~ ~

Alex climbed in her 1981 Jetta and hoped to God the thing started. As the engine sputtered to life, she let her breath out a little.

A knock on her passenger window startled her and stopped her escape. Assuming it was one of the girls from the sauna checking on her, she began rolling the window down while preparing to fend off their unwanted concern. Her hand stopped midway when she came face to face with the weirdo from the sauna instead.

Before she could get a word out the woman said, "I thought I'd check on you in private. I've never noticed you before and that's strange. I usually know everyone."

She made Alex nervous. "I already told the other ladies that I'm fine. I appreciate you checking on me again but I'm just going to go home and chill," she clipped out in an effort to cut the conversation short.

But the other woman leaned in the passenger window. "So, which one are you anyway?" She put her hands on the car and her eyes flashed silver.

Fuck, fuck, fuck, fuck, fuck. Alex shook her head. The last thing she needed right now was another episode.

"You know what? I need you to back the hell off." Alex sat up taller in her car and stared the woman down. She made it a rule to never show fear to anyone no matter who they were or what they threw her way.

The woman eyed her. "I don't think that's gonna happen."

Alex took stock of the situation—*blue hair, wannabe Goth, maybe twenty-one. I can take her.* She turned the car off before climbing out the driver's side. She glowered at the girl. "You need to leave . . . now."

But Goth girl smirked, put her hand on the hood of the car, and slowly pushed the vehicle out of the way so there was nothing between them. "I don't think so, Red."

Wide eyed, Alex backed away. Fire started climbing inside her again. "What the hell are you on?"

Crazy cocked her head. "Not enough. And I want what you have."

Her foot was burning. "I don't have anything. I'm drug free, honey."

"Oh, that's cute." She laughed. "It's just my luck I ran into you today. Don't worry. It won't hurt. One little snap of your neck before your transition and I get to keep it."

"What are you talking about? You're insane. Get away from me." Alex looked around for help but the parking lot was empty. How the hell could a parking lot be empty at ten in the morning? Wasn't anybody late for work anymore?

Alex slowly backed away. Around her, steam spewed from cracks in the pavement. The engine in her car roared to life and started revving.

The girl rubbed her hands together and said, "You *are* powerful. This is a good day for me." She edged closer.

Alex prepared to fight. She'd been fighting since before her parents died and could hold her own against anyone. It was either the Barbie's poisoning people against her when she was a kid, or when she started in journalism, politicians in positions of power trying to scare her off a story. She hadn't been in a fist-fight since she was twenty, though, and this chick looked ready to destroy her. For once, Alex wished she knew what her fire could do.

She backed into the alley, keeping her eyes on the Goth freak. Maybe if she could reach the back door to the gym, she'd be okay. Rivulets of sweat poured down her back. Whether from fear or the heat screaming under her skin, it didn't matter.

"So, I have a theory. Want to hear it?" Goth girl questioned as she advanced.

"Is it going to stop you from threatening me?"

"It's not a threat, Red. I'm taking what you got."

Goth pushed Alex further back into the shadows, and Alex knew she was done for if she didn't stand her ground. It was too much like the night of the tragedy. She didn't know how she'd made it out; only her dad yelling at her to run. She listened; they died. Alex had never run again.

Goth girl reached down and picked up an old pipe. "You're an orphan, right? Mommy and Daddy got popped and left you all alone to figure it out." She smirked and slapped the pipe against her palm.

"Something like that."

"Yeah, it happens that way a lot with half-breeds. Though you don't smell like a half-breed. You smell like power." She glanced around, and smirked. "No one's here to help you, Red."

Alex bumped up against an old garbage bin. The metal was soothing against her back. "Are you going to make your move sometime soon?" Sneering, she dug her heels into the concrete that was beginning to ooze beneath her feet.

Still smirking, Goth bitch replied, "Just waiting for you to get ready. I like a fair fight." She launched herself in the air.

Ms. Freak came down hard, landing a blow directly on Alex's shoulder before she could get out of the way. Her bone cracked as she fell to her knees on cement that had melted beneath her feet.

Trying to get her footing, Goth slid in the wet cement. Alex rolled into the back of her knees before she could swing the pipe again. Goth landed hard on her ass, screaming as the hot liquid burned into her flesh.

The alley came to life around them as they fought. Light bulbs exploded against buildings—manhole covers flew off the ground.

Alex dug her nails into the other woman's arm, trying to dislodge the fingers gripping her hair. With a hard twist, she slammed her left elbow into the woman's stomach. Goth girl held on, but Alex knew she'd done some damage. Alex fought harder than she ever had. Her life was at stake.

Refusing to give an inch, the woman dug her heels into the earth, dragging them both out of the scalding cement.

She tightened her grip, kneed Alex in the back, and hauled her further into the shadows.

Alex's heart raced, her body on fire, knowing the only way she would survive was to embrace the heat. She concentrated all her thoughts on her attacker, stirring the flames under her skin, directing her rage and pain at the woman trying to kill her.

The world exploded around them. A car detonated, throwing out twisted pieces of steel. Shards of glass and metal pierced her opponent.

Falling forward, the woman screamed as a pipe impaled her gut. As chaos rained down, Alex pulled Goth over her torso, shielding herself from the worst of the debris.

Fire and molten metal pelted them and cut into their flesh. Beneath Alex's back, metal bubbled, turning to lava. Later she would question why it didn't burn her the way it did her adversary. When the shower stopped, she rolled them over. Alex spared a moment to compare her soft pink flesh to the woman who lay in the dirt covered in angry burns and cuts—her flesh melted to the bone in some spots. Goth chick writhed in agony, moaning incoherent nonsense, trying to dislodge the pipe from her stomach.

Alex leaned in and placed her good hand around the wound to try and stop the bleeding. "It's okay, I'll call for an ambulance."

She shouldn't have let her guard down. With supernatural speed Goth reached out, grabbed Alex's neck and twisted.

Alex tore at the hands, struggling to breathe. Exhausted, her energy used up, it was too much for her. As Alex began convulsing, she pictured her aunt's face. In the last seconds before losing consciousness, something inside her shifted. Something dark. On her final breath, over and over in her mind, she chanted the word *Rise*. Over and over. *Rise*.

Instinctively, Alex knew the fire inside her wouldn't

let her die. She felt it clawing its way out, and for the first time she embraced it . . . gave it control. As unconsciousness inched its way forward, the fire finally broke free.

When her killer burst into flames, Alex smiled as she succumbed to the darkness at the edge of her mind.

~ ~ ~

"Come on. Wake up. Get in the car," Quinn yelled in her ear.

Alex shot up with a start, slapping at her flesh, trying to put out a fire that was no longer there. Ignoring her aunt, she glanced wildly around, searching for her would-be-killer, knowing she'd find nothing.

All the while Quinn pushed at her. She let herself be hauled along in a daze until Quinn slapped her face and yelled something about moving her ass.

"Quinn?" She stumbled over her words as her aunt dragged her through the chalky earth. "Some lunatic tried to kill me. Where is she? How did you get here?"

"We don't have time for that right now. Move! Get in the car."

"I think I killed her." Alex cradled her face in her hands. "Oh my God, something is really wrong with me."

Quinn pulled her hands away from her face and continued to force her toward the car. "Nothing is wrong with you."

Allowing herself to be dragged along, Alex looked around her, confused. There was no body, only black earth covered in cement dust and shards of glass. "I don't understand."

"We can't be out in the open like this. You're in shock. We'll talk at home." Quinn pushed her into the car and slammed the door before climbing in the other side of her vehicle and starting the engine.

"How did you get here?"

"Alex, we'll talk at home. Please, honey, I need to focus." She cupped Alex's cheek and sighed before calmly saying, "Now shut up."

The drive was frenetic and quicker than it should have been. Quinn checked the rear-view mirror every five seconds, the entire way. What seemed like only minutes later, they pulled into the driveway of a modest rancher hanging over the Georgia Straight between Vancouver and Victoria. Quinn jumped out of the vehicle and dragged Alex across the lawn, through the front door. She slammed it behind them and turned the deadbolt.

Quinn hadn't said a word since they'd left the parking lot, but she turned to her now. "Alex, we have a lot to do and not a lot of time." Quinn grabbed her shoulders. "I need you to go upstairs and take a shower.

Alex felt the burning of the tattoo against her foot and wondered if she was losing her mind. Like a child, she nodded to her aunt and turned to climb the stairs to her bathroom. Still in a daze, she reached the top of the stairs and noticed her reflection in the hallway mirror. Her hair was matted as usual, but now the ends were charred black. Her face was covered in soot, and she had a bruise on her left cheek from where the woman had smashed her face into the ground. She'd won though—in the end the fire saved her. She liked it. Her body wanted more. Tears filled her eyes and she turned from her image. That wasn't her.

Closing the bathroom door behind her, she stripped out of her sweats and leaned half naked against the wall. She straightened her shoulders and flexed her hands to physically brace herself before looking at her foot.

There it was. Alex slumped to the floor and bent over to inspect the mark. It looked like a tattoo. Small bumps and ridges against her skin made the design appear freshly inked. The flesh around the mark, slightly pink and tender, the color of the flame an intriguing hue of pale lilacs, red and tangerine. Oddly, she noticed the lilac matched the color of the bathroom wall. She lifted her foot to her face. Her toenails were black and the bottom of her foot was covered in blisters. *I killed someone.*

Wrapped in her towel, sitting on the floor, Alex twirled her hair around her fingers. *Maybe if I could get the tangles out and cut off the ends . . . I killed someone.*

She wanted her Mom. Much of her childhood was a blur, but her parents had always been there. They'd been open with her about the adoption. Alex hadn't cared who her birth parents were. She figured if they didn't want her, she didn't want them. The night of her eighteenth birthday her parents were murdered. Robbed at gunpoint in a back alley and left for dead. Their killer had never been caught.

Fire had been part of her life ever since.

It wasn't like she'd tried to be different; she just was. At five foot ten inches, with a tidal wave of flaming red hair, a shit kicker boot collection, and a huge attitude, she was definitely not in line for homecoming queen. Before her parents' deaths, they'd told her to always be herself. Afterward, she didn't know who "herself" was anymore.

The dreams and voices started once she moved away from the family home. Her shrink called them grief voices. She never told him she sometimes talked back.

Fifteen minutes later, Quinn found her in the bathroom crying.

As she opened the door, Alex looked up from her spot on the floor and said, "I killed her and I think I'm okay with it, Quinn. I had so much power running through me. You have to tell me what's going on. No more half answers and no more stalling."

Quinn reached down and held her close. "Oh, honey. I'm sorry. We should've had this conversation a long time ago. I shouldn't have waited, but I was hoping, well . . . it doesn't matter now does it?"

Quinn visibly forced herself to relax, helped Alex stand, and wiped the tear-streaked soot off her face. "Please have a shower. You won't get another chance for a while. I'll be downstairs making tea and we'll talk. I promise."

After Quinn walked out, Alex pulled herself together. She went through the motions of her shower; quickly washed her hair, ignored the burned spiky edges.

Alex ran her hands over the bumps of the tattoo on her toe before rinsing off and stepping out of the shower. Grabbing a towel off the rack, she dried quickly, and rammed fingers through knotted hair. With a last tentative look at the tattoo on her foot, she smashed her feet into slippers that had seen better days, pulled on her favorite yellow housecoat, and headed to the kitchen.

Chapter 2

Collum woke up with a headache. Too much fighting and Diplomatico rum the night before hadn't done him any favors. He swung his six-foot six-inch, two-hundred and fifty-pound frame to the edge of the bed, and pushed his hands through inky hair before massaging his temples. He was big enough and dangerous enough that he was generally left alone. Which made his line of work a little easier . . .

He walked to the window and closed the blinds. His condo was on the top floor of a building that overlooked Stanley Park and the Pacific Ocean. A view most people would kill to have. Collum didn't give a shit.

Pulling on his track pants, he turned to study his reflection in the full-length mirror. Eyes a mix of shadow and steel stared back at him. Eyes that looked tired and cynical. His muscled arms were covered in tattoos that told the story of a time forgotten. A time that had shaped mankind. He worked hard saving the world from shit on a daily basis, with no thanks. He'd stopped looking for thanks a long time ago. His father made sure of that.

He did his job and looked after his people. That was enough. Just because he'd managed to cheat the reaper for a while didn't mean shit. He could meet his match today as quick as the next.

Being a guardian wasn't for the faint of heart. As the leader, Collum spent less time getting his hands dirty than in the past. He was still what he was, though, and if you asked around you'd hear you didn't want to mess with him. Collum took orders from no one and very few people ever risked pissing him off. He only had one real friend. In his position, he couldn't afford to like too many people. It was easier to remain solitary. Dragons didn't make good friends.

That didn't mean he didn't like pleasure. Two thousand years of sex makes you pretty good at it, and Collum liked being good. He liked watching the ladies faces when he hit their buttons just right. He liked hearing their screams of pleasure in place of the screams of death that usually followed him. Collum loved soft skin and waves of silky hair, and tiny toes that curled when he brought them to orgasm. Sometimes, a night with a woman was the only thing that reminded him of why he chose to protect this world.

The knock on his bedroom door was quickly replaced by Glenn walking in with the paper. "It's about time you woke up. It's almost noon."

"I don't recall asking you to be my father—only my housekeeper."

"Yes, well, when you killed him, I decided to take on the role. So, I guess you're stuck with my paternal instincts, like it or not."

The two men glowered at each other for a minute before Collum backed down. "You were more of a father to me than he ever was."

"Precisely why I agreed with you that he had to die."

Collum turned his back on the man and grabbed a gray T-shirt out of the dresser in the corner of the room. He didn't want to think about that right now. "You have any coffee?"

"You're going to have to talk about it at some point you know."

"Why? She'll still be dead, won't she? The bastard still lived longer than he should have." He stared hard at the old man in front of him. "Coffee?"

Glenn stiffened slightly before masking his face with an air of indifference. "Of course. It's probably cold by now. I'll make a new batch."

As he walked out of the room, Collum frowned but didn't call him back or apologize. He wasn't a child, and didn't need to talk about what happened. It had been twenty-five years and he'd done what needed to be done. He always did what needed to be done.

Collum was halfway down the glass stairs of his condo for that cup of black coffee when his cell rang. Addicted to knowledge, he had played a large, if silent role in the advancements of many technologies humans took for granted. His iPhone was never out of his reach.

"Yep. What?"

"Hello, is this Collum Thronus?"

"How did you get this number?" was his terse reply.

"This is Quinn Taleisin. I'm Kaylen's daughter. Her granddaughter was attacked today right after the mysterious appearance of a flame tattoo on her foot. We need your help."

Collum sat on the stairs, the coffee and Glenn forgotten, and let his head drop. "Tell me where you are. I'm on my way."

Chapter 3

Alex found her aunt in their kitchen. Sunlight poured in through the big bay windows. The room was comfortable but not cluttered. It had cream walls and blond oak cupboards, and a dolphin cookie jar. Her aunt stood at the butcher-block island pouring them apple spice tea. When Alex entered the room, Quinn gestured for her to take a seat at the little white table in the corner. As Alex sat, Quinn placed chipped mugs on a paisley hot pad before sitting herself.

"I knew we would have to have this conversation eventually. We probably should have before now, but I guess I was weak and hoping to spare you for as long as possible."

"Aunt Quinn, I was attacked by something not-quite-human this morning. I think I killed that not-quite-human thing, and I'm pretty sure I melted the YMCA parking lot so forgive me for being rude here, but can you tell me what you think is going on."

"Very well, I'll get straight to it then. I'm asking you to believe in me, Alex, and to remember that I love you." She rushed on. "Your family, our family is . . . complicated." Quinn sighed and rested her heavy arms on the table, her tea forgotten. "It took me twenty years to locate you, Alex, because someone much more powerful than I am, made sure you disappeared. You were never supposed to be found."

Alex studied the room, aware of how quiet everything had become; like the house itself held its breath. "What are you talking about?"

"You are special Alex, more special than any of us. As it turns out that was too risky.

"You aren't making sense. Who are us?"

Quinn talked over her niece. "Your birth mother was special too. She'd always been advanced. Her skills were stronger than most of us. Father loved that about her. She could control her element almost from birth. That's unheard of among our people. Eventually, she became one of the strongest of us."

Alex trembled—lifted her tea with shaking fingers and held the cup against her mouth as she waited for Quinn to finish.

"I was never a warrior, but I've worked hard to keep the balance. As a record keeper, I protected the world in my own way. By keeping this secret. By protecting you . . . I've done what I could to protect our family. Our family is always first. Remember that over the next weeks and months. Family—this family—comes first."

Alex grabbed the edge of the table to steady herself. She considered her aunt's eyes. "You're starting to scare me."

Quinn clutched her arms across her stomach. "Now that your tattoo has appeared you are a secret that can only be kept for a little longer. You are the daughter of one of the strongest Elemental to ever exist, Alex . . . and . . . you are something a little bit more."

Alex snorted; a crazy sound that echoed off the walls of the kitchen. "Good one, Aunt Quinn. You had me freaking out there for a minute. I have no idea what an Elemental is, but I think you've been reading too many fairy-tales."

"First," Quinn said. "I never tell stories. I deal with facts and truths. Even in the mystical world, there is fact and truth. Second, there isn't a lot of time for you to get on board with this. If others are already sensing you, then we can be assured the elders will hear about it soon. We need to move you. You'll have to absorb it as you go."

"Others sensing me? What others?"

"The woman in the gym this morning was really bad luck on our part. Non-humans can sense each other all around. I should have thought about that, but I hadn't counted on you transitioning so quickly."

"This is insane. I can't believe we're even having this conversation."

Quinn poured more tea before saying, "Alex, think about this logically. Think about your episodes, and how your dreams strangely seem to predict things. The tattoos appearing on your skin. The way odd things happen to you. And how fire bends to you."

At the mention of fire, Alex tugged at her housecoat collar.

"All Elemental have an ability to control an element. Yours is fire. My element is wind. Water was your mother's." Quinn quickly added, "It's normal Alex. At least, it's normal for us."

"Are you seriously telling me that all these years you've known why fire takes over my body? Every time I've had an episode you've known exactly why. Why wouldn't you tell me?"

"I thought I was protecting you. That's my only excuse." Quinn wrung her hands. "I don't know who your father is. I don't know what else you can do. Your grandmother told me about you on her deathbed and made me swear to protect you and keep you a secret as long as I could."

"Jesus, Quinn, this is fucking nuts."

"Believe me I know. But it's true. I swear it on my life. Hell, right now I swear it on your life. Because your life is in danger."

"And that freak this morning?"

"That was a raider. They steal powers from other immortals. Thankfully, your element kicked in and somehow you were able to control your fire enough to save your own ass. Because of our family connection, I knew immediately once you tapped into your full element. That's how I found you. But that also means others will sense an element awakening."

Alex slammed her cup on the table. "This is bullshit. You want me to take you at your word when you still haven't explained exactly what an Elemental is. And what the hell do you even mean by—I'm a little bit more?"

Quinn stood, stretched out her hand and the two blankets off the living room couch flew into her hands. "You looked cold, dear. Wrap up in these so you don't go into shock."

Alex's jaw dropped, her eyes blinked. "What the hell? . . . What are you?" She pushed the chair away from the table and slapped Quinn's outstretched hand away.

"I'm fast, dear, very fast. It helps to have the wind at my back." She placed the blankets on the table and sat down again. "Now, I'm sorry to have done that, but as I said we don't have a lot of time to play around with this. I've called your guardian and he should be here soon. You need to be prepared. I've never met the man but I hear he isn't very patient."

Exhausted, Alex followed her Aunt's lead and sat. Her head fell into her hands and she mumbled into her palms, "Now I have a guardian? Maybe I'm losing my mind."

"Stop being melodramatic. You aren't losing your mind. This isn't easy to explain, but I want you to know that I never knew. Not until years later. Not until my mother died. I hate having to tell you now. I hate that this is happening to you. But there is so little time. I need you to listen and trust your instincts." Ashen faced, Quinn continued. "Your mother disappeared a lot. She was a fighter, a warrior, a golden goddess to our people. We knew she was in love with someone. She'd make comments here and there, but never revealed who it was."

Teary eyed, Quinn took another sip of her tea before continuing. "There are four elders of our race, one for each of the elements in the world——fire, water, earth, and wind. They make the rules we all live by. They agreed to mate your mother to a dragon. The elders thought it was a way to solidify relationships with the dragons."

"A dragon?" Alex studied her aunts face, tried to find something real in her gaze. "Maybe you're losing your mind, not me."

"Shut up and let me finish. When your mother found out, she fled. I remember hearing her screaming at our parents that she already had a husband." She sighed deeply. "The rest is brutal. The dragon found her and her lover. He killed them and locked himself behind his walls before we could seek revenge." Quinn checked her watch before saying, "That's the official story. That is what I always knew. Would you like to hear the true story—the confession your grandmother made to me with her last breath?"

Morbidly fascinated, Alex nodded.

"Your mother did not die right away. The dragon's son found out what happened and interrupted his father's savagery. Unfortunately, he was too late to save Gray's husband. But this friend to our family, this son, realized Gray was pregnant. He brought her back to die in her mother's arms, rather than on a cold rock. Your grandmother— Kaylen—delivered the child." She smiled faintly at Alex. "Kaylen gave that child to the son to hide. That child was you, my darling."

Alex swallowed the tears at the back of her throat. "But why kill my mother? What purpose would that serve?"

"Our family is very, very powerful, sweetheart, and we have been viewed as a threat by other families for many years. Mother had suspicions about why Gray was offered to the older dragon in the first place. She believed there were elders among us that wanted to prevent her from bearing a child."

"So, who am I? Who is my father?"

"I'm sorry, darling, Gray carried that secret to the grave." Quinn's voice quivered. "The moment you were born, Mother knew she had to hide you in plain sight, until she could discover who your father was and who orchestrated your mother's murder. So, she took you to someone who could make you disappear. She took you to the son who saved you—the Dragon King. He brought you to your adoptive family. Made sure you'd remain hidden to all but him."

Alex's tea waited, cold and forgotten. The scent of apples ignored. Surprisingly, though, with everything that had been going on, she began to believe her aunt. Now what did that say about her?

"When you say Dragon King, I assume that's an honorary title, right?"

"Oh, sweetie. You should feel very, very lucky right now that it isn't. Collum Thronus, King of the Dragons and Guardian of the Races, may be the only one strong enough to protect you now that your transition has begun and the barriers protecting you from detection, have fallen."

Quinn ended the conversation. "Now, as I said, there is very little time, and I expect he will be here any minute. I'm going to pack a bag for you. You drink your tea. Maybe make some toast too. I'll be back in a minute."

As her aunt walked out of the room, Alex tried to steady her heartbeat. She was left with a ton of new questions, and a cup of cold tea. The toaster mocked her from across the room until she stood up and grabbed the loaf of bread off the island.

A knock sounded at her door, but before she could answer it some guy barged in. An exceptionally large guy.

Alex's mouth hit the floor, the loaf of bread dropping from her limp fingers.

He wore tight-fitting black cargos and a gray T-shirt that showed off muscled arms covered in intricate tattoos. His hair was tousled, and he had three days' worth of stubble on his handsome face.

The look in his eyes promised the kind of sin angels dreamed of.

Her nipples tightened. He smelled like dirt and muscles and rough sex. She inhaled deeply. Had the urge to jump up on the kitchen counter, spread her legs, and beg him to take her.

Chapter 4

Collum could smell her . . . He walked into the room completely unprepared. This was only a mission. Talk to the girl to find out how far along she was in her transition, make her see reason and then get her out. Except, she was more than he'd prepared for. She wore a shabby yellow housecoat and slippers someone's dog had obviously chewed the shit out of. A knot of fire red hair framed her freckled face. She had a dazed look on her face. She was an utter mess. She looked like sunshine and courage and rebellion.

He'd begun walking toward her when her scent stopped him in his tracks. Instinct and arousal warred with duty. If he couldn't taste her, he didn't know what the past two thousand years were for. He stalked closer, silently challenging her to turn away. When she stood her ground, the dragon inside him roared. He snarled. She swallowed. Then blushed. That blush pissed him off. Or maybe it was the way his hands kept clenching, reaching for her. He didn't have time for this right now. He didn't want her—couldn't want her.

He stepped forward, crossed his arms across his chest, glanced at the kitchen clock.

A female muttering in the distance alerted him to the fact they weren't alone.

"You're the granddaughter?" he asked sharply.

"I'm Alex," she said and licked plump cherry lips.

"Where is your aunt?"

"Why don't you tell me who you are and what you want?"

Collum almost laughed. *Fuck she was sexy.*

"I'm here to save your life," he replied before leaning down to meet her eyes. "Unless you wanted something else." His large hands rested on the counter table and brushed against hers.

"Yeah, well. That doesn't answer my question does it. I'm not really in the mood to go fishing so maybe you could try and be a bit more forthcoming."

His lips curled. "I'm your guardian."

"And does my guardian have a name?"

"We don't have time for useless questions, little girl."

"You know, Quinn tells me we don't have time either, but I'm inclined to disagree. Name?" she prompted.

Grudging respect mixed with arousal as he replied, "Collum."

"Collum." She held out her hand. "Nice to meet you."

A magnetic current thrummed through his body as their fingers touched. Heat pooled in his gut. Flames, a mirror image of his own, danced in her violet colored eyes. Fire exploded inside him. He blew a stream of smoke at her mouth to watch it tickle her lips.

Collum picked her up and held her against his body. Inhaling deeply, he growled, "You smell like mine."

Chapter 5

Alex refused to break eye contact. Something inside clawed at her flesh—reaching for the man in front of her. Desire crawled through her chest as he pressed his face to her neck. She gripped his shoulders as he placed her on the kitchen counter, and stepped between her thighs. The whole time he kept breathing in like he was trying to absorb her. His hands were brands on her skin. One palm stroked her back, the other found its way into her hair.

She pressed her body against his, trying to take on his heat. Her breasts crushed against his chest, and she whimpered in the back of her throat. Things like this didn't happen to her. She usually dated journalists with very un-dragon like qualities or weekend mountain men with annoyingly trendy facial hair. She did not get ravished by drop dead, slam-dunk, gorgeous alpha males, in her aunt's kitchen.

After this morning's revelations, she was ready for a bit of sinning. She nipped at his neck. His grip tightened as he growled low and deep. Somewhere in the back of her mind, Alex realized she was ready to have sex with a stranger on her aunt's kitchen counter, with said aunt in the other room, perhaps even on her way back to this room. Awareness crashed in with a resounding thud.

He stepped back and shoved his hands through his hair in jerky movements before drawing a ragged breath. "I'm sorry. That shouldn't have happened. You're at a critical point in your transition, and that makes your heat difficult to ignore . . . It will likely get worse as it grows." His jaw clenched. "I should have been more prepared."

Alex blinked, her mind jumped from one thought to the next.

"Did your aunt tell you what's happening?"

"What?" She shook her head. "What the hell? Aunt Quinn," she yelled, jumping off the counter to back away. Pulling her housecoat tighter around her neck, she snapped, "Are you kidding me? You can't do that. And I'm not sending out heat, asshole."

He held up his palms in surrender. "I said I'm sorry. We don't have time for this. There are people who will hurt you if they know you're still alive. I need to get you somewhere safe."

A panic attack pushed at the edge of her temple. Confused and turned on, she needed a goddamn coffee. She refused to give control of the situation to him. "So, you're some kind of dragon thing? And I'm supposed to go away with you?"

Collum sighed and gritted his teeth. "Yes, something like that. Your enemies will make a move soon. As soon as they find out you live, they'll come after you, and me for my part in it. We hoped your element wouldn't surface."

"I'm expected to believe everything Aunt Quinn said was real. Just like that?"

"Yep." He blew more smoke at her mouth, his gaze intense. "Just like that."

She stumbled back. "Wait, do you know who my father was?"

"I don't. But now that you're transitioning, we need to find out before the elders do. They tend to dislike things more powerful than them. And if I've guessed right, you kid, are about to be far more powerful."

He pulled at a stray thread on her housecoat, right above an old coffee stain.

"You need to put some clothes on." Collum reached for her hand. "We have to go now."

Alex yanked her hand back. She knew if she let him touch her they'd be on the floor. She didn't know if she trusted him, but she'd learned over time to trust herself. Aunt Quinn hadn't told her enough, but it was enough to know she wanted to find out more. Now she had to figure out why her parents were killed.

If sex dragon guy could keep her alive long enough to do that, then she'd go with him. She took a steadying breath. She didn't usually feel small around men, but this giant dwarfed her. Instead of being frightened, she wished he'd lean down and cover her mouth with his.

He grinned like he knew what she was thinking, took her hand in his larger one, and rested his other on her hip.

Alex almost purred with the echo of his heat. She reached to touch the smoke pouring out the strands of his hair. Quinn walked in before she had a chance.

"Honey I have . . . oh."

Alex wished she could sink into the blue wall paper, but Collum simply raised his head and took one step back.

He gave his head a slight nod. "Quinn, I presume."

She responded the same. "Dragon King."

"You have her things ready to go?"

All business, she handed the bag to him. "Everything is here; passport, extra clothing, all her necessities."

"Good. We won't have time to stop. I won't make contact again for a few days, but I assure you I'll let nothing happen to her. I promised Kaylen, and I never break a vow."

Alex interrupted them. "Um, hello. I'm right here you know. How about you both talk to me, instead of over me? Besides, I haven't agreed to go anywhere yet."

Collum stiffened, and glared at her.

She stomped her foot. "I'm not a child. I'll make my own decisions, thank you very much."

He snorted and turned back to Quinn. "Say your goodbyes. I'll be in the car."

He strolled out of the kitchen like it was any other day of the week—not like her life had been ripped to pieces.

Quinn dropped the bags at her feet and rushed toward her. "I told you he was impatient. You really have no choice, my darling. I swear on my life that we're telling you the truth. This must happen. You'll be safe—he can control your fire."

Quinn handed her a yellow tank top and a pair of sweats. "Now put these on. You can't run for freedom in a Hudson's Bay housecoat. It's undignified."

"But I haven't said yes yet. It's—"

"No, Alex, stop." Quinn hugged her. "I love you with all my heart. But you have no say in this. You must go now."

Alex held on to her aunt as tight as she could for a final minute, then stepped away. "I love you too, Quinn."

Five minutes later they walked out to Collum's vehicle. After a final kiss to her aunt, Alex climbed in the vehicle and looked at her would be saviour. "Okay, Dragon Boy. Let's go find out who Daddy is."

~ ~ ~

Alex stretched out in the car beside Collum. All her limbs pulsed with electricity. She was running into the unknown with a stranger. A very rich stranger if the car had anything to say about it—although that wasn't saying much. I mean, who drives a Hummer anymore? Especially in the environmental haven of Victoria BC. If they weren't careful, they'd get lynched by the green-movement mob before they made it to the ferry to get off the island. He was losing a few cool factor points driving this thing.

She gave him her most formidable look of disapproval, to which he smirked and replied, "You wanna die, you drive a Prius. You wanna live, you drive a Hummer, baby."

Alex knew she had to run and she knew it had to be with this man, but he pissed her off. She turned to look out the window, intent on ignoring him. It would be a lot easier if she weren't picturing herself jumping him. She prayed he booked separate rooms at whatever hotel they found for the night. "So, you are a king in your world, right?"

He shrugged. "I suppose so. A few of my kind listen to me."

"So why risk it? I mean, I don't understand why you would risk your future, your life, for me?"

"Your grandmother was my friend. She was one of the very few friends I've had in my long life. Hell, I even had a thing for her for a brief amount of time until she let me down easy. She became my family, both her and your grandfather."

"My grandfather? I had a grandfather?"

"You still have a grandfather. Only you don't want to meet him. Domhall changed over the years. Too many wars, too much death. He isn't the same. He's an elder, Alex. Your grandmother tried to save him, but in the end, nothing was enough."

She ignored the scenery flying by them. "Why does he need to be saved?"

"Watching your mother die messed him up. She was always his favorite and her death did a number on him. Immortals the world over think he's as close to turning dark as any being can get without going over to the other side. All of the council recognizes it."

His voice quieted. "After everything happened, your grandmother wanted to take him away, remove him from the council, so she could try and bring him back to the light, but they wouldn't let her. The fucking elders liked him where he was—half mad. It didn't do them any good—he disappeared for ten years after Gray died. These days he's mostly a rambling idiot. But don't let it fool you. He's still more powerful than any of the other elders, probably than any Elemental alive or dead."

Alex stared out the window. "I never knew my grandmother, and she died not knowing what happened to me."

"Don't think of it that way. You lived. That's all that mattered to her. She gave you a chance. It's more than the goddamned council would've ever done."

"Who are the council?"

"They are the four elders and other statesmen for the Elementals. It's like the human parliament."

"Where are you taking me?"

"My place in England for now, until we can regroup and find a way to locate your father's family. I've heard of a witch that might be able to help."

Alex closed her eyes. She couldn't take much more. It seemed every time she asked a question, more shit landed in her lap. She just wanted to sleep, and they were almost at the ferry. Once they were on the mainland, things would get riskier. She had to take the time now.

~ ~ ~

Alex woke up to Collum's thumb delicately rubbing along the edge of her thumb. Their eyes met. Her tongue darted out from between her lips. When she sensed him about to pull away she tugged his head down to taste his tongue.

The moment his mouth touched hers, desire ignited in Alex's stomach and she clenched her fingers in his hair. She needed to hold on to something. Something that would keep her from drowning. His tongue was making her whimper again. She tried crawling over the seats. Surely the pressure in her gut would ease if she could lie on top of him. Her skin ached everywhere. Her hands were on fire. Alex ignored the ache, struggled to help him undo her shirt buttons.

How long had he been kissing her? A minute? A day? Nothing mattered but his gorgeous mouth. Except her hand wouldn't stop itching and it was getting worse and it was seriously affecting her ability to be in the moment. Annoyed at the pins and needles, she shook her hands. Out of the corner of her eye she saw it. On the tip of her right finger was a velvet orange flame. All thought of flesh and fantasy fled.

Collum grabbed her before she could jump out of the car. "Wait a minute, babe. Don't stop yet."

"Really? Look." She shoved her hand in his face.

Smoldering eyes dropped from her face to her hand. He exhaled slowly. "It's okay, Alex. We knew this would happen. We're on the ferry now, and have a little breather. It's only one flame. I promise, you'll eventually grow to love that tattoo. Now, let's go use the bathroom, wash our faces, get a coffee, and regroup. It's a short trip. Once we hit land we have a long way to go before we can stop."

She yanked her hand back to examine the tattoo. "Maybe you knew it would happen, but I sure didn't." She noticed the people in the other cars. Nausea climbed up her throat. She wanted to be one of them. "I can't do this. I have a job, and a deadline coming up. They'll fire me. I worked really hard to get this story."

"Your aunt will let them know you're sick. It's all covered."

"How can you be so calm about this?"

"Honestly, babe? Because this isn't the bad part. You're turning into who you are meant to be. Evolving. Go look in the mirror, Alex. Besides, in a couple of days we will be so knee deep in shit, it'll make this look like a walk in the park."

"Right—good way to keep me from freaking out. And why do you keep kissing me? You have to stop doing that. I mean, I'm in a state of serious stress right now. I can't be held accountable for my actions around a guy like you. You are supposed to be making sure I'm okay, not ravishing me in the front seat of the car."

Collum laughed. "Sweetheart, if I can figure out a way to not want you, you'll be the first to know."

Alex punched his shoulder, hopped out of the car, and wound her way through the other vehicles to the ladies' washroom. After taking care of business, she washed her hands and studied herself in the mirror.

Collum had been right. She could see the transformation taking place, and it wasn't just about a tattoo. Her skin glowed; her hair was thicker and more crimson in color. Not that it stopped the tangles. She pushed her fingers through the mass wishing she had silky hair like her aunt. The color of her eyes was shifting. Her lips were fuller. Her cheekbones seemed higher. It was subtle but Alex could see it all. She could feel it. Everything seemed firmer, healthier, stronger. She felt powerful.

In the mad dash from her aunt's and the insane connection with Collum, (a fucking dragon thank you very much) Alex hadn't had time to connect with what was happening to her. Now, here it was, staring her in the face. Of course, there were questions. She needed to know what she'd be capable of. She needed to know what her father's blood would bring to the table. Would she be able to control whatever urges bubbled to the surface? And how would it manifest itself physically? After the ferry trip, they'd head for the airport hopefully find the witch that could answer some of her questions. With any luck, she'd make it to her twenty-sixth birthday.

~ ~ ~

Collum knocked on the bathroom door. "C'mon, Alex. I picked you up a coffee and it's getting cold. We'll be docking in half an hour. It's time to suck it up and get back in the Hummer."

She pierced him with an annoyed glance as she exited the restroom.

"Check you out," he drawled. "Those eyes are ready to spit flames."

She arched a brow. "Yeah, I've decided to seize the moment and go with it."

His lips quirked. "Stick with me, baby, in case you need someone to reel you in. With eyes like that, you'll be sending out death rays pretty soon. Try to not to get pissed at anyone, okay?"

Alex grabbed her coffee and weaved in and out of the vehicles parked on the dock to follow him back to the car. She refused to notice the number of appreciative female stares Collum was getting. "Ha, Ha, warrior guy. I think they look cool. Where are we going anyway?"

"England, The Isle of White. Don't worry. The irony of leaving one island for another isn't lost on me, but you'll be safest there while we figure a few things out. No one would dare try to take you from a dragon's home. Our best chance is to hunker down there while we look for the witch. I'm hoping we can get the two of you together before any of the Elementals figure out what's going on. For now, we have to get to the airport in one piece." He smirked. "I hope you like private jets. I only travel my class."

"A Hummer and a private jet? Why don't you just tattoo environmental disaster on your forehead and be done with it."

"Ah, don't act out, little girl." He tapped her forehead. "Remember—Lava Eyes—try not to burn me. Besides you'll get used to it soon enough. And we immortals, play by a different set of rules. I've been saving this planet for longer than you've been alive."

"How old are you anyway? You had a crush on my grandmother?"

"I'm a little over two-thousand years old. Your grandmother was six-hundred when she died. Elementals stop aging when they reach their full immortality. Which for you should be in about six months, unless your father's blood affects you differently."

"And you descended from dragons?"

He straightened to his full six-foot six-inch height. "I am Dragon, Alex. For the first one thousand years of my life, I was only Dragon. Over time, I evolved to be able to transition to a human body. Now I am a blend of both. The beast lives inside me and I control the power of the dragon at will."

Heat pooled in her stomach as he spoke.

They'd reached the car and he leaned over her to get the passenger door latch. He covered her body with his and exhaled hot air against her neck. "Any more questions?"

Alex pushed him back before they made fools of themselves again. When she saw the burning red in his eyes, she changed the course of their discussion. "Yes, you said my grandfather was really old? How old is that?"

He sighed. "Domhall is over fourteen hundred. There are only a few of his age left. Domhall's time in battle and your mother's and grandmother's deaths scarred him deeply. He stays very secluded now; always wary that someone is out to end him."

"Does he have a reason to feel that way?"

"Partly yes, I suppose he does. The power he has amassed during his life is immense. He's an unstable threat, not only to the Elementals, but to other immortals as well."

"What if he isn't as far gone as . . ."

"He is, Alex. Do not attempt something with him. He's a zealot and half insane. He's not your tie to a family torn apart. I don't trust him."

"Do you trust anyone?"

"I trusted your grandmother and she's dead. And during the last years of her life, the man who was supposed to protect her was too busy getting lost to give a shit. He isn't worth your time."

"Is that why Aunt Quinn never told me about him?"

"I don't know. Today is the first day I've ever spoken to your aunt. My time with Kaylen was before your birth. As far as the world knew, our friendship ended hundreds of years ago."

They climbed in the vehicle and prepared to depart the ferry. A slow silence grew as Alex became lost in her thoughts. They were in serious trouble.

Too soon, Collum started the Hummer and pulled off the boat onto the dock.

The moment they touched land, a vibration began to pulse around Alex. Whatever it was, she was sending off waves of energy. There was no way the council wouldn't sense her. They raced to the airport, ignoring all mortal speed laws. When they pulled in the parking lot, Collum snatched her out of the vehicle and they raced to the terminal.

Alex knew that if they made it to the plane they'd be lucky, very lucky.

Chapter 6

Lachon Findel stood outside a cave entrance in the heart of the Rocky Mountains, mentally preparing himself for the meeting he was about to have. The air was cooler here than in Vancouver and he was dressed in hiking gear. The wind blew his hair in wild waves around his face and he had a five o'clock shadow at nine in the morning. The mountains suited him.

Getting to the entrance to the cave was no small feat. He'd had to park his Range Rover two miles down the road and hike up the rest of the way. The two Elemental's inside preferred solitude. They relied on others to bring news of the goings on in the outside world.

Time to get this over with, he thought, as he squared his massive shoulders and walked into the cave to find Ealian and Taurin Gondien. You'd think as the oldest living Elemental he would be over getting the creeps. He'd seen it all—done it all, yet something about where these two lived still freaked him out. Because they were twins, they shared their elements.

This fact made the pair a thorn in his side he couldn't pluck just yet. He'd been telling himself that for thirteen hundred years. If only he'd removed them as a threat a thousand years ago, he wouldn't be in his current predicament. But hindsight is twenty-twenty, isn't it? At one-thousand, seven-hundred and thirteen years old, Lachon had outlived every member of his race. Taurin and Ealian rounded out the council of elders. After losing Domhall, it was important to keep the council strong for the race.

The council were the soul of the race, and in addition to their elements, each member represented a part of the soul. Lachon represented Justice and Water. Taurin was Choice and Earth, and Ealian was Passion and Wind. There should have been a fourth to balance them, Domhall. Domhall represented Love and Fire, but he'd walked away after the death of his daughter. Once, Domhall and Lachon had been the best of friends, but not for a long time, not since the night they'd all agreed with Taurin's choice to wed her to the dragon. After Domhall left, Taurin and Ealian changed. Domhall's departure altered their ability to feel true love. Ealian's lust turned into something ugly and Taurin's choices became increasingly harsh. Lachon was left with law to keep them balanced.

He rounded a sharp curve and entered the largest cave. He'd never understand why they lived here. The damp cave was lit by beeswax candles that left every corner in shadows. Fires around the rooms sat in old metal brassieres. Thick pillows and blankets lay everywhere to try and stave off cold. He supposed it lent an air to their mysteriousness—if you went in for that sort of thing. Lachon didn't. As elders, they had more money than the human gods could dream of. They could have purchased a castle and lived like kings. But for some reason the two of them liked living in the shadows. That was also part of what creeped him out. Over the years, the siblings had gotten darker and darker. Lachon felt ill around them. They cast a pallor over everything they touched.

"Greetings old one," Taurin said as he entered the room from a smaller cave off to the side.

That was the other thing that annoyed Lachon. Just because they were old, didn't mean they had to act ancient for God's sake. No one was interested in the overblown persona Taurin and Ealian kept up. Taurin entered the space dressed like every Hollywood pirate over the last twenty-five years.

His dirty blond hair left streaks of grease down his back and his frilled cream shirt was as grimy as his tan slacks. He wore varying amounts of leather cuffs on both wrists, plus scuffed riding boots. Lachon wondered if the man was trying out for a Jack Sparrow cabaret part. Having been around to meet some of the worst pirates in history, he couldn't imagine why Taurin thought he could pull this off. If he'd come face to face with Hayrettin Barbarossa looking like this, he'd have lost his head. Lachon almost pitied him, then remembered he'd stopped pitying others over a thousand years ago.

Ealian flowed into the room behind her brother, naked except for a pale green silk housecoat. It never ceased to amaze Lachon how similar the two looked. The fraternal twin's hair, eyes, and bone structure were eerily close. Even their body type was the same.

Ealian inched toward him. Each step made Lachon's skin crawl as he watched her hip-bones sway under the silk of her dressing gown. She'd taken to wearing only wraps about ten years ago and he wondered, not for the first time, if the brother and sister had resorted to drug use to try to add excitement to their lives. The two were private and thick as thieves.

Ealian reached him and rested her hand on his chest as she crooned. "Lachon, darling, you've come to visit us. Why, it has been ages since we last had the pleasure of your company."

Lachon noticed her tongue was slightly blackened, her speech slurred, and knew he needed to tread lightly. "Ealian, I miss the company of you and your brother greatly, but you know how business takes me away for long times."

"Ah business," Taurin said. "Why do you insist on carrying on business in the human world? You don't need to run that business. You contaminate yourself by exposing your body to the humans."

"I know you feel that way, Taurin, but I don't. I believe it's important for me to understand human ways and laws so that I can better serve our people. Though I respect your choice, it is not mine." Lachon bowed his head slightly and glanced into Ealian's eyes as he spoke, as a sign of respect. He knew she was the one who held the power of the siblings.

"Of course, dear Lachon," she said. "We respect your opinion on the matter. I'm sure you must find all kinds of wonderful things to ignite your passions by interacting with the humans. Though I personally wouldn't wish to have my body infected by them."

Taurin spoke up from across the room. "Don't concern yourself, sister. I would never let anyone unworthy come near your sacred body."

"Of course not, brother," she said while continuing to stare at Lachon and stroke his chest. "I know you'll always protect me."

Lachon held his ground and his tongue, until Ealian tired of her game and moved away from him. He was going to have to take one hell of a hot shower tonight to wash the stench of her touch from him. "There are items of importance we need to discuss."

Ealian lay her slight body in a pile of pillows by one of the fires. Her legs stretched out free of the gown she wore. Her tiny breasts were almost fully bared. Taurin sat closely beside her, motioned Lachon to a pile of pillows directly across. "Of course, what is of such import?" he asked as he absently began to pluck at the loose threads on his shirt.

Lachon slowly lowered his six foot, three-inch body down to the pillow and tried to arrange himself in such a way he didn't feel like he was lounging in an opium den. "My sources may have discovered something. There have been rumblings of an emerging Element."

Ealian and Taurin appeared only mildly interested. "What sources, dear friend? We have heard nothing."

"With all due respect, your sources are not mine. The Oracles have felt a shift. Someone is coming into power. Only they can't see who it is."

Ealian sat up. "Who do we know that is of age to come into their powers?"

"None of our people, Ealian. I've discreetly checked."

"Well, check again. Go ask your record keeper. She would have the answers we need. The Oracles talk in riddles. The record keeper knows facts."

"We could do that but I fear we cannot ask her." Lachon paused. "She called the dragon recently."

Lachon braced himself for their reaction. Taurin finally stopped playing with his shirt to give Lachon his full attention. Ealian began to shake. Control over her passion was never held too tightly. He didn't want to be stuck in the cave with her if she came undone.

"Why would our record keeper call the guardian of the races? She's never met him. Why would someone from that family be reaching out to the dragon?" Ealian jumped up to pace. Her dressing gown and need for seduction forgotten. "What are they playing at?"

Lachon remained seated so as not to add fuel to Ealian's questions. "I don't have the answers yet, Ealian. I've sent rangers to see what they can learn." He leaned forward. "It is puzzling though. Domhall's been quite quiet of late."

Taurin walked over and rested a hand on his sister's shoulder which she shook off with a look of disgust. He spoke with a deceptive mildness. "We need to gather all the information before we begin to guess what is going on, sister. Lachon is right in this. You are gathering to storm for no reason."

"Do not tell me to calm, brother dearest." A sneer curled her lip. "That family has been an inch from treason for years. Look what almost happened. A daughter with too much power betrayed her kind and Domhall left us." She practically shrieked the last bit out. "Lachon, find out why she contacted the dragon. Or speak to him yourself if you must. He understands law."

Finally, Lachon stood. His immense size dwarfed Ealian. "As I said, I'll find out everything I can. I've never walked away from my duty to our race. I do not need you to tell me how to do my job, Ealian. Keep your temper. I came to you as members of the council to let you know of the strange power shift. I will take care of it—whatever it is."

Chapter 7

Alex exited the Starbucks in the airport, thinking they were home free, when she felt eyes on her. Collum told her to wait outside the men's washroom and she hadn't listened. All she'd ingested that morning was herbal tea. After all the crazy revelations and what she suspected awaited her, she wanted a Caramel Corretto from Starbucks. It wasn't that she didn't recognize the danger she was in. She did. Completely. But the caffeine addiction had taken hold. If she were entirely honest with herself, the little voice inside always pushing toward rebellion was screaming at the top of its lungs—*They wanted to kill me. Screw them.*

Of course, now she regretted her impulsiveness.

Her stalker was impossible to miss, wasn't even trying to hide. He walked toward her with a casual indifference.

Easily six-foot four-inches tall, he sauntered, more than walked. A devastating angel, he looked like he was carved from gold. His hair flowed down his back in a cascade of white silk. His ice—green eyes pierced her from across the room. He was lean, and perfectly, impeccably, dressed. His chiseled jaw (that of an old English aristocrat) and his bearing practically screamed Old World. Maybe he was forty? As he stepped closer, she swore she heard Eminem's *Monster* blasting from his iPod. Maybe not as old world as she thought then.

He stopped inside the boundary of her personal space and removed his ear buds. "Hey, Alex. Crazy day, right. It's time to go home. Where are your bags?"

The words slid like butter through the chaos in her mind. "Excuse me?"

A single eyebrow raised on his unlined face. "I'm Domhall—your grandfather. I'm sure you've heard all about me by now. Don't worry, I'll fill you in on everything Collum screwed up, once we are on the plane. Now where are your bags? We have to move before the others show up."

Alex closed her mouth, blinked her eyes, looked him over and promptly turned around to hightail it to wherever the hell Collum might be. Only, he stepped in front of her before she'd barely moved.

He raised his hands in a symbol of surrender. "Come on now, don't be like that. No games okay? I'll pour you a whiskey, top grade. We can catch up on the plane."

Alex stopped before slamming into him and looked up. It was a long look up. "I don't know who you are, or what game you're playing, but there's no way you're my grandfather and I'm not going anywhere with you. Now, I'd rather not make a scene in the middle of the airport. And if you know Collum's name, I'm sure you know what he's capable of, so back off."

The guy laughed. "I knew you had spirit. But c'mon, you're made of smarter stuff than this. Take a second look at me before running. No matter what that dragon told you, I'm here to help. That overblown jerk tried stealing my wife four-hundred years ago and now he thinks he can take you too? Pompous ass. I'm sure the tales of my insanity have been incredibly detailed, but he can go screw himself. So, how about we get moving?"

"Do you think I'm stupid? Isn't my grandfather one of the oldest Elementals alive? How can you be my grandfather? You were listening to Eminem."

"What? An old guy can't get into RAP? What can I say—I've aged well, like that fine whiskey I have on the plane."

Alex burst out laughing. She was standing in the middle of the airport, having an absurd conversation, with a man claiming to be her possibly insane, possibly out to kill her, grandfather, and no one was paying them the least bit of attention. She felt no fear. He was simply . . . weird.

"Still not convinced, hey? Okay, if you want me to fit a mould, try this on for size." The man adjusted his posture. "I have followed you for your whole life my child, though all fought to keep me from you. I've known, in all ways, where to find you. I grieved the passing of your mother and grandmother with my whole heart. Yet, I knew in order to protect you and your aunt from the wrath of the council, I must keep to the silence. I come to you now because the Guardian Collum, thinks he is strong enough to protect you. He is not. We have but minutes. I beg of you to come with me, now, before we are found."

Domhall stepped closer and gently placed his hand on her shoulder. "Is that how you want me to sound, kiddo? Old? Stoic? I've been many things in my life. But however, I sound or look, you can be certain of who I am and that I will never harm you."

The heat from his palm soothed her. The only thing that made any sense to her anymore was her gut. And her gut said to believe him.

"Well, Grandpa, I might or might not believe you. If you truly want to help you can come with us, but I'm not going without Collum. We aren't leaving him, or my clothes behind."

"Are you kidding me? I'm not taking that ass anywhere. Who do you think you're bargaining with?"

"I think I'm bargaining with my grandfather, who told me he loves me beyond all measure and wants to keep me safe. So, let's quit jabbering and go get my guardian."

She prepared for him to argue with her but instead he

took her hand, gifted her with a lazy smile and said, "My fierce blood, I would never dream of telling you no. Let's go find the ass. I can't believe he left you alone this long anyway. Sorry bloody excuse for a guardian if I ever saw one."

Chapter 8

Collum searched for her as he exited the gift shop. Of course, she hadn't been waiting outside the men's room when he finished. Not that he'd expected her to listen to him. He'd seen her walk into Starbucks for a coffee, felt no danger and took the minute to pick her up something for the flight. He couldn't say why it mattered to him. The reality was he knew nothing about her or how her powers would eventually manifest. Hell, she could wake up tomorrow with horns, or an insatiable need to suck his bone marrow. Getting emotionally entangled wasn't smart and Collum prided himself on being smart.

As he considered the stuffed animal in his hands, he admitted that wasn't entirely true concerning the women in her family. He'd made a fool of himself with Kaylen years ago; prancing and preening, like an untrained whelp just entering transition. Making moves on a married woman. Kaylen treated him with respect while turning him down. In the end, he'd loved her like a sister. He'd never stopped making stupid choices for her though. With Domhall, he'd crossed a line he shouldn't have.

A wave of unease hit him on the walk back to the Starbucks. He shoved the bear in his jacket and started running when he sensed them. He felt their intentions, knew they were between himself and Alex. He rounded the corner at a dead run, ready to kill anyone in his way. His diversion was about to cost Alex her life.

He skirted around the corner with raised hands, ready to strike—only to be confronted by the site of Domhall holding Alex's hand. Those entwined fingers were the only thing that kept Collum from losing control. He skidded to a halt, watched as Domhall directed pulsing blue energy at two Elemental soldiers. The scene was oddly soothing, yet ultimately terrifying.

The humans felt nothing, saw nothing, but what Domhall wanted them to. Whoever sent these soldiers had had no idea Domhall would be at the airport, or entirely underestimated the old man's power. His eyes glowed with the fires of Valhalla as he chanted in the old language. The Elemental soldiers were young and unschooled and had no hope of blocking their minds to him. Collum almost pitied them. Within seconds their eyes glazed over and they vanished.

Collum notice a third soldier approaching the couple from behind. A sword bulged under the man's jacket. He swung behind the fool on silent feet. Death was on the soldier with one twist. A slight crack. A moment to break a neck and quietly place the body in the nearest chair. It was over within seconds and no one around them noticed a thing. Collum hardly broke his stride. A second later he stood next to Domhall.

The old man nodded slightly. "Well, it's about time you fucking showed up. I told her we didn't need you, but she insists we drag you along. We better move before dumb and dumber," he nodded to the corpse in the chair, "and even dumber's, friends return. The next group might not be so easily swayed by my charms."

Collum gritted his teeth. He pointed to the dead man in the chair and said, "Do you want to cloak the body to buy us a bit more time?"

"See," Domhall said to Alex as he cast a cloaking spell over the dead Elemental, "the man has no couth whatsoever." He grinned triumphantly. "My plane is waiting, let's move."

Collum refused to give him the satisfaction of a thank you. He stared directly at Alex, waited for her nod of approval and said, "I have my own plane," before adding quietly, "If you damage her, Dom, I'll kill you like I did him."

Domhall laughed and plugged his headphones back in. Above the sound of Nirvana blasting out his ears, he replied, "Same goes here . . . beast."

Collum led them across the tarmac to the waiting plane. He trusted Domhall about as much as he trusted . . . well he didn't trust him at all. Too much had happened, but they needed to reach Europe quickly and he knew Alex would never leave without the man now. Maybe his power could cloak them until they reached his land. As soon as their feet touched his estate Domhall's interference would no longer be tolerated.

Domhall strode forward holding Alex's hand. "Quit making stupid plans. I can feel your eyes burning into my back and you're making it hard for me to concentrate on my music. You aren't taking my granddaughter anywhere without me. Get used to it."

"Your granddaughter?" Collum sneered. "Kaylen worked hard to keep her from you. You expect me to believe that you've suddenly changed into a doting grandpa?"

"You're so goddamn pompous. Kaylen didn't tell you everything, you know. I was her fucking husband. You were just some guy who kept getting in the way. Get in my way now and I'll take you down."

"Don't forget who you're dealing with, boy," Collum growled.

"Oh, oh big man on campus. Losing your constant cool, are you?" Domhall laughed. "Don't forget who I am, lizard—who I was."

"You know what, you crazy shit, I've changed my mind. You aren't coming anywhere with us."

Alex finally wrenched her hand out of Domhall's. "Stop. Both of you, stop! I don't know, or trust, either one of you completely at this point. I'm literally betting my life that you are both here to help me. I'm trusting my instincts. I'm not going to listen to this crap for much longer though. So, can you both get back to the job of saving my life and deal with your personal issues later? God, for two guys who are supposed to be so old and powerful you are acting like children. Now, would you shut up and get me to England, and to whoever can tell me what I am."

Alex stomped to the plane, while grumbling something about boys, and egos, and why did she have to get stuck with these two.

Domhall followed quickly after her, smirking at Collum. "You heard her, get on the plane and quit acting like such an infant."

Chapter 9

Alex flopped into a seat as far removed as possible from Domhall and Collum. As the adrenaline from the day wore off, she dissected everything that had happened, studied the two men she shared the plane with. What her grandfather had done in the airport was unbelievable. She wouldn't have thought things like that were possible twelve hours ago. When he'd grabbed her hand, she'd been afraid, until he pushed her slightly behind him and winked at her. He'd calmly told her, "Don't let go of my hand, kid. I got this," before obliterating the two soldiers sent to kill them.

Alex hadn't noticed them—they simply appeared out of nowhere. Domhall protected her with an energy field before the two men had a chance to verify her appearance. She'd felt the energy before she saw it, which was utterly amazing. The energy glowed the same color as her grandfather's eyes. The power felt impenetrable. Alex hadn't even noticed Collum or the third assassin. Apparently, Domhall hadn't either. That confirmed her choice to stay with Collum, no matter what Domhall said.

Her instincts had proven right most of her life. But right now? She had to remain vigilant. Couldn't leave her future up to these men, no matter how much she wanted to be sure of them. Maybe good ol' grandad was playing her. She was also self-aware enough to recognize that her desire for Collum could easily be clouding her judgment. But her aunt vouched for Collum and she was the one-person Alex trusted completely.

She studied both men under her lashes. They were doing their best to ignore each other, while giving her the space she desperately needed.

Looking at Collum made her belly ache. She wanted to climb on top of him and beg him to kiss her until she screamed. She had no idea what the full extent of his powers were, but there was no doubt he'd kill anything in his way.

And then there was Domhall. Her grandfather was a fourteen-hundred-year-old warrior, who controlled the elements and who could disintegrate men by looking at them? She rested her head against the window and drifted off. There would be time to dissect more in the morning. The journey had only just begun.

~ ~ ~

Alex smelled oranges. It was a strong and tangy scent. It smelled clean, healthy. She opened her eyes to find herself in a garden surrounded by citrus trees. The light was intense. A slight breeze wafted crisply, yet her body felt heavy. Alex tried to raise her hand to her face. Everything appeared clean and clear . . . except her. Alex was weighted. She knew her body remained on the plane while her soul traveled here, wherever here was.

"Hello, Alex, welcome home."

She observed the man standing a few scant steps away. He was the blood pounding under her skin, hot and fluid. There was feline presence to him. She had the distinct impression that he belonged to her. He was easily as tall as Collum, but in place of Collum's muscle there was a lean and composed strength. She sensed he harnessed a dormant savagery. His yellow eyes glowed with secrets she didn't want to know.

"Where am I?"

"You are home, Alex. We are waiting for you to join us."

Alex weaved, tried to steady her mind. "Who are you?"

He approached her with ease, a slight smirk on his lips. "I am Neeren."

"Why am I here, Neeren?"

"In England, I'll be coming for you. Your fathers' people want you home. When you see me, come to me."

"Who are you, Neeren?" She shook her head, tried to clear the cobwebs. "I know you."

He grinned. "Your family awaits, Alex." He reached his hand to her arm and laid his fingers lightly against her skin.

For a mere second, Alex became corporeal. He leaned in and stared directly into her eyes. A half-moon glowed inside his eyes. A jolt reverberated up her spine and a tingling sensation flowed behind her retina.

Neeren gently kissed her forehead before stepping away. "Come willingly to me, Alex."

~ ~ ~

Alex woke up crying. Tears poured down her face.

Collum was at her side in an instant, touching her, questioning her.

She hesitated, overwhelmed with a desire to keep her dream secret. More often than not, Alex's dreams were premonitions. Who was to say this wasn't a new manifestation of her powers. The dream had felt more real than any before—like she was on the verge of pushing her body through a mist to another side. A fiery sensation burned up her leg to her shoulder but she kept silent. She knew she'd see a tattoo engraved on the flesh that burned. It pulsed under her hand as she rubbed her arm. She understood she'd been branded. The burning sensation stopped where Neeren's had touched her shoulder.

Alex grasped Collum's hand while looking to her grandfather. "Domhall, can the Elementals speak to each other telepathically?"

"What did you dream, Alex?"

Both men stared at her with concern, but also, curiosity.

She might trust them with her life, but she wasn't ready to trust them with her strange introduction to Neeren.

"I'm just wondering. There's so much about myself and my family that I don't know. We've been so busy running that I haven't had a chance to assimilate anything. Or to ask all the questions I want."

"You're right," Domhall said before glancing at Collum. "We have the time now and the girl deserves to know more about what's going on. For that matter, so do you."

He settled in the seat closest to them. "Gray, was fierce from the moment she was born. A true warrior. In our culture, Alex, women are revered for their strength. We place no distinction between men and women when it comes to the ability to protect our race. Most immortals feel this way."

"This is true for dragons as well," Collum interjected. "Most female dragons are better warriors than their male counterparts."

Domhall nodded. "I was already an old man before Gray came along. I taught her everything I learned during my many years on earth. Your grandmother thought I was starting too young with her, but I knew she was born to be a leader. And she had so much passion, I didn't want her to waste it. I was a thousand years old and taught her all I knew. It was too much." He smiled. "She'd always been a trouble maker. As a warrior, though, no one worried much. She would take out her aggression on whichever mission she was assigned to. Once, we lost track of her for almost two years. I'd had a thousand years to learn to temper my abilities to those around me. She thirsted for knowledge; much as I did and still do. You all think I've gone insane, but, don't you see? That touch of insanity is all that holds me together. I need to forget who I am and what I'm capable of from time to time."

"But if you are so powerful, why didn't you stop her?" Alex asked.

"Cause, kiddo, she was my daughter and I loved her. I would deny her nothing. I also don't think it was so terrible for her to have so much power. We've been fighting wars for longer than I've been living and where has it gotten us? I no longer see in black and white. My world is colored with my experiences. Not all the Elementals are as perfect as they present themselves. Collum knows that. Your grandmother knew that. That's why she hid you." He petted her curls before saying, "If I'd stopped Gray, you wouldn't exist. That would be too great of a tragedy for me to live with."

Alex leaned over and kissed her grandfather's cheek. "Thank you for telling me more about her. Now, I need to learn more about who I am. Can the Elementals talk to each other telepathically?" she asked again.

"No, Alex, they cannot." Collum replied without hesitation while stroking her fingers absently. "Are you ready to tell us what your dream was about?"

Neeren's face appeared behind her eyes. Nothing was black and white, she told herself before shaking her head. "It was nothing. It's probably fear of the unknown cropping up. Look, I'm exhausted and I need to use the bathroom. Can you guys give me some space please?"

The men moved away in an uneasy truce. As they found their seats, Alex marched to the bathroom.

In the tiny room, she stripped before the mirror and studied the tattoo coiled around her body. There was no room for fear now. She'd have to get a grip and deal with it. Flames wound around her leg, hugging her muscles. Fire settled on each rib, dropping bits of red ash. The flames floated up her side, along her shoulder blade, over her shoulder, and ended where Neeren had touched her. Who was he? He'd said her family was waiting. For a moment, Alex couldn't breathe.

She closed her eyes until the chaos calmed. Until she was ready for more.

Her red hair glistened and her skin glowed. As she stared, the tattoo shifted against her skin. She had no idea what the flame did, but the power of it echoed through her body. It connected with her muscles and pulsed against her nerve endings. A yellow half-moon shimmered in the centre of her violet eyes. She inhaled raggedly.

She wanted to know. Needed to know why her eyes now matched Neeren's. So, this was it. The decision was made. She would go to Neeren when he came for her.

Chapter 10

Neeren sat in his garden a moment, composed himself before heading into the house. They'd found her and soon they would have her. So many years of loss and waiting. They almost had Alex and she was perfect. He forced himself to let go of the past.

Entering the library, he found her sitting in a pool of light, in front of the ceiling high windows. "It is done."

Lifting her head, she dropped the book she was reading onto her lap and nervously twisted her hands together. "Did you tell her about me?"

"No. Only that I would be coming for her."

"Good, she can't know about me yet. Meeting you will be enough of a shock."

"I agree but soon it will become apparent."

All around Neeren lay the trappings of wealth and ease. Every need, every want, had been his. The home, designed with his every desire in mind, had been built entirely from glass and steel. He wanted no shadows in his house or his life. Artwork from the greatest modern painters covered the few walls he had. The rest lay in piles around the room. His home sat on the edge of a cliff, the ocean on three sides of him. No matter where you stood, thanks to the glass, the sea was there to meet you. His grounds were heavily guarded and his estate was vast. He was surrounded by beauty—as he should be. He thought of Alex. She truly knew nothing, and those who sought to keep her from them had taught her nothing.

Neeren poured himself a glass of spiced rum, as he thought back to his upbringing. His people had called him special. Capable of more than any of them, power had been his birthright. Such had not been the case for Alex.

"Don't worry," he said. "I will help her find her way. And I will bring her home."

Chapter 11

The plane reached England at three in the morning. Unable to relax his guard, Collum had been awake for hours. He and Domhall had taken turns watching over Alex during the twelve-hour flight. Domhall fell asleep around one in the morning. Through his headphones, the whole plane could hear a bass beat. How the man's hearing was still intact, was anyone's guess.

Tense from the hours of listening to Alex's mewling sleep sounds, Collum leaned over as the plane began its descent. He stared in fascination at the freckles along her nose.

"Hey, we're about to land." He chuckled as she scowled in her sleep and rolled over. "C'mon, wake up, babe." Bending closer, he whispered in her ear, "You're whimpering sex sounds in your sleep. Are you dreaming of me?"

He watched, fascinated as her eyelids fluttered open and she reached for him. The hair rose on his arms, his nerve endings flared to life. Ignoring common sense, he pulled her fingers to his mouth to suckle them. Kept his body between her and Domhall. The guy still appeared to be sound asleep; the Deaftones *Leather* blasted out his headphones and he hadn't moved in hours. Still you never knew with Domhall.

When he saw the moon in the centre of her violet eyes, he almost climbed on top of her. Domhall be dammed. He pulled her fingers from his mouth and reached for her mass of hair. "I'm gonna turn those whimpers into moans."

The captain's voice welcoming them to England brought him back to earth with a re-sounding crash.

"Fuck," he whispered as he started to back away. "We're going to burn so good together."

He turned away before either of them did something even more stupid, to see Domhall glowering in his direction.

"Could you use a little more discretion," Domhall flung out, music still blaring.

"I'm trying man. I really am." Collum walked away scolded, but too worked up to care.

He'd felt the heat rising off Alex. He'd seen her eyes. Her transition was reaching explosive levels. When the time came that they couldn't hold back, and it was coming soon, they'd be lucky if they came away whole.

Chapter 12

Alex watched Collum walk down the aisle. Her grandfather followed him off the plane. Domhall was loudly singing *Beat It* by Michael Jackson so she figured it was smart to leave him be.

Why the hell did Collum have that effect on her? He'd practically had her begging him to rip her pants off. She shoved herself out of the seat and followed the men off the plane, steam rising from her hair.

As she pushed passed Domhall, she heard him grumble something about luggage and being nobodies errand boy.

"Hey," she blasted as she reached Collum on the Tarmac below. "You can't just do that you know."

"I'm on the edge here," he warned without turning around.

"Look at me. I mean it. You almost jumped me in front of Domhall."

He spun around, steel in his voice. "Look, sweetheart, you reached for me. Now move away or I'm throwing you to the ground, and I don't give a shit who's watching. Christ, look at you. Your hair is almost on fire. I can see that fucking flame glowing beneath your clothes. And your eyes are shimmering. You want me to find out what fire tastes like? Keep pushing."

The ends of her hair burst into flame and she grabbed him with both hands. "I dare you to try," she half screamed.

Collum stepped forward so that their bodies were touching. "You're going to kill me, Alex. Can't you feel how close to the edge I am? I'm going to go get the car and you are going to stay away from me. You're going to sit in the back seat and not say another word to me until we get to the house. Soon, I'm going to come to you. You will let me into your room and I'll take you up on your little dare. Taste every inch of you until you're screaming my name, begging for more. And then, I am going to make you mine. Do you understand?"

As she stared at the man in front of her, the feminist in her screeched in rebellion. She dropped her hands from his shirt, took a step back, and burst out laughing.

"Oh man, you really are two thousand. Do chicks usually dig that macho crap? Do you ever have me pegged wrong. Take your archaic, do-what-I-tell-you attitude and shove it. You're hot, I'll give you that—but fuck off." She snapped her fingers, said, "You gotta work a little harder for a piece of this," and walked away, hair on fire, strutting like the warrior she was.

The heat of Collum's lust-filled gaze at her back nearly burned her up, until she reached the car and slid inside, still aching with desire.

~ ~ ~

Alex sat fuming in the back seat of the vehicle, when Domhall appeared ten minutes later, their bags in tow. He nodded at the Land Rover. "I'll drive."

"Not a chance," Collum quipped as he jumped in the driver's seat. "I still don't trust you. I appreciate your help in the airport, but it's my car, and I'm driving."

"You would risk my anger?"

"When are you going to get it? I'm not afraid of you. I never have been. I was killing your kind before you were born. So how about you don't forget who I am. The mission, and Alex's protection, are my responsibility."

Alex watched the two men eye each other up. She rubbed the back of her neck in irritation.

Domhall snorted and turned his golden head to the side. "Whatever, but I'm with you every step of the way. And if I feel you aren't up to the task, I'll take the choice away from you."

"I wouldn't have it any other way," Collum snarled.

They traveled further inland on a series of nondescript roads. Despite everything, Alex appreciated the beauty of the surroundings. Gentle, sloping hills flew by, heather dotted the craggy landscape. The earth felt raw and relentless, as though the land itself held immense power; power it would never relinquish to a mere human.

They drove through a modest village in a green valley, bordered by the ragged mountains. As the vehicle climbed, the air became thinner, seemed to shimmer. As they turned a corner an ancient estate appeared out of nowhere. At the wrought iron gate, Collum leaned out to punch in a security code. Soundlessly, the gate swung open.

Alex marveled at the ancient magic pulsing around her. The castle was carved out of the face of the mountain. "This is your place?"

Collum shrugged, "My family has owned this land for as many centuries as the Ilse of Whyte has existed."

Alex wasn't sure what she'd expected, but it wasn't this place of shadows and magic. The sun rose over the mountains. Energy glowed all around the house. Clearly Collum only had one foot in the mortal world. His control and strength told her much about him. But seeing his home showed her who he was in ways his mannerisms never would. This home, this land, was where he belonged. She was certain of it.

"Don't think about it too much, Alex. It's only a house."

"Only it isn't, is it? It's you and it's beautiful."

They locked eyes. She forgot the sway of the willow trees. The music of the underground springs faded under the roar of desire churning in her ears. Her breasts ached. Desire bubbled in the back of her throat as his eyes scored her.

His lip curled. He stepped toward her.

Domhall's voice brought her back to reality. "Hey, do you have any staff here? Any food? A pretty water fountain isn't going to feed me."

Her face heated as Collum shook his head, said "Shit" under his breath and turned to her grandfather.

"I sent Glenn a text from the airport. There should be a light meal ready for us in the dining room. The wards around the outer property keep it hidden from outside eyes. I'll add more today. That should keep us protected for a few days at least."

"Good," Domhall replied. "The elders will send out scouts. When the scouts can't find us, they will come themselves. Even with your wards, we have three days here at most. Contacting the witch needs to be your first, and only, priority."

~ ~ ~

Inside, the castle looked like what Alex always envisioned a castle would. Every inch of it gleamed with old wealth. Alex followed Collum down the hallway, feeling like she'd stepped back in time to the sixteenth century, but with HBO and high-speed Internet. When she tried to ask him about some interesting art on the wall, he replied, "Ask Glenn. He runs the place. I only live here."

He showed her to a room without looking at her, threw her bag on the bed and told her to be down for breakfast in twenty minutes before backing out the door with Domhall on his heels.

As soon as the two men left, Alex rushed to the bathroom for a desperately needed shower. She'd been up for almost twenty-four hours at that point and the stress she'd experienced throughout the day was enough to give anyone

BO. The huge bathroom was carved directly out of the rock. The sink and counters floated slightly off the wall. The toilet was hidden behind a separate door. The sunken tub-slash-shower took up half the space. When she stepped down on the base of the tub, the floor warmed to her touch. In the shower, a rain stream fell gently on her skin from the ceiling, while a natural spring poured out of the mountain wall. For ten short minutes she luxuriated in the steam that rose as the water hit the heated floor.

Conscious of the time and starving, she forced herself out of the shower, and into the bedroom to dry off. The room was decorated entirely in shades of yellow, from soft butter tones, to the deepest wine-gold. The bed was so high she had to jump on to it. Pillows of all sizes covered the bottom half. A flat screen TV jutted up from the foot of the bed. A massive fireplace filled one entire wall. She allowed herself one moment of pretense—that she was on vacation—before brushing her teeth and dressing in a new pair of sweats, a fresh sports bra, and clean tank top. She desperately needed a run to clear her head but knew the chance of that happening was nil. Maybe after breakfast she could talk Collum into letting her go . . . if she stayed on the estate.

With a final look at the bed, she shoved her hands through her hair, tried to work out the tangles, and headed for the dining room.

Chapter 13

Collum lounged at the mahogany table, drinking a coffee, and reading the news when Alex entered the kitchen. He tossed the paper aside to study her. "You're late. And you don't have socks on.

The flame on her toe mocked him. Bits of fire creeped around the edges of her tank top. Her hair was wet and wild around her face again. "Are you kidding me? I rushed as quickly as I could. Plus, I like going barefoot."

He stood, walked to her, and stroked the edges of fire on her shoulder. "When were you planning on telling me this had fully emerged?"

She shrugged. "It happened on the plane."

"After you woke up crying, you mean?" Collum stroked the tattoo. Waves of heat wrapped around them. His eyes glowed.

Alex leaned into him. "Yes."

He concentrated on the lines of the tattoo. Danced his fingers along the edges. Let his mind reach for hers. "Why didn't you tell me?"

"Because of my dream."

He ran his fingers across her cheek. Breathed deeply. Wondered how far he should go. "You'll tell me about your dream soon. Won't you?"

"Yes, always yes."

"Have the Elementals reached you?"

Her eyes glazed over. "Elemental? No. Not them."

Collum released her shoulder and stepped back. He'd gotten the answer he wanted.

"The mark shouldn't have happened this quickly. You still don't want to tell me what your dream was about?" She almost fell as he stepped away.

Anger jumped at him from her accusing eyes. "You know what? Screw you. I don't know what you did there, but don't ever do it again. I don't have to tell you everything."

"You do if it affects my ability to keep you safe, sweetheart."

"Quit calling me that. I'm not talking to you anymore. I'm hungry. I've hardly eaten, and had even less sleep. So back off and shut up."

"Do you know what it means?"

"What?" she asked, exasperated.

"Your tattoo. Do you know what it means?"

She sighed but refused to look at him. "You know I don't."

"It means you have fully transitioned into your Elemental state. That tattoo holds your power. It's a part of you and will react, and respond with your emotions. It feeds off your element. You will use it to protect yourself."

"I've never seen one on Aunt Quinn."

"Quinn's element is wind. Wind is easy to disguise." He leaned back on his heels. "Do you understand what I'm telling you?"

He witnessed the struggle on her face. Held his tongue as she rubbed the tattoo where he'd touched her moments before. Let her come to the truth on her own.

"I'm immortal."

He opened his mouth, blew smoke over her tattoo, watched it writhe against her skin. "Yes, babe, you're immortal."

He leaned in, intent on licking Alex's tattoo to show her what immortality meant just as Domhall entered the room, and headed straight for the cinnamon buns on the corner table.

"So," Domhall mumbled around a mouthful of pastry, "when you mentioned Glenn earlier, were you talking about *the* Glenn?"

Collum stepped back, moaned under his breath, "Fucking guy has the worst timing," before turning to Domhall. "Excuse me?"

Domhall removed his headphones. "Glenn, *the* Glenn. Is that the Glenn you mentioned earlier? 'Cause if it is, I might forgive the totally inappropriate shit with my granddaughter I walked in on. Get a bit of control, dude."

Bearing his teeth at the man, Collum replied, "Yes, it's *the* Glenn."

Domhall rubbed his hands gleefully and two-stepped to the coffee pot.

"What's he talking about? Who's Glenn?" a red-faced Alex asked.

Collum threw his hands up, headed for the coffee pot himself, and simply replied, "Have a cinnamon bun and cup of coffee. Then let me know if I need to answer that question.

Chapter 14

Later that night, Alex emerged from her second shower, wearing an oversized, forest green, cotton robe. Breakfast had been awkward. Domhall had shot weird looks at Collum all through the meal while Collum acted every inch the dragon. Eventually, Domhall noticed her growing tattoo and said, "Cool" before grabbing more of Glenn's coffee. Her grandfather was one strange guy.

Collum was right of course. She'd only needed one bite of the cinnamon bun before thinking Glenn must be an angel. Not even an immortal could bake like that.

Their discussion centered on strategy and location spells. Alex alternated between feelings of guilt, frustration, excitement, and exhaustion before finally excusing herself and crawling into bed. Eight hours later she'd woken up, still exhausted, and made her way downstairs for dinner. The two men were still there. She doubted they'd even slept.

After more talk about locating the witch and her father's people, it was all she could do to get away before she made a fool of herself. All she'd wanted was to crawl into Collum's lap, have him rub her back, and tell her everything was going to be okay.

She left the kitchen. Decided to snoop around the dragon's castle for a while. Collum caught up with her as she opened the door to what she assumed was the study. His hand covered hers. His warm breath against her neck.

"I can give you a tour if you'd like."

His scent, his voice, were aphrodisiacs. He dripped sex and something else she couldn't yet name. It was obvious why he turned her on physically. It was his barbaric attitude she could do without. And she really had to figure out what he'd pulled in the kitchen earlier.

She turned the doorknob under his hand and pushed into the room to gain a little distance. "I was really hoping for some alone time."

"You had alone time all day, sweetheart, while I was stuck talking strategy with a guy who'd rather talk about Glenn's cinnamon buns."

Alex perked up. "Well they are absolutely incredible."

"Oh God. Not you too."

"Where did you meet him?"

He advanced toward her. "Glenn? I don't know. He's always been there."

She shoved her hands into the pocket of her sweats. "What about your dad?"

At the mention of his father, Collum stopped his pursuit. His eyes turned cold. "What did Quinn tell you?"

"That he killed my mother and that you killed him. Is that true?"

He picked up a book off the shelf, his stance rigid. "It's true."

"I'm sorry you had to do that."

"I'm not." He closed his eyes for a moment. "The man was a killer of women. Your mother was not the first."

When he opened them, she noticed a red glow under black pupils.

"I'm The Guardian, Alex. He didn't get a free pass because he was my father."

The air in the room tightened. "And with his death you also became king?"

"No, I was king long before." He placed the book back on his desk and flexed his shoulders. "He lost the right to lead when he killed my mother."

"He killed your mother?"

"He broke her wings, she committed suicide. Same thing."

She took a step toward him but his raised voice stopped her.

"Don't. You don't get to comfort me. I don't want it or need it. I'm not heartbroken."

"But . . ."

"No. My life wasn't yours. There were no cuddles. No lullabies." He shook his head softly. "I'm a dragon, sweetheart. Warm and fuzzy don't come with the territory."

Alex couldn't imagine not being adored by her parents. Even after they'd told her about the adoption, she'd never, for a second, felt unloved. She couldn't fathom having such a cold upbringing. But she also knew what it felt like to have people intrude. Collum was right. They weren't friends. She didn't have the right to question or comfort him.

She straightened her shirt before nodding. "I would like to thank you for getting my mother out. Somehow because of you I survived."

He'd already made his way to the door.

When she spoke, he turned. His eyes burned through her. "You're welcome. Your life," he growled, "was worth saving."

Chapter 15

Sunshine poured into her room. The clock on the nightstand flashed six in the morning. Alex groaned and shoved her head under the pillows but sleep eluded her. She climbed out of bed, shoved her feet into pink flannel socks, and wrapped up in her favorite yellow housecoat. People made fun of the housecoat, but her adoptive father had given it to her and she refused to give it up. Plus, it was nice to have a piece of home with her. Thankfully aunt Quinn knew her well enough to pack it. She stared out the window for a while, watched the world, marveled over everything that had happened, before making her way downstairs to the kitchen.

As she rounded the corner, her stomach rumbled loudly. The smells wafting out the kitchen door were heavenly. She inhaled as much of the smell as she could before saying to the older man sprinkling sugar on wicked-looking pastry, "You must be Glenn."

He dusted his hands on a blue, rhinestone embroidered apron and replied, "That'd be me. You must be our new addition, Alex."

She smiled. "Your cinnamon buns are incredible."

"Well, dear, I'm always happy to accept a compliment." He reached for a fresh bun, put it on a plate, and passed it to her with a wink. "You should probably test this one and make sure it's up to snuff. Now, can I make you a coffee?"

She nodded while shoving pastry into her mouth.

Glenn reached around her, grabbed a cup out of the cupboard to fill. Her mouth watered as he placed the cup on the counter and motioned for her to take a sip.

She wiped her mouth on her sleeve. "Thank you. I hardly ate last night and I'm starving."

"Would you like another one?" He scooped up a second cinnamon bun and put it on her plate before she could say no.

She laughed out loud. Pushed her hair out of the way as she accepted the second bun. Sighing with contentment, she said, "Collum tells me you've been with him forever. Did you know my grandmother?"

"I'm afraid not my dear. Collum is," he clicked his tongue, "very private about his friendships. Dragons usually are."

"Are you an Angel?"

Glenn laughed out loud. "Oh no, no. Valhalla forbid. I'm a raven my dear."

With a blank look, she repeated, "A raven?"

"I'm a shifter. The raven is my true form. It's a bit of a gift from Odin."

Alex thought back to her basic knowledge of Norse mythology. She might not know much but everyone knew about the Ravens of Odin. She gulped down her coffee. "Wow, so, shifters and Odin's Ravens, exist? For real?"

"Yes, we're all for real. That's likely the case for everything you think is unreal."

She bit her lip as Glenn laughed again. It was a kind laugh, though. "Can I have another coffee please? I think I'm going to need it today."

As Glenn plucked the cup from her hands, Collum walked in. Surprise lit his face. An entirely ridiculous giggle embedded in her throat. She climbed off the counter. Tried to smooth down her hair without him noticing.

He inclined his head to her. "Good morning, did you sleep well?"

"I did thank you. The bed is very comfortable," she stammered, feeling like an idiot.

"Your paper is on the dining table. Your steak and eggs are almost ready," Glenn said as he handed a coffee to Collum.

Fascinated, Alex watched as Collum took the cup and slapped the other man on his shoulder affectionately. She'd never seen Collum touch anyone, well other than her. He appeared completely at ease. She recognized all too clearly that she knew absolutely nothing about him.

"You have icing in your hair, Alex?" Collum said.

"What?" Alex pulled at her housecoat.

"I said—you have icing in your hair."

"Oh." She grabbed her hair, found the offending piece and shoved it in her mouth to suck the icing off.

Rushing to cover her embarrassment, she said, "I'd like to go for a run. Do you have any trails I can use or should I run the road?"

Collum shook his head. "You can't go for a run."

"Excuse me?"

Glenn began banging pots and pans, but Collum talked right over the noise. "I said—You. Can. Not. Go for a run."

"I beg to differ. You told me this place would be safe. My back is aching and I need to release some pent-up energy."

Collum gave her a sinister look. Behind him Glenn began coughing. She ignored them both and carried on, "I need this Collum."

"Nope. Not happening."

"Look, buddy, I don't think you get it. I'm going for a run. I'm only asking you the best route to take."

Her tattoo tingled against her skin as she stepped into his personal space. She could smell the shampoo he used. He smelled good in the morning. She inhaled. Why did he have to smell so good when he was acting like a cretin.

His eyes narrowed. "You can't protect yourself if something happens and I don't have time to follow you. Go work out in the gym on the lower level."

"I can't what? Maybe you haven't heard, but I can protect myself just fine. I've already saved my own ass once. It's not like I'm talking about leaving your precious estate. Man, you're being a total jerk."

She glowered at Collum but the jerk refused to give in. Behind her, Glenn interjected. "I can follow her."

Alex clapped her hands. "There, see, Glenn will follow me. You can drop the male chauvinist act now."

Glaring at Glenn he retorted, "Fine, you fly behind her and keep an eye on things. But you two had better not leave the fucking property. I don't know who else is out there, and I can't bloody well protect you if you won't listen."

He stormed out of the kitchen with his coffee in hand.

As soon as his footsteps faded in the hall, Alex hugged Glenn. "Thank you. Is he always so grumpy?"

"Well, actually yes, though he's usually not so talkative or accommodating," Glenn replied with a confused smile.

Alex snorted. "You call that accommodating?"

"Trust me dear, that was very accommodating. Now why don't you go get changed while I finish up here. I'll meet you out front in twenty minutes."

"Done." She gulped down the last of her coffee before rushing out of the room.

~ ~ ~

True to her word, Alex was waiting on the front steps when Glenn showed up. They went over a map of the surrounding property before agreeing on a five-mile trail that looped past the river near the back of the property. As Alex tightened her laces and stretched, Glenn disappeared around the corner of the house to shift into his raven form. Within minutes a gleaming, deep purple bird cawed at her from the tree.

As she jogged through the trails she felt the raven's steady flap of wings behind her. How odd it was, to feel such calm with his presence. What a fascinating and bizarre world she found herself in.

She heard the lapping of water not far off. Other sounds joined in. Grasshoppers and woodland bugs talked in the underbrush. Dew on the tress and ferns sparkled. It was cooler here in the shade. As the sweat ran down her back, she was thankful for the shadows. Small animals rustled nearby. If she didn't know better, she'd have thought she was home on Vancouver Island with Quinn waiting up at the house with hot chocolate.

She was still angry with her aunt for not telling her everything years ago. It could have saved her so much pain and confusion. If she'd known, perhaps she'd have started this journey long ago, before she was in danger. It certainly would have been a lot easier in college if she'd known why things frequently combusted around her or why her dreams seemed to predict the future. She'd been a freak. She would've like to not be a freak.

She brushed off thoughts of the past. None of that mattered now. It was ridiculous to complain when more important things needed her attention, like the sun and the trees, and a hidden fresh water lake she'd noticed on the map earlier. It was within the boundaries of the estate. Glenn said it was the perfect place for a rest before heading back to the house.

She slowed to a walk as the trail grew thicker. The scent from the water hovered in the air. Alex checked her timer. Thirteen minutes to run two and a half kilometers. Not bad but certainly not her best time either.

Ahead of her, Glenn perched on a low branch. She pushed through the foliage and came upon a small clearing with an emerald lake. Large boulders created a wall. She scrambled down to reach the water.

"I'm jumping in, Glenn," she shouted as she pulled off

her socks and shoes, and dove in the water. Behind her the Raven shrieked.

She squealed with unconcealed delight as her head broke the surface of the lake. "Glenn, get your feathered ass in here. It's perfect."

~ ~ ~

"I sent him home."

She shrieked. Frantically shoved the mass of wet, red tangles out of her eyes to see Collum standing next to her shoes. He was in fine form, dressed head to toe in black. Black track pants that hugged his quads. Black T-shirt that hugged his chest. She lost her breath for a minute.

"What are you doing here?"

"You told me you could save your own ass so I decided to see if it was true."

His arms were folded over his chest. Tattoos covered his muscled forearms. "Get out of the water, princess."

"I don't think so. Not with that look on your face I'm not."

"I don't have a look on my face."

"You sure as hell do have a look on your face."

"Get out of the water and show me what you know about protecting yourself."

"Yeah, cause that doesn't sound at all ominous. I'm good right here."

He growled at her like the predator he was. "I can see you shivering from here. Get out of the water. I'll give you a head start."

"Head start? What do you think's going to happen here?"

"You need to burn off some energy. I need to know if you can protect yourself. We're going to find out."

"I can't believe Glenn left me. Traitor." Her teeth chattered. She took perverse pleasure in seeing Collum grimace.

"He isn't a traitor. He's following orders. Now get out of the water before I come in and drag you out by that hair of yours."

Alex had forgotten about her hair and groaned at the mention of it. Goddamn hair would take hours to dry. "Well at least step back. You're blocking my path."

A wicked smile curled his lips. He retreated three steps before handing her a towel from behind his back.

She pulled herself out of the water and on to the rocks. Practically launched herself at him to get the offered towel. She was so cold she felt like her bones were going to crack.

"You know you're made of fire, right?"

"So you keep saying."

"You're standing there shivering so hard you look like you're having a seizure and I'm reminding you that your element is fire."

At her blank look, he stepped close and traced his finger along the flame tattoo that wrapped up her body.

"You are fire, Alex. Warm yourself."

He stroked the flames on her shoulder. Alex thought she might faint from his touch. He leaned down and licked the water off her skin. Her tattoo writhed, strained to reach him.

"Why is it doing that?"

"I'm fire. It recognizes itself in me—even if you don't yet. You aren't human anymore, Alex so stop acting like it. Stop pretending this is a holiday."

"I'm not pretending anything. This is my life. Stop treating me like I'm a child."

He ignored her. "Try to hit me."

"I'm not hitting . . ."

"Hit me, girl."

Finally, angry—really angry—she pulled back her fist and swung.

He blocked her, easily twisting her arm behind her back.

"I'm a dragon, Alex. You can't hit me with your fist. Use your fucking flames."

"Let go of me. You're hurting me."

"It doesn't hurt. You're an immortal. Now wake up and let your fire out."

"I don't know how," she cried.

Collum released her and stepped back. His voice was gentler when he spoke again. "You do know how. You fought off that raider in the parking lot. You've been dealing with this since you were eighteen, right? Channel it. You know what you feel like when the fire is rising."

She squared her shoulders. He was right. She never backed away from a fight and she wasn't going to now. But she wasn't going to let him off that easy.

"You're an asshole."

"He grinned down at her. "Babe, you ain't seen nothing yet. You ready?"

With a big breath and last long look at the boulder baking in the sun, she shoved her feet into her runners and replied, "I'm ready."

"Good, now put your hands out."

"Why?"

"Just put them out and stop asking me questions."

"Fine. Here." She thrust her palms up to his chin and stared defiantly at him.

He clasped her hands in his own. Alex felt the rush of heat flowing between them. He pulled her hands up to his mouth and blew little sparks onto her fingers.

"Quit flirting and do it," she grumbled to hide the catch in her throat.

"I'm showing you how simple this is, channeling energy into something I want. I want to burn you, Alex. I want to singe your flesh and taste your heat. That's what the beast in me wants because he knows you can take it."

The tattoo burned against her skin, squirmed with need. She pulled her hands away as a shiver raced up her spine.

"Let the flame off your flesh."

She thrust her chin out. "How?"

"Talk to it. That tattoo is more than a drawing. It exists to serve you. Visualize letting it free. Can you sense what it wants?"

Digging deep inside herself, she focused on the intensity of the feeling flowing from the tattoo into her. It wasn't alive, more like a manifestation of who she was now. Alex pictured the flame travelling to Collum. She closed her eyes. Ignored the noise around her. Felt the fire climb off her flesh. Felt it touch Collum as though it were her own hand. Startled, she opened her eyes to see fire wrapping around his hands, crawling up his chest.

His jaw was clenched. Sweat glistened on his top lip. She watched entranced.

"Call it back now," he said through gritted teeth.

"I don't want to yet. I like how this feels. I feel powerful."

He curled his fingers through her flame. Caressed the blaze crawling against him.

"Call it back now, baby," he said as he closed the distance between them. "Or I'm taking you right here and now."

She let him come. *I should have had this feeling from birth.* Fuck them for keeping her from it. Alex tested the heat. She reached into the flames climbing over Collum. Let them cover her skin. She could feel what he felt through the flame. It was agony. It was more pleasure than she'd ever thought to feel.

He grabbed her arms. Leaned down and smashed his mouth onto hers.

Their tongues met. Fire exploded behind her eyes. Her legs gave out.

Collum ripped his mouth away, drew himself back. "Take your fire back, Alex."

"No."

He planted himself firmly in front of her. "Do you want this?"

She matched his posture. "You know I do."

"Good. Use that to learn to fight," he growled. "Call your fucking fire back now."

She did as he asked. Focused on her flame and visualized it crawling back to her flesh. A little piece of his fire seemed to follow.

As soon as the flame retreated, he grabbed her hands and pulled her along behind him to the edge of the clearing. "Now, throw it at that tree."

"Throw the fire?"

"Yes. You can't outrun Wind. Water can drown you. Earth will try to swallow you. You must be able to control your flame, and your emotions, to defeat them."

She furrowed her brow, focusing her energy on the flame still crawling along her arms and legs. Visualized drawing it into her palm. Sparks ignited against her flesh. She pictured a ball. Commanded the sparks to join. Used the passion ignited by Collum to control her fire. Within seconds a fireball rested in her hand, waiting to do her bidding. She launched it at the coniferous tree Glenn had sat in earlier. The fire connected and shattered into the base of the tree like a lightning bolt. Bark flew in the air and the tree toppled over, smoldering at the base.

She jumped in the air and twirled around to high five Collum. "I did it. Holy shit. I can't believe that. Did you see it?"

"Glenn's gonna be choked. That was his favorite tree."

She smacked his chest. "What? Are you kidding me?"

He actually laughed. She almost begged him to kiss her again.

"Ow. Take it easy, I'm screwing with you. Keep that control and you'll do fine. But remember the tattoo is only a tool." He tapped her forehead. "You *are* fire. And this today," he swept his hand at the downed tree, "is only the beginning."

"I know, I know. Can't you let me have this little bit of excitement?"

"Keep practicing." He turned away.

"Where are you going?"

"I'm leaving."

Alex couldn't believe it when he started walking away. "You're actually leaving?"

He swung back around and his dark gaze pinned her. "Glenn will be right back. I can't stay out here with you all day, sweetheart. I have things to do."

"But I thought . . ."

"What did you think? That we'd play in the flowers all day?"

"Wow, okay. I get it."

"I don't think you do. I'm not your college buddy or your girlfriend. I'm a dragon, Alex, and my instinct is to score your flesh with my claws until you beg me to claim you. That's what *my* fire calls to in me." He turned as Glenn flew into the clearing. "So, I am going to leave you with the only being in the world I won't kill for being near you right now."

She gaped at him. "What if I want the same thing?"

He replied without looking at her. "I'm not having sex with you in a field. That isn't what we're going to be."

"We're going to be something?"

"You know as well as I do that we are," he said before leaving the clearing, and her, behind.

Chapter 16

Alex took her time heading home. What started out as a quick run at eight, dragged until after noon. She was proud of herself, annoyed at Collum, super turned on, and confused about how she could be, with everything else going on. She refused to look at Glenn, angry at him for ratting out her location to Collum. Thankfully, he didn't try to engage with her. When he shifted back into his human form she noticed his purple silk shirt and matching dress shoes, but refused to give him the satisfaction of complimenting his outfit.

She ran into Domhall on her way back into the house.

He looked at her wet hair and said, "So, how was the run? Tempting?"

She ignored his jibe. "It was fine. I'm on my way to take a shower."

"Doesn't seem fine. You know, we can leave anytime you want, right?"

"What are you talking about? I need to be here to find the witch."

"Maybe. Maybe not. Collum isn't the only one that can teach you. Some of us may have methods far preferable to his."

She dripped water on Glenn's perfectly polished floor and studied her grandfather. "Why did you agree my mother should marry the dragon? Why are you here, Domhall?"

"Who told you about that?"

"Aunt Quinn. If you hadn't interfered, none of this would've happened and I might know who I am."

His face twisted. Electricity in the room flickered on and off and a blue light surrounded him. "I'm here because you are my flesh and blood. *You* shouldn't be here with him. No dragon should be near my blood."

"But you agreed. You're an elder. Quinn said it was the elders who forced my mother to be with that killer."

"That's all they are you know. Killers. Every one of them." He spun around pointing at the walls. "This was his house too. She would have lived here—in this hovel."

"You haven't answered my question."

He shook his blond hair around his face. "You naïve thing. This isn't even about you."

Alex retreated from the crazed light in his eyes and stepped right into a hard chest. Heat formed a wall around her.

Collum spoke quietly. Placed comforting hands on her shoulders. "Dom, you're frightening your grandchild. This isn't the time or place."

"You, you're nothing but a beast."

"I know, but I'll keep her safe."

"From who?"

"From you. Take a breath for me, buddy."

"You aren't the saint the world thinks."

"No, I'm not."

Domhall shifted and the light around him changed to a pale aqua shade. "She doesn't have to be kept safe from me. I'm her grandfather."

Collum slowly pulled her behind him before replying, "Then stop scaring her, Dom. Get your shit under control."

The light around Domhall faded. He backed away from them both. "I . . . I'm sorry. It's this place. We shouldn't be here."

Collum simply nodded. "We'll leave soon."

Alex watched her grandfather leave without looking at her. She placed her face against Collum's spine.

He let out a breath and stepped away from her. "Are you okay?"

"I'm okay, but what was that?"

"That was Domhall. I told you he was close to the edge. Promise me you won't be alone with him again."

"I can't believe he would hurt me."

"Maybe not intentionally. But he's unpredictable. While he is inside the wards, it will prove . . . difficult for me to stop him if he loses it. Maybe hang out in your room until dinner."

"I don't want to be alone."

"Yes, you do."

She breathed in the scent of him. "I think I'd know what I want."

He placed his hands on her hair and curled his fingers around the wet strands. "Do you? Because I do. I knew the minute I saw you in that ugly housecoat in Quinn's kitchen." He nudged her toward her room. Said, "Now, go away before I do something I regret," before pulling his cell phone out of his pocket and walking away from her, again.

As she hurried down the corridor to her room, she realized their time was inevitable. He was demanding and pompous, infuriating and bossy. And she was incredibly, unabashedly, excited by the prospect of being with him. She closed her bedroom door, wondering if she was ready.

Chapter 17

The knock on the door came at eleven that night. Alex had spent the day in her room. Glenn found her earlier and mentioned both men would be unavailable to join her for dinner. He'd brought her a tray of chicken and steamed asparagus. She'd been glad for the reprieve.

She'd fantasized about what she'd say when Collum came to her. About what she'd do. But fantasy was altogether different than reality. In her fantasy, she retained some control, but Alex knew he would not be the guy to let her lead. He'd sweep her away until all that was left was her core melting.

She opened the door. He stood there looking larger and more beautiful than she thought a man could. It was in his eyes. The way he looked right into her. It was haunting.

"I can't do it," she told him when he moved to come in.

He stood before her with his legs parted and his eyes taking on the red glow again. His voice ragged. "Don't say no, Alex. Let me kiss you, like you want to be loved."

Her breath caught in her throat and she backed into the room. Collum followed. Stalking. Predatory. With a wave of his hand, the door shut and the fireplace roared to life. He backed her into the wall, placed her arms above her head.

"Tonight, you're mine . . . One night, Alex."

He covered her entire body with the length of his, driving heat over her skin.

She leaned in.

"That's it, baby." Collum dipped his mouth and licked her lips. He held both her arms in his one hand. He grabbed her hair and brought it to their mouths. "Catch fire," he exhaled on to her tongue.

Alex erupted. Jolted against him and moaned. Her tattoo writhed against her skin as sparks burst along her flesh.

Collum stroked the pulse at the base of her neck while grinding his body in a steady rhythm against hers. Her arms still held tight above her body, his tongue still tasting her. He hadn't even kissed her yet and Alex could barely think. His hand moved lower, pushing aside the fabric of her bathrobe.

She moaned louder, breathless. There was no way she could speak. The ends of her hair caught fire.

"That's it, let go with me. I've been thinking about this all night. Thinking about your little sounds."

Collum pulled the robe off her body. She felt the muscles in his arms clench against her. His eyes turned completely red. He gripped her waist. Hands dipped to her thighs and back up. She shivered as he lightly traced over the fur at her core. His palm rough as it continued up to cup her breast. His teeth scratched against her flesh before taking her nipple in his mouth.

Her strength gave out just as Collum placed his knee between her legs. He let her arms go. She clutched his shoulders like a lifeline. Each suckle on her breast drew fire up from her core. She gripped the tattoos along his chest and arms.

When he raised his head, he was a man possessed. He smashed his mouth to hers and fit both hands in her burning hair. Their skin burned each other. As their tongues fought and their mouths fit together, Alex ignited. Liquid flame poured from her flesh.

She screamed into his mouth. Collum dragged one hand from her hair to stroke her passion higher. It was almost brutal—the intensity, the need to join. He pressed his fingers inside her and rubbed his thumb across her clitoris before letting go of her tongue to rake his teeth along her neck and push her harder against the wall.

Alex was lost to everything but his hands on her and the fire raging over her body. She knew nothing but the need to be claimed and to claim. Abruptly, he lifted her into his arms and laid her on the floor as he removed his clothing.

She watched greedily, took in the specimen before her. He was dark, untamed. His arms and legs thick with ropes of muscle. His chest carved from dragon bone. She'd never seen anything as brutal, as erotic.

"Alex," he said, in a guttural, inhuman voice. "You are mine."

She looked at his glorious, battled scarred body—a fallen angel who was going to take her to the edge of insanity. "I want this as much as you. Don't stop."

He fell to his knees and traced the outline of her flames with his finger. The fire followed his touch.

"You're going to come for me now." He leaned down and took her clit in his mouth.

She thrashed on the floor. Her nails scored his scalp.

His hands forced her hips into place, as he tasted more. Thrust his tongue deeper.

Alex was burning up. Her blood turned to lava. She screamed in agony as she came. Waves of fire poured from her body on to Collum's tongue. He sucked harder, breathing in her fire, consuming her. As her final waves pulsed onto his tongue, he lifted his head and roared. She reached up to grab his face and he thrust into her body. Ecstasy raged through her as their bodies joined.

As she pushed her hands into his hair claws exploded from her fingers. Flame climbed from her to wrap around them. Smoke from his body covered them.

"Collum?"

"Let it happen, baby. You can't hurt me." He slowed

his thrusting to match the tempo of her tattoo. It had begun crawling against him the moment they joined.

Nothing had prepared her for the sensuality of what was happening. Her blood was lava beneath her flesh. She ached. Breathed into his sinuous strokes. Could feel the waves of another orgasm beginning in her toes.

"Easy love," he said. "I need more of you yet. Let me take all of you."

Alex stared hard, lost in him.

"Give me your mouth, Alexedria."

She leaned into him, confused for a moment, waiting for his lips to touch hers.

"Don't think Alex . . . feel." Collum drew her tongue into his mouth and blew smoke from his body into hers.

The smoke moved inside her, found the nerve endings of her tattoo. She felt the aching, a calling to her fire. Her flame pulsed against his flesh, bit in, branded him.

With a final thrust they both shattered. As Alex lost control the room around them caught fire, their skin singed in the heat. For a moment, it seemed they were nothing but molten energy in a room aflame with their passion.

As they came back down, Collum pulled his hands from her burning hair, and pushed through the flames to touch the floor. She watched him, fascinated as he closed his eyes. His breathing calmed, a blue light flowed from his hands. The flames on the floor faded. Alex's tattoo slowly released its hold on his skin and curled back to her body. Her skin cooled.

She reached up to touch his shoulder where the tattoo of a perfectly formed flame lay seared into his skin.

"What just happened?"

"Our fire claimed us."

"But how did you stop the fire in the room?"

He shrugged. "I envisioned what I wanted to happen."

"Is it always like that?" She groggily curled into him.

Collum stood, lifted her into his arms and carried her to the bed. "No, babe, it is never like that." He stroked her hair and lay beside her.

"But how did you know I wouldn't hurt you? Did you know my fire would brand you?"

One side of his upper lip curled. "I am where fire began. Flame will always reach for me."

Collum stretched out, caressed her. She let him, finally feeling safe and utterly full.

As she let go of the night, she remembered what he'd called her. "Wait, why did you call me Alexedria?"

She caught his grin as her eyes drifted shut.

"Because, baby, it's your name."

Chapter 18

The woman climbed out of the lake; moonlight bounced off her glistening skin. Vines of ink twisted themselves around her body. They started at the base of her toe, crossed the foot, wound around the muscled calf of the right leg and skimmed her leg up to the edge of her abdomen, where a small flower dropped off and waited to be tasted. The tattoo continued around her hips, encasing them in a caress, before it whispered across the flat of her pelvis and small of her back. Each rib was covered in living art. Buds folded under the breast. More flowers dripped delicately down the arch of the breasts. The vine rested against her heart, traveled up to kiss the side of her neck and hide behind her ear. Then slid down the back of one shoulder, wrapped ever so delicately around her bicep, licked her elbow, and gently fell to her wrist where one final leaf slept. Waiting with practiced ease on the base of her finger.

She had ice-blond hair that glistened as though blue fire lapped at its edges. She was tall with a lean, muscled physique. Her skin was alabaster. Her eyes were a deep rich plum, too deep to be black.

The figure smiled wistfully and caressed her tattoo. Slowly she began to unwind the vine from her arm, pulling it away from her skin, in a dance that was both sensual and terrifying. She moved toward Alex loosening the vine as she walked. Her look felt warm and soft. It felt welcome. Like love.

She studied Alex for what seemed like hours before

walking away. Though she wanted to beg her to stay, Alex knew it would do no good.

Alex woke to the sound of a heartbeat and the remnants of her dream. Felt the body of her lover pressed against her chest and smiled into his skin.

"Good morning," Collum hummed as he kissed her head. "Did you sleep well?"

"I think so. I had strange dreams all night. Some of them involved dragons in the dark and wings encrusted in black onyx. Others were of a woman? Maybe an angel?" She shook her head and stretched beside him, arching her back. "And you?"

"Well, some little thing kept kicking me all night. I'm quite sure somewhere between three and four a.m., her tattoo did something super inappropriate to me."

"It did not. You're making that up."

"I never lie. It's one of the rules of being a guardian. C'mon, we better get up before Dom comes looking."

Alex splayed her fingers over his chest. "I'm a grown woman. And it's not like he's a typical grandfather that needs to be worried about my virtue. Who cares if he finds you here?"

Collum reached for her hand. "It's easier if we don't have to answer questions right now."

"I thought you didn't care what people thought of you." She curled her fingers into his chest hair. "I don't mind answering questions. Not that I have any answers. I haven't had time to give what happened too much thought yet. Only that it happened and it was beyond anything I've ever experienced."

He leaned back. "I simply prefer to keep things private. I'm not interested in an inquisition."

Alex sat perfectly still for a moment before she collected herself. "You came to me remember? I didn't realize I was something to deal with." She whipped the blanket around herself as she climbed out of the bed. "I don't need this, Collum. I don't know what all that fire and smoke shit meant to you, but I thought it meant we were more than a discussion topic for a grandfather I barely know."

"You're acting childish. There's no conspiracy here. I'm not interested in dealing with your grandfather right now. Can't you respect that? See the wisdom in it?"

"All I see is a guy who is having second thoughts and I'm not interested in that. You can act as calm and mighty as you want, but I see the truth."

She stumbled in the mass of blankets pooled around her ankles, pushed her hair out of her eyes, and yanked the blankets higher.

"And you can call me childish all you want. What I see is someone who, even at two thousand years old, doesn't know how to be a grown man. But you're right. I have too many other things to concentrate on right now, like how to stop my bloody hair from starting on fire every time I get pissed off." She gave him a scathing look. "I almost forgot, the women of my race are warriors, not toys. I'm not playing your game, Collum. Get out of my room—now."

She swept into the bathroom with all the glory she could muster and refused to look back.

~ ~ ~

After a twenty-minute shower Alex returned to find the bedroom warmed by a fire Collum had started. She fingered the robe he'd left on the bed for her and felt her resolve strengthen. The big guy was an idiot and she didn't have time to deal with that right now. She dressed in jeans, (the good ones that made her ass look phenomenal) and a knit gray sweater Aunt Quinn had given her last Christmas. She fluffed her hair and headed out of the room to find breakfast. She wasn't about to let some guy get in the way of her and Glenn's cinnamon bun, even if he was a Dragon King. She'd simply pretend it had never happened. She wouldn't think about her toes curling or her flames caressing his skin, or the fact that she could still feel him inside her.

Oh Christ, she thought as she wandered out in to the hall.

She found Domhall in the kitchen filling his plate with a mountain of eggs and fruit.

"Morning, kiddo. I ah, I'm sorry about yesterday. It was a bad day for me. I get them sometimes, but I'm tip-top today. Glenn made Eggs Benedict this morning. Want some?"

Alex refused to ignore her grandfather no matter what Collum thought so she walked over to him and kissed his cheek. "Good morning. Yes, thanks. I'm starving and would love to eat."

"Good, glad to see the events of the past few days haven't affected your appetite. It's important to keep your strength up." He winked at her. "Well, you look gorgeous. Trying to impress someone?"

"Nah, I just happen to be gorgeous," she teased him back.

"Thank God for small favors. There is no one here you need to impress. You come from one of the strongest blood lines in our world."

"Except that I'm only a half-breed, right? And I might be a dangerous one at that."

Domhall responded with a slight nod. "Right, we can't know. But I know my daughter and she'd never let someone unworthy near her. You can trust in that child."

"Can't you tell me anything else?' Don't you have any ideas about who my father is? I mean if you are so powerful, shouldn't you be able to figure this out?"

"Trust me, if, and when I can tell you something, I will. Things come to us in time. Patience my dear, is a virtue when you live forever."

Domhall handed her a plate of food piled as high as his and gestured to her to join him at the table.

Moments later, Collum walked in and headed over to the platters of food left out by Glenn.

She was secretly thrilled when he gaped at her in her jeans.

"Close your mouth man. That's my granddaughter."

"I don't have time for this," Collum mumbled. I'll be in my office." He rushed out of the room without a backward glance.

"You really shouldn't tease him, Alex."

"I'm going to have nothing to do with him for a long time. You can trust that. Look, I saw a beautiful garden on the way down from my room that I missed last night. I'm going to go sit out there and enjoy the sun while I eat."

"Be kind kid. We're only men. And that one, even if he is a twit, will protect you with his life. He took an oath. And you, you are perfection, like your mother and grandmother. Be gentle."

"I'm the new one here, remember. You two are so busy talking about protecting me. How about if you learn how to talk to me? And, like I've been reminded since we arrived, you aren't only men." Alex allowed Domhall no time to reply as she stomped out of the room.

~ ~ ~

In the garden the smell of heather lingered in the air. She'd never been much of a gardener. That was Aunt Quinn's forte. She could imagine reading a book and drinking tea there on another day, in another life. Alex found an inviting table and chair in a corner half hidden by English Ivy. The late morning heat soaked into her skin through her sweater.

She savored the flavors of the morning meal. Glenn had outdone himself. As she relaxed, she thought about how strange it was that she was eating Eggs Benedict while sitting in a castle garden. Then again, how weird was it that she'd had sex with a dragon and that she was a descendent of an immortal race. If she'd had any girlfriends, this would make for one hell of a phone session.

She studied her hands. They looked normal. She pulled her sweater sleeves up and focused on her arms. The tattoo lay quiet against her skin. She blew on it, hoping for a reaction. Nothing. Played with her hair. Tasted it. Nothing. She removed her shoes and curled into the patio chair. It was warm and luxurious, like everything else of Collum's. The sun slowly lulled her to sleep. Let her protectors find out what they needed to. Maybe tomorrow they would set off for the witch.

Chapter 19

"Wake up Alex. It's time."

The voice echoed on the air. Alex pushed tangled red tresses out of her eyes, prepared to forgive Collum.

"It's time. We are waiting. Are you ready?"

The echo was different. There wasn't laughter in it. There wasn't annoyance either. She sat up, startled out of her sleeping state.

"Neeren? You can't be here."

"I can be anywhere. You'll find out soon. Are you ready? All you need to do, is take my hand. There is no place for you here. You belong with me."

The hand reaching out to hers was sculpted with short, clean finger nails. The air around him shimmered with intensity and . . . something else. Was it ease? He was standing in a dragon's home like it was his right. In a moment of clarity, Alex understood that this was a man who was never told no. Not because people feared him, but because no one would think to say it.

"You need to leave. Collum could come out here at any moment. Or Domhall. Look, you might not know who they are, but it would be safer for you if you left now. Besides, I'm not ready."

Neeren offered a languid, lazy smile. "You can be assured that I know everything I need. Now, we are all waiting. It's time to come with me. Take my hand."

The desire to reach out to him almost overrode her good sense. She shook her head to clear her mind but the need to go to him remained. It wasn't sexual. More like spirituality?

Was that it? Her fire didn't reach for him the way it did Collum. It was deeper—a force in her gut—something trying to push through her skin, through her bones.

"Look, I want to know more about myself and believe you have the answers. I probably will come with you, but this is not the best time. There are things I need to figure out. Can't you wait a little while?"

"No, this is the time. There is nothing more important than coming with me. I hold your answers, not some witch."

"How do you know about the witch?"

"I told you already. I know everything I need to."

"But . . ."

"Alex?"

Alex turned to see Domhall stride in to the garden.

"I was coming out to see if you wanted some juice," he said.

She jumped in front of Neeren to block him from Domhall. She couldn't bear for him to be hurt, even if she didn't know why. "You have to go now."

The same quiet smile remained on his face as Neeren said, "It's okay, Alex, he won't hurt me."

"Are you nuts? I may not know everything about this world, but I do know that he is one immortal you don't want to mess with."

"Agreed. I don't and I won't. Will I, Domhall?"

Before her grandfather could respond Collum ran in to the garden. In his palm lay a ball of fire. He stopped beside Domhall. Alex cringed as he said, "Step the fuck away from her."

Neeren smirked. "Oh for Creator's sake. This is getting ridiculous. I won't take her against her will, but I will take her. You are, The Guardian, I presume?"

Collum nodded. "And you would be?"

"Neeren. I am here for Alex. She belongs with me."

"Well, Neeren, you can't hope to take her from me here. This is your last warning."

Beside him, Domhall stood quietly.

Alex stretched her arms out in front of Neeren. "Stop it. Please, Collum, I'm okay. I believe he won't hurt me. Neeren, can't you give me more time?"

"This is our time, Alex. Say goodbye to the dragon."

Before Alex could react, Domhall flashed to her and pulled her away from Neeren. Chaos erupted around her.

Collum hurled a blue flame at Neeren. The man dodged left. Collum lobbied fire balls across the garden. Neeren evaded each one. Launched himself at Collum, releasing a stream of ice into the flame as he did so. The ice knocked Collum backward. Neeren grabbed his wrists. Collum flipped his hands out, twisted Neeren's head down and smashed the man's skull into his knee. Neeren dropped, then rolled away shooting another stream of ice at Collum.

Alex clutched Domhall's hand. She stood frozen. It was too much like the morning she'd been attacked. She tried to scream at them to stop but the words lodged in her throat. Choked her.

"You might be bigger, Dragon. You will tire faster."

Collum snarled, said, "You wanna tell me how you're controlling that water, boy? Not that it matters. No creature will take her from me while I live."

Neeren grinned. "Then I guess I better kill you."

Alex stood paralyzed as the two men advanced on each other. The garden was awash in flame and ice and she wondered if either would come out alive. An array of heathers, ferns and tulips lay at her feet—their beauty destroyed by chaos. A tremor began in her stomach, rolled up through her chest. She found her voice then, begged for them to stop, but neither man listened. Maybe it was in her mind.

Domhall laid a hand on her shoulder. "Settle, Alex. Collum is letting off steam. He hasn't even let his dragon loose. That's how little concern he has that Neeren can take him. Super cocky of him, but dragons are known for being cocky. Anyway, Neeren's having fun. He hasn't had a good fight in years. Let them go at it for a minute."

She shook her head. Her voice rang out. "What are you talking about? They're killing each other."

"They're not killing each other. If it eases your mind, I can tell you that Neeren is incapable of hurting you and he knows you care for Collum. Yet, in the end the choice is yours to stop it."

She whipped her head back and forth between the two men and Domhall. "What are you talking about? Why aren't you stopping it? Why aren't you helping Collum?"

"Really? That dragon doesn't need my help. He's Collum Thronus."

He said it like she was supposed to know what the hell he meant.

"Besides, I don't want to help him. There's something bigger at work here, granddaughter. Don't you want to find out more about who you are? All you have to do is tell me."

She studied the two men locked in battle. The idea of either one of them being hurt ripped her gut in half.

Both men felt like home.

Collum made her laugh. He annoyed the hell out of her. He also made her toes curl and she wanted to wake up next to him again. She knew without a shadow of a doubt he would protect her with his life.

But something inside woke up the moment she met Neeren. A light that felt like a thread pulled her to him. Or to what she suspected he meant to her understanding of who she was. She refused to try and figure out Domhall's angle. No one could figure out Domhall. All she knew was that she couldn't risk one of them dying.

She glared at her grandfather. "Stop them. I'm asking you to stop them."

Domhall waved his hand. The flames and ice dissipated. His voice rose above the ferocity around them. Took on a hollow sound, like the earth rumbled inside him. "You will end this now. It is over."

Both men fell to their knees.

"Dom, you fucking idiot," Collum bellowed.

"Sorry, old man. Alex is leaving with Neeren. It's time. You will let it happen."

Collum fought against invisible bonds. "I knew you couldn't handle this. I never should have trusted you."

Domhall waved his hand again. The bonds holding Neeren fell way. He stretched out to his full height.

"It is better to only trust family," Neeren said before walking to where Domhall and Alex stood. "Isn't that right, Grandfather?"

Alex spun between the three men. "What are you talking about? What is going on?"

Behind her, Collum continued to punch at the energy field holding him in place.

Her grandfather spoke. "Collum, stop before you hurt yourself."

"You piece of shit. Your own wife wanted her hidden. How can you do this?"

"My wife wanted her hidden from the other elders, not from her own family. Do not judge me. It took me years to find Neeren. I will not leave the care of my family to those corrupted by power."

"You're the corrupt one, Dom. You've lost the fucking plot man. I found the witch. She can help us."

"We don't need the witch, Collum. I have my family. I need no outsider to help Alex learn her powers. Her family will do that."

With a final strike, Collum smashed through the energy field holding him. He advanced on Domhall and Neeren. Alex noticed the incredulous look in their eyes. The death looming in Collum's.

"You will not take her from me," he growled. "We are claimed."

Even the air in the room froze as all eyes turned to Alex. She pushed the hair back from her face and said, "Oh sure, now you decide to tell them?"

The men all began talking at once—The fight forgotten.

"Are you kidding me?" Domhall asked.

"It matters not. She is still coming with me. Take my hand, Alex," Neeren demanded.

"I'm sorry, lover. I can't let them take you," Collum whispered while walking toward her.

"All of you. Shut up now," Alex shrieked. "Collum, stop moving. First you call me yours, then you push me away because you don't want complications, and now you decide to tell my grandfather we had sex! Considering I don't even know what claimed means, I'm declaring I don't give a shit about it. None of you get to decide what to do with me. I do. I'm taking some of my power back."

Neeren chuckled. "You made the right decision."

"Shut up, Neeren," she yelled.

Collum advanced. "Alex, you cannot trust these men. I won't let you go with them."

Domhall interrupted, saying, "If you don't allow it, I will rain fire down on your home. There is no choice left here."

"Try it asshole. This house was built with fire."

Alex stared at Collum while admonishing her grandfather. "No one is raining down fire on anyone. I won't accept Collum being harmed." She turned to Domhall. "Are you listening, Grandfather?"

When he nodded she turned back to Collum. Prayed he

would understand. "Collum, I'm sorry but I'm going. I need to do this. I believe that he is worth trusting."

She turned to Neeren and grabbed his hand. "Take me home."

Before any man could make a move, Neeren grinned, and they disappeared.

Chapter 20

Collum lunged for the space where Alex stood, grabbing only air. He whirled on Domhall. Landed a solid left hook to the man's jaw. "You son of a bitch. Do you even know what you've done?"

The punch rocked Domhall off his feet for a moment. "Of course, I know what I've done. I take care of my own," he replied while rubbing his jaw.

"Like you took care of Gray?"

Domhall leaned down. Plucked a tattered daisy out of the filth. "Exactly like that. We're no longer a concern of yours. I release you from the request Kaylen made of you."

"Tell me where he took her."

"Not a chance. And he didn't take her. She left you of her own free will. Did you honestly think you'd be able to keep her? She's a Taleisin."

"I'm a fucking king. I have every right. No matter what game you're playing, we've claimed each other. Even you can't stop that."

"You lost. She's gone. Don't forget that she was raised as a human. To her, this claiming means nothing. If it had, she would've never left you." He crushed the daisy petals in his hand. "Look around you, Coll. I'm leaving you to your lonely and old existence. I hope your rocks can keep you warm at night, for Alexedria never will."

Domhall swept his hand out. Power lifted Collum off his feet. He flew back against the concrete wall of the garden. The concrete crumbled beneath the force. Landed in a pile on top of him.

"That's for touching my granddaughter," Domhall said. He straightened his jacket. "I'll be off now. No need to worry about me. I've already called for a car to take me back to the airport. Places to go you know."

Collum, pushed the rubble of his back. Watched Domhall leave. Insane as he was, Domhall was also right. She'd left him. She'd chosen to go with this Neeren. Family? If that were true, it meant Gray had sinned far more than any had guessed. He wondered if Kaylen had known.

Chapter 21

Alex clung to Neeren's hand and refused to look back. She knew it was a small act of betrayal on her part to leave Collum the way she did. But, they hadn't talked about a future and they had no past. She only knew that this was the time to find out more about who she was. Collum had been right that morning. It wasn't time to create more confusion in her life, or to complicate it with a relationship.

"We are here."

Alex looked around. "How did you do that?"

"We came through a portal."

"I need to sit down. And maybe rum. You have any rum? I'm beginning to think I'm gonna need a lot to drink today."

Neeren grinned. "Good idea. It is a celebration. You are returned to us. I will pour and we will talk. Then I will introduce you to the others."

Alex regarded the room. A glass wall opened out to the ocean. The space was bright and light. Palm trees dotted the distant cliffs. "Are we hanging over the ocean here?"

"Stunning, isn't it." Neeren strolled to the corner bar and poured them two glasses of rum. "Have you tried this before? Zaya Rum? It's a bit sweet, but still a rich, textured rum for sipping."

She sat on the edge of a graphite colored leather couch in front of the window. "Don't do that yet. I don't want to have a conversation about your taste in alcohol. Tell me what you and Domhall were talking about. You called him grandfather. For some reason, I believe you're telling the truth. Who are you?"

Neeren adjusted his long frame to sit beside her. His movements were lithe, graceful, unhurried. Alex wondered if he always moved like that. Quiet, self-assured, self-aware. He turned his yellow eyes to her and raised an eyebrow. He said nothing, just let her look at him until she understood.

"You're my brother, aren't you?"

Light lit his features. "I am, though, much older. I knew about you when you were born. We all did, but they took you. We spent years looking for you. Even with all our power and persuasion, we couldn't find you. I am happy to finally meet you, sister." He reached up and stroked her cheek affectionately. "You cannot imagine what it was like. Knowing you had been ripped away from us."

Alex gulped the Zaya. "You're right, I can't imagine. I thought everyone assumed when my mother died, I died with her."

"We knew. We felt you. We couldn't find you."

She sunk into the couch. "Oh God— This whole time? Can you tell me why I'm believed to be such a threat?"

"I cannot speak for the Elementals, sister. I can only speak for myself and for what Domhall has told me. I won't tell you lies. I won't hold anything back. Are you ready for a long afternoon?"

The sun rested high in the sky. Water reflected light onto her skin. The warmth soothed her and she focused on Neeren. Every part of her existence had been encased in tales, fabricated by people wanting to protect her, hide her, hurt her.

"I want to know who I am. Tell me."

"I knew you were strong." He settled beside her on the couch. "Domhall found me ten years ago. You are correct when you say he is not to be crossed. He is the most powerful being I have ever encountered. I doubt any of the Elementals truly understands this. No creature outside of my people has been able to find this place before. Yet, Domhall simply walked in the front door one day and introduced himself to me. Much like you and I sit today, we poured a drink and chatted about all that had come before."

"Ten years ago. And none of you reached out to me? Do you know what the past ten years have been for me?"

He reached for her hand. Smiled gently. "Yes, sister, I do. You needed to grow up. You needed to experience life and death, love and loss. How could you comprehend this world before now? You needed lovers, you needed to defeat bullies, you needed to struggle and survive. If we had brought you here earlier, you would be a very different person, one likely to make mistakes. Do you see?"

Alex thought about the night her parents died. "I don't yet, but I'm listening."

He chuckled. "You are hot blooded. You chose a dragon for a lover. What did I expect?"

"Why don't you start by telling me what we are?"

"That is complicated. We are many things. We are Immortal. We are Elemental. We are Parthen. The tattoo you carry on your skin and the fire that is such a part of you is something I cannot claim to have. I was gifted with power over water and I control it. However, I must live by it. It feeds me. I suspect this is why you are drawn to your dragon—the fire and all." His eyes sparkled as he looked at her.

"Are you teasing me? How can you tease me right now?"

"Why not? You are immortal. You are power. You are about to get everything you desire. It is a good day, sister. Embrace it."

It was impossible to miss his complete yet humble satisfaction with himself and his life. "You are so . . . different. Why are you so at ease about all of this?"

"Now comes the part about the other half of who we are. Our father was the King of the Parthen. Like all good fairy tales, when he met our mother they fell passionately and violently in love. After she stopped trying to kill him, they married. It had to be kept secret of course. The Elementals would never allow the union of the two. But it was true love. For over a hundred years, they lived and loved and led our people. I was raised to be a King. My life was easy, sister. Then came the day we found out Mother was pregnant again. Our people came from across the globe to celebrate the news. The pregnancy was easy. Mother was strong—a warrior. I was a proud son—soon to be a brother."

"How old were you?"

"I had been alive ninety-seven years when you were born, Alex. Mother's pregnancy was one of the greatest and scariest times of my life. We all knew what it meant. I had been hidden from the Elementals. You would have to be too."

"But why do they care so much about this. What are the Parthen? I'm sure there have been others who have loved other races?"

He tossed back his rum before saying, "We are Dreamwalkers and seen as a threat. Though the Elementals have powers far vaster than we do, they are afraid of what we can do to their minds. To have a child who holds the power of the elements, who can come to you in your dreams? Imagine what they could do? Imagine what we can do? Imagine being able to use your fire to kill your enemy while he slept. This is what they are afraid of. This, is why you were hidden."

"And we are the only two in the world who can do this?"

"We are the only two in the world who are half Elemental and half Parthen. It is our Elemental side that allows us to enter their dreams. The Elementals carry a natural ability to mind block. While we can freely walk through others' dreams, none before us have been able to enter an Elemental's mind. Another Parthen who might try it would be sensed trying to enter the subconscious. Our mixed blood allows us to walk through those barriers."

"So, they're right. They had no idea what I even was and still, they were right. We are dangerous."

"They could be right. They are not. We are not killers. Remember this, sister. You are a warrior yes, but there are rules. These were taught to me as a child. We do not kill the defenseless, even if they have wronged us. A death, a kill, is only honorable when they can fight back."

Neeren grinned again and uncurled his frame to stand. "Would you like more rum?"

Alex handed him her cup. Watched as the sun slowly descended. The ocean below was quiet, the surface as clear as glass. "That's strange. I thought the ocean would be rougher."

Neeren handed her a glass, refilled. "It follows my emotions and I am at peace right now. Today my sister came home. It is a peaceful day."

"Why didn't our mother tell her family about you, about any of this?"

"Perhaps it was an attempt to protect me. Perhaps she assumed there would be plenty of time after you were born. Our father ignored all caution and rushed to her when he found out she'd been given to that monster."

"And he was murdered."

Waves crashed below them for a moment, the only indication of Neeren's inner turmoil.

"You must hate them all," she said. "I hate them right now. And Domhall was a part of this. You know that right, that he's an elder?"

Neeren grinned mischievously. "Indeed, I know this. But today isn't a day for hate, little sister. Our parents knew the risks. I'm only sad you didn't get a chance to know them."

The rum eased the tears at the edge of her throat. Two lives lost because of hatred, because of her.

Neeren sighed. "Please don't blame yourself. I felt the same for a very long time. That my life had somehow led to this outcome, but they made their choices. They would have changed nothing even if they'd known what would happen."

"I'm jealous of you, you know. You had all those years with our parents. I had nothing."

Neeren walked to the toffee colored lounger on the other side of the room. He retrieved a thick cream cashmere throw, shook his head again, and returned to lay the blanket over her.

"And I, little sister, am jealous of you. You grew up knowing nothing of war and hate. I was trained from birth to become a shadow. Was reminded daily that it was my duty to protect my people by staying in the dark. After father died and I became King, I climbed out of those shadows. Refuse to have them bind me any further. I choose now to protect my home and my people by my resolve and my strength. I am not a dark being and I refuse to live like one. As should you. That's why I brought you here. Enough hiding."

"But the Elementals will come. Eventually they'll find out about us. I was being tracked before. It was only Collum and Domhall that kept them at bay."

"So, let them come. We *are* power. The Parthen are a strong and vast race of shifters. Our grandfather will come too. He will let no-one harm you. And let us not forget about your dragon."

As the sun set, Alex burrowed beneath the blanket. It was warm here, wherever here was. "He isn't my dragon." She ignored the voice inside telling her, she knew he already was.

"He has protected you since before your birth, Alex. All immortals bow to Collum Thronus. He would have taken me in that fight if Domhall hadn't stepped in. The dragons don't appoint Kings lightly. Plus, he's been Guardian to all the immortals longer than either of us have been alive. This has nothing to do with bloodlines and everything to do with power. And he holds it all." He shrugged and smiled at her. "Whether you are ready to accept it or not, he is your dragon."

"I don't want to talk about him right now." Alex stood up and swayed slightly. The blanket was still wrapped around her shoulders. Her hair lay in a tangle around her face.

Neeren laughed. "As you wish. Come with me. I'll take you to your room so you can sleep off the rum. Are you hungry? I'll have someone bring you dinner. Why don't you take the time to rest and we will talk again later? The nights are long and beautiful here. I'll walk you by my ocean and you can meet your people."

Chapter 22

Collum paced in front of the fire in the great room, watching the twilight with a bottle of whiskey by his side. *She left me.* She'd taken another's hand and walked away. He wanted to stand on the roof and tell the moon to fuck off. Instead, he tipped the bottle to his mouth, chugged, and swore at shadows.

He thought back to the day he'd first met Alex. Kaylen begged him to save the baby. She'd been a fragile bundle of blubber and he'd been terrified. He'd never held a baby. He'd been trained to kill things, to exact punishment. She'd been his chance at redemption. Look at him now—all the work he'd done to make her disappear and he'd failed. Been too cocky. Then again, he'd planned on fighting off Elementals, not a man who could open portals.

Somehow, Domhall had known. Fucking Domhall. He never should have trusted that lunatic.

He silently raged to the wind and the dark. She was gone. After two thousand years, he'd found her in the most unexpected place and she'd left him. Collum pitched the empty bottle into the fire and reached for another. Steam poured off his body. His wings tensed, shifted beneath his skin.

He barely had a glance for his ancestral home. The history that usually burrowed into his bones to calm him had no effect tonight. His body ached to fight and kill. It's what he was good at. What his father trained him to do. He threw the second bottle at the fireplace to watch it shatter. To rain liquid over fire. He failed. He never fucking failed. When he found the son of a bitch that took her, he'd break him slowly, and relish every goddamn second of it.

~ ~ ~

The knocking on the door barely broke through the haze in Collum's mind. Glenn entered without waiting for an answer.

"Before you bite my head off, you should know you have a visitor."

"Get out. What part of don't disturb me don't you get?"

"You may have most of the village terrified of you. You may have most of the dragons bowing and scraping to you like you're some kind of king or something. You don't pay me enough for that."

"I am a king and I pay you a goddamn fortune."

"Yeah, funny how it doesn't matter." Glenn laughed. "As I said you have a visitor."

Collum snarled low in his throat and turned back to pick up the fourth bottle. "Get rid of him. I have nothing to say to anyone."

"Well, I could do that, but I'm not going to. I suspect *she* isn't one who takes no for an answer very often."

"He's right, *mi amour*, I don't."

A tiny creature pushed past Glenn and strode into Collum's hall like she owned it. Her waist length, mahogany hair flew out behind her. Hazel eyes framed by lush black lashes, filled with laughter. She strutted into his home wearing knee high black stiletto boots and red leather pants, and flopped in the chair closest to his bar.

"Hey, big guy, chill. You called me. Any more of that whiskey hanging around? It's been a long flight and my feet are killing me."

Glenn cleared his throat. "My lord, may I present, Maria Del Voscovo—The Witch."

The woman lounging on Collum's chair said, "Ah, Glenny, what a great intro. You should get a raise. But you guys can just call me Mar."

Collum remained silent. He blinked. The woman in front of him walked in looking like sex on a stick and knew it. Her perky breasts pushed up and spilled over the bustier she wore. Leather pants moulded to her flesh like a second skin.

"So, what do they call you? I mean I can't keep saying big guy, can I? Though it does have a certain ring. Have you looked in the mirror lately?" She winked. "Taking steroids, are we?"

Collum choked on the mouthful of whiskey he'd just swallowed.

"Woo there, you might want to slow down. Can't hold your liquor? It's okay, not everyone can. Speaking of which, I'll take mine with two ice cubes."

Glenn burst out laughing and shut the door behind him as he left.

Collum gaped at her. This couldn't be the powerful witch he'd been told of. "Who the hell are you? I sought a great sorceress, not a wet behind the ears, party girl."

"Yeah, I get that sometimes. Stereotype much? We can't all be about fire and brimstone. I like my life a little less bloody, thanks."

He covered his face with his hands. "I can't deal with this right now."

"Sure, you can. Now go ahead and pour me that drink. It ain't going to pour itself you know." She winked at him again, pulled the boots off her feet and wriggled her toes in front of the fire. "Holy shit that feels great. My toes were starting to ache. You know how much those heels hurt?"

He snorted with disbelief, thinking of the crumbling wall in his garden and the mass of bruises on his back and torso.

"Witch, I no longer need you or your complaints. You made the trek for nothing."

She replied, "Dragon, I doubt it. You need me more than you know." She patted the cushion next to her. "C'mon let's chat. I figure you aren't done drinking and I haven't even started."

A she lifted her face to the darkening sky outside, her voice quieted and took on an earthy quality. "The nights are long and beautiful here. Maybe you'll take me for a walk by your ocean later."

The air in the room shifted and Collum rose to tower over her. Even in his drunken state he recognized magic. "You know something."

The witch reached out and took the bottle from his hand. "*Carino*, I know more than something."

Chapter 23

Alex followed Neeren through a maze of hallways. She was surprised at the ease she felt around him. The only time she'd felt close to this level of comfort was in Collum's arms. Even with the fighting and bickering, he'd never made her feel awkward or different. There were questions though, answers that Alex needed. She couldn't have walked away from Neeren and the answers he offered no matter how much she wanted Collum. Maybe, given time, they could've been something more, but maybe that wasn't in the cards for them. Right now, Alex needed family.

"Wait. Does Aunt Quinn know about you?"

He shrugged indifferently. "No one knows about me."

"I'm sorry. You've lost as much family as I have. She's wonderful. You'll have to meet her."

Neeren continued walking. Occasionally, they ran into a housekeeper or another staff member who tried not to stare openly. Neeren offered a slight smile to everyone they passed.

His castle was nothing like Collum's. It was made almost completely of glass, metal and bronze. Sculptures lined the walls. Everywhere she turned, lay piles of priceless art. Occasionally, a piece hung from a metal beam. He led her through a vast open hall and into a different wing of the house where hallways branched off in different directions. Stairways appeared from nowhere to lead to sitting spaces bathed in sunlight. Modern chandeliers hung from ceilings. Tropical flowers filled steel vases everywhere she looked. Alex's head spun from the fragrance.

"We are here. Your room overlooks a private beach. I thought you might like the view. You also have a fireplace in case you need access to fire." He pushed her hair from her face. "I wouldn't want you to feel lost. This is your home now."

Overwhelmed by an urge to hug him, she threw her arms around his neck and squeezed. Neeren squeezed back, then gently set her into her room.

"I'll be back in a couple hours to take you for that walk. There are clothes in the closets. All will fit you exactly. I hope you like the styles chosen, but if not let me know and I will have a stylist brought to you so you can tell her what you like. There will be a servant in the hall if you need anything before I return. Just push the intercom button here." He motioned to the sleek system on the wall inside her suite. "And she will bring you whatever you require."

Chapter 24

Neeren headed for a suite in a private wing at the far end of the house. The staff retreated as he walked. Neeren was king here. He pushed open a set of bronze doors covered in etchings of panthers. This was his sanctuary. Only one other person was ever allowed inside. She stood patiently by the window. He strode to her.

"I have brought her home."

Her ice-blond hair glistened in the light from the windows. It skimmed her shoulders and accentuated the muscled strength of her bare arms. She wore white today. She wore white every day. He studied the vine wound around her arm. It shimmered with plum petals the same as the color of her eyes. She focused those eyes on him now.

"How is she? Is she taking it all well?"

"She is taking it well. She is strong—like you."

"No. If she is strong, it is like you."

He smiled. "The dragon claimed her. He will search for her. I fought him and he is stronger than me."

"No one is stronger than you, my love. Did she ask about me?"

"Only vaguely. Domhall helped a great deal. I'm not sure she would have come if he hadn't been there." He walked to stand beside her. "When do you want to meet her?"

She leaned onto his arm. "I'm not sure I'm ready yet. I've dreamed of this for so long, but I'm terrified."

"You are terrified of nothing."

"My darling, you make me so proud of you. I am terrified of many things. I made so many mistakes. You suffered so much because of them."

He shook his head, stroked her back. "Tonight then? I will walk her along the ocean, to the spot we love. You can meet her then." He kissed the top of her head. "I have much to do. Do not fear coming to the ocean tonight. I will be there to protect you."

With a final embrace, he left and made his way back through his home. He shifted into panther form on the way. Required the ease of the feline body and the release he could only feel in his true form. He understood the dragon more than any suspected. Neeren had had to learn to control immense power at a very young age. Remaining at ease, at all times, was paramount. He couldn't afford anger.

He stalked through his castle until the tension left his body. It was getting harder to talk to her. She wore her guilt like clothing. Neeren suspected she wouldn't hold on much longer if she couldn't shake the burden of it.

He sauntered into the sun and slowly made his way to the beach. He stretched his long body along the sand, and surveyed all he owned by birthright. The ocean before him, the land around him, his castle on the cliff—all his. Soon he would share it with Alexedria. Below him, the ocean sang.

Other panthers joined him after a time. They always came to him in this form. Four lay at his feet to kneed tired muscles with their claws. The fight with the dragon had taken some of his strength. They sensed it. In panther form, all his people sensed the needs of each other. He let them rub their bodies against him. He was their king.

~ ~ ~

Later that night, Neeren knocked on Alex's door. He entered without waiting for a response. He'd showered and changed into a beige T-shirt, and black slacks. Around his wrists, he wore leather cuffs. Bare feet stuck out from beneath his pants.

He found her resting in a butter-yellow, leather chair situated by the window. She stared at the moon as it lit the ocean below. She too had changed and was dressed in a flowing, silk violet dress. Her tattoo was visible. The flames followed her movements.

"You look content, sister. The dress is beautiful. It suits you."

Alex rose and hugged him. "Thank you. Everything in that closet is beautiful. I've never worn anything like this before. I feel like a princess."

"You *are* a princess. Come." He reached for her hand. "Let us go for that walk. People want to meet you and then I want a little more time alone."

"About that? Do I have to meet everyone right away?"

"Of course not, but you don't want to hurt their feelings, do you? Be brave. You have made it this far, you can manage a few introductions. Don't worry, I will not leave your side. No one will bite." He winked and led her out of the room as he talked, without giving her a chance to change her mind or think of refusing him.

"Where exactly are we anyway? I mean, it doesn't feel like we're in England anymore."

"True. Such a wet and dreary place," he said, shuddering. "We are on my private island near Mylos, in the Greek Isles. Most of the Parthen live here. There are, of course, some that decide to explore other places. Some that have second homes in North America. Many are educated off island, but most choose to return here where it is safe and we don't have to hide what we are. We are a tight knit and private people."

"And the portal that brought us here? Is that another one of our special gifts?"

"No sadly. Though the Island is cloaked, we travel as most do. The portal was a one-time offering from Domhall. A magic he gave me that would open only twice. Once to get me to you and once when you took my hand to come home. Ah, here we are now."

He placed Alex in front of him. A steel staircase opened to a hall below. Hundreds of men and women filled the room. When they saw her, they erupted with cheers and laughter. Neeren tightened his grip on her hand. Tears streamed down her face. Together they walked down the steps and into the crowd below. He eased them through the throng, while speaking with each person individually. The crowd reached out to stroke them both as they walked by.

He leaned down, whispered, "We are feline, Alex. Touching is natural for us. However, if you are uncomfortable, I will tell them to stop."

"No, it's okay. It's a bit strange, but I don't feel fearful. It feels reverent. I'm not sure I'm worthy of that."

Neeren rested his cheek against hers. "Of course, you are worthy, my sister. You are their princess. It is expected that they treat you with love." He straightened, raised his hand, and the room fell into an easy silence.

"Today my sister, Alexedria is returned to us. I will protect her with my life. I ask that you do the same."

One by one each person in the room sank to their knees and shifted into panther form. A low hum filled the room as they purred. Beside her, Neeren remained in human form to ease any concerns she may have. There would be plenty of time to show her his panther and to find out if she could shift.

He thought back to the day his father had been killed, his mother lost to him, and the sister he'd never met ripped away. He never thought the day would come when they would stand united among their people. Together, they were unstoppable. The Elementals would pay for what they'd done. For their cowardice and malice. Now that he had her back, he would be unrelenting.

He smiled at his sister. "Come, it is time to show you my ocean."

Chapter 25

Collum refilled Mar's whiskey glass. "You didn't travel here to play games. Tell me what you know of the asshole who took her."

"Well, first off. I love to play games. You should probably know that in case you want to get kinky later." She laughed at his raised eyebrow. "What? No go? Well, if you change your mind, I'm sure you know where to find me. I do like an extra hard mattress by the way. I know you wouldn't think it to look at this amazing body of mine but . . ."

"Enough," Collum roared. "Tell me what you know, witch."

"Okay," she roared back at him. "Keep your shirt on. Or better yet, take it off." She raised her hands. "I know, I know, I took it too far. Sorry, I can't help myself sometimes. So, the man that took her. Let's rephrase that. The man she left with," she paused, "was her brother. Turns out mommy dearest had a secret marriage for over a hundred years. You guys are pretty dense not to have figured that out, like, forever ago."

"One hundred years? How did you learn this? Did you have a vision?"

"Nah, Domhall found me at the airport and filled me in. Don't be too hard on the immortal. He might be a little insane, but I think he likes you."

"Get out." Collum stood, ready to drag her out of his home. "Get out of my house."

Mar took another gulp of her whiskey. "Ah man, I was warned about you . . . always the tough guy. Just chill. I can help you find your girl. It'll take some time though, and you'll have to decide if it's what you want. Domhall offered a few clues. Turns out he's a little on your side. He didn't kill you, did he? That's gotta count for something."

He sat down. "I must be drunk. It's the only explanation as to why I'm letting you stay."

"I grow on people."

He grimaced. "You can find her?"

"I can. I'm not one to tout my own horn too often . . . Well, actually I am."

"Get on with it, witch."

"It's Mar, remember caped-crusader."

"Oh, for Odin's sake. Get on with it, Mar."

"He—the brother that is—is a Parthen. You know of them?"

"Everyone knows of them. Feline Shape Shifters and Dreamwalkers. That changes things. Are you sure?"

"Why do you think Kaylen wanted the baby hidden? No way the elders were going to let that baby live. Don't let anyone tell you they didn't know what they were doing when they gave Gray to your nutso dad. Nice digs by the way. I especially like the whole dragon cave, danger, stay away thing you have going on. Not big with the locals much, huh?" She took a hearty swig of her whiskey and wiggled her toes closer to the fire. "You know, Glenny was telling me there's an awesome market on Saturdays in the village. You might want to check it out."

"I'm going to strangle you. I really am . . ."

She raised her hands in surrender before continuing. "Soooo, if you know of the parthen, you know their old king died a mysterious death a bunch of years ago. The new king no one ever sees? Any guesses?"

Collum threw his glass in the fire. "Fuck."

"That's right Lord O' the Rings, that would be your lover's brother. The solitary king of the Parthen is the grandson of the most powerful Elemental in the world."

He grabbed another bottle of whiskey. At this rate, Glenn would be going on a booze run soon. "You want another drink?"

"Do I? Man, do we have loads to talk about. Pour another round and join me by my fire, Dragon Balls."

"It's my house, Mar, and my name is Collum."

"Whateves. So, right now, the king is making cute and snugly with sis. But don't fool yourself. I hear he's super aloof. There've always been rumors. Hardly anyone gets to meet him and those that do, generally keep their mouths shut after. Out of fear or loyalty, couldn't tell you."

"What are the rumors you've heard?"

"Oh, you know, an amazing lover, has a harem of feline groupies, can seduce you just by looking at you, keeps a ghost locked in his tower. The usual."

"Will you quit messing around and tell me something more important than Friday night gossip."

"You don't listen do you? Keeps a ghost in his tower. Rub my feet and I'll give you three guesses who that is."

Chapter 26

Alex walked hand in hand with her brother down the cliff to the edge of the sea. He pointed out parts of his land that were now hers. He picked seashells for her. The moon lit their path as waves gently tickled their feet.

She curled her toes in the warm white sand. "I see why you go barefoot now. This feels amazing. The water is warmer here than what I'm used to in Victoria. Am I dreaming?"

"You are not. This is your home. We are your family. With us, your life will be easy. Everything will be taken care of. You only need tell me what you wish and you'll have it."

"You make it sounds so easy. I'm not used to this. It doesn't feel real to me. Shouldn't there be struggle?"

He curled a finger under her chin. Raised her face to look at his. "Why? We have had enough struggle, do you not think? You'll never hurt again, sister." He paused, took a deep breath and said, "There is a final gift I wish to give you tonight. Come."

They walked further along the narrow and private path. Evening scents and sounds surrounded them. Cicada bugs serenaded them. It was peaceful, yet with every step they took, Alex felt tension mount in the grip of Neeren's hands. She grew anxious. The ends of her hair sparked in reaction. Until now, she'd only felt a controlled, easy comfort around him. As if he quietly mocked the world, confident in his every moment. That man wasn't with her now. Her confidence slipped. She wondered if she should turn back.

Waves crashed around them. He kept walking, taking her with him to a moment in time she sensed he'd been waiting for forever. When he finally stopped, he stared into the clearing ahead. The look in his eyes almost brought Alex to her knees.

A figure waited in the shadows.

The world quieted as he released her.

"Your past and your future wait in that shadow, Alex. It is everything. It is why you are here."

He smiled. A devastating smile, that reached his eyes and transformed him. Cat. King. Alpha. This was her brother. United, they walked to the other end of the beach. To the hidden figure.

With each step, Alex felt a sense of completion. Something was about to end. More was about to start. She felt Neeren tremble and squeezed his hand. He pressed back gently. The figure, closer now, turned. Alex witnessed a woman's shape tremble as well. Neeren hurried them.

When they reached her, Neeren fell to his knees. Raw emotions tightened Alex's throat. Tried to claw out of her lungs. The woman came out of the shadows and rested her hand on Neeren's hand. She reached for Alex, years of loss and yearning etched on her porcelain skin. Alex fell to the earth beside her brother.

The three of them collapsed on the beach together, cried like babies. Held on to each other like lifelines. For hours they were like one. Alex, unable to let go, fearing she would disappear.

The woman raised her head first and wiped her eyes. "Look at me. My darlings. My Alexedria, can you ever forgive me?"

Alex dashed the tears away and searched the woman's eyes. Eyes so much like hers. "Mother," she finally said, "I forgive you anything."

Chapter 27

Collum recoiled, the past twenty-five years shattered by that one flippant remark. "You can't be about to tell me what I think you are. She's dead. Everyone knows she's dead."

"Well duh, of course they do," Mar replied. "Funny how everyone will believe what they're told isn't it. Who told everyone she was dead?"

She climbed off the plush chair and wriggled her fingers in front of the massive stone fireplace. "I felt the same when I finally figured it out. Domhall is good at keeping secrets. He's even better at manipulating them. I only clued in, 'cause he wanted me to. The players are about to shift Dragon-Mine and I'm more than happy to be one of them."

Collum studied her frame in the fire. She chugged her whiskey, with a devilish smile.

"You're enjoying this," he finally choked out.

"I always enjoy a bit of intrigue. It keeps me fresh." She scolded him, "Oh, come on, you're a dragon for Christ's sake. Dragon's get off on intrigue. The only reason you might not be enjoying this as much as me is because you've fallen for the reason we're all playing the game."

He cursed. The world turned on its axis. He'd lost Alex. He'd never get her back now. "Domhall."

"Yep, good old insane, Domhall. Loving husband, loving father, loving grandfather. You know, I'm beginning to suspect that dude ain't as nuts as you all think he is. This is going to start a war, Collum. I don't know about you, but I sure as hell know whose side I want to be on."

The whiskey glass in his hand felt like lead. "Gray is alive."

Mar patted his muscled arm. "Gray is alive."

"Can you find her?"

"I'm pretty damn sure I can." She rubbed his muscles beneath the black cashmere sweater. "You know, I thought you'd be meaner. Folks warned me about you. Don't cross him, don't piss him off, don't let him near your daughters, blah, blah, blah. If you weren't in love with the girl, I'd totally have a go with yeah."

He ran an exasperated hand through his hair. "For Christ's sake, Mar, take this seriously for a minute."

"I am. I'm totally serious. I'd be all over you in a heartbeat if it weren't for the smell of the lust you have for Alex, all over you. Honestly, it's not fair. But, I don't go in for being turned down, so, you know, *no toques*." She flipped her hair back and swept her hands down her body before tossing back the final slug of whiskey in her cup.

"I'm just going to ignore you," he said.

"That might be best."

"And I don't love Alex. I barely know her."

"Uh huh. You keep telling yourself that, oh master-of-denial. You reek of claiming smoke. Don't dragons only claim the one who is to be their mate?"

"It's different. Alex isn't a dragon. The rules don't apply."

"Yeah? Bullshit, Obewankanobe. Just 'cause you don't want to be claimed, doesn't mean you aren't. Smoke that logic. Oh, and you better hope you are claimed because I hear tell it's the only way to find her."

He grabbed her shoulders. His dark eyes filled with blue fire. "Quit playing games with me, witch."

Mar shook him off. "Easy, big guy, not sure if you noticed, but this skin is perfect. No bruises, okay."

He released her immediately, moved to the other side of

the room, studied the ancestral paintings that lined the wall of the library. Each face was as dark and harsh as his own. Each face, a descendant of dragons. Humans thought dragons were a fable, a legend like unicorns. In reality, they'd simply evolved to walk among the humans. They were a fierce and passionate race, led by instinct to conquer.

Collum was the one among them with the power and control to lead. Most hid on their towers of rock, with little desire to be near other beings. Spread across the world, they came only when called. They came when he called.

He rejoined Mar by the fire, placed his hand gently on the small of her back. "I apologize, witch. I shouldn't have grabbed you." He rubbed her skin with tender affection.

She turned her brilliant white smile on him and retreated from his touch. "None of that now. I told you, I'm not into you okay."

He smiled fondly at her. "Ah, yes, I forgot. Now tell me what you meant. How can I find Alex?"

"Right. This keeps getting better and better. Another rumor, of course, but I'm fairly certain it's true. Tell me, is it true ancient dragons could call to their mates across time and lands?"

Collum studied her. "That is the rumor."

"But is it true?"

"We are not ancient anymore so I fail to see why it matters. Those old ways have been lost. And Alex is not my mate."

"Sure, sure, but you claimed her."

He nodded. "But she is not dragon, was raised human. She is young and unschooled and we were together but once. The bond isn't strong enough to find her, even if the ancient ways still existed."

"Well I disagree with you and I want to do a spell. I've studied the ways of your people. I'm, like ninety-two percent certain I can find her, or at the very least get within a close range. I only need you to be willing to try."

He sighed, felt a moment of weakness. "She's found her mother."

"Who cares. You swore to protect her. That vow isn't kaput. Domhall has his own game plan. My sense is she's going to need you. Sorry, but you better suck up the fact that she traipsed off with another dude and try this."

The brand on his flesh ached. Moved under his sweater. Called out for its other half. He nodded. "What do we need?"

"Cool—Your blood, a strand of her hair, a dragon's egg. I have the rest."

"A dragon's egg. Are you out of your fucking mind? It's against every law of my people to touch dragon eggs. They are sacred."

Mar doubled over with laughter. "I sort of figured that. Thought it was worth a shot. Those goddamn things are worth a fortune."

He growled again. Felt like all he did was growl around this child.

She giggled. "Take it easy. Ha, you should've seen your face. Gosh, I love how *volátil* you dragons are. Easy pickins, easy pickins."

Collum took a menacing step toward her.

"Stop. Stop. I'm funny, remember? You like me." She jumped over the back of the lounger and grabbed her boots. "It's just the blood and hair, promise. You have to be willing to let me cut you and you have to be willing to stand inside the life circle I create."

Collum retreated. "Very well. When?"

"Tomorrow. It's like one in the morning and I'm totally wiped." She bounced out of the room. "Don't worry about me. Glenny showed me where I could put my stuff. We took care of that while you were down here throwing good whiskey in the fire. He deserves a raise you know. Tots for now, *carino*.

~ ~ ~

Collum sat by the fire for a few minutes after Mar had left. The revelations for the night were almost too much for him. Kaylen had lied. There was no way she hadn't known who Alex's father was. It surprised him that he wasn't angrier. But truthfully, he respected her strategy. Goddamn he missed that woman.

The clock on the mantle read two o'clock in the morning. He forced himself to leave the den. Morning was coming soon. His feet carried him to the room he'd shared with Alex. The covers were still rumpled from when they'd made love. Glenn had wisely chosen not to make up the room. He picked up a pillow, inhaled her lingering scent. He sat on the edge of the bed and placed his head in his hands. Her mother was alive. She had a brother. Knowing everything he did, he couldn't see how she'd possibly wish to return to him.

"Fuck," he muttered, raking his hands through his hair as he straightened.

He'd been charged, however, with keeping her safe and she wasn't safe yet. Not with the war coming their way. The war her mother and brother were sure to crave as much as their enemies.

He had vague memories of Gray Taleisin. He'd heard the stories. The woman was a fierce warrior who loved knowledge and destruction as much as any dragon. She must be chomping at the bit for payback. Whether Alex liked it or not he was bound to her for a while longer. That meant he had to find her before they all did something stupid.

Chapter 28

Alex wept openly. Held on to her mother like she was a lifeline.

Gray wiped the tears from her eyes. "I am so very, very sorry, my beautiful child. Sorry for everything. I could hardly bear living, knowing you'd been taken from me, knowing I had to stay away from you."

"Why didn't you bring me here before now?"

"I didn't know where you were. Your guardian hid you well. Please don't hate me, Alex."

"I don't hate you. I just don't understand all of this. I don't understand why I wasn't sent to you right from the start."

Gray held her tightly. "I can only assume your grandmother thought asking Collum Thronus to make you disappear was the right thing to do. That she was protecting you from the elders. She thought I was dead. Everyone did. Truthfully, I almost was. Domhall saved my life, weaved a spell to keep me alive until he could get me to a healer. He knew the elders would steal you and agreed with Mother that you should be hidden for your own safety. He told her I'd died while she was cleaning you in the other room."

Alex swiped her arm across her face. Sniffled on the last of her tears. "Why would he do that? Lie to his own wife?"

Gray replied, "I learned long ago not to question my father. He has knowledge and foresight none of us can claim to understand. I'm certain he knew of Neeren and your father Daylen almost from the start." She weaved slightly in the sand.

Neeren steadied her. "It is all right, Mother. We're together now. Father knows you loved him."

Jealousy surge through Alex as she watched the interplay between the two. She might never have the same bond.

"Daughter, look at me please," Gray said as she brushed her cheek. "I love you with every breath in my body. What Domhall did, I believe he did to protect us all. He afforded you the chance at life. He afforded me time to grieve my husband. Neeren had time to learn how to lead. War will find us soon. I'm happy it didn't find us twenty-five years ago."

"What about Collum? He's the one that hid me from you."

"Your dragon is a worthy mate. I have no quarrel with the beast. He only did as Kaylen asked. In truth, if not for him, we would be dead, slain by his father. Collum kept you hidden from those who would hurt you. There is nothing to avenge. We will not harm him." She laughed then, a real laugh filled with joy. "Not that I think we could."

Alex remembered the feel of his skin on hers, his lips on hers. "Why does everyone keep calling him mine? There was no commitment between us. He's an infuriating man. In fact, he's a bit of a bully."

Gray laughed again. Then turned to kiss Neeren's head. "My darling boy, please leave me with my daughter. We have so much to catch up on."

Alex examined the reflection of the moon on the water. The Parthen lived in paradise, attuned to the sounds of the tropical birds that shared the island with them. Fig trees lined the upper beaches. The delightful musk of honeysuckle vines filled the air. Gray's voice brought her back to the present.

"I hated your father when I first met him. He was pompous, so self-assured. It drove me insane. We met in battle. I'd taken out one of his cats. He almost beat me that first time. At the last second, he pulled back and told me I was too pretty to kill. He shifted into a giant panther and took off before I could finish him. He assumed no women could ever hurt him." She laughed. "The second time we met, I slashed his face open with my vine. He hated me then. We were mortal enemies. But we couldn't stop chasing each other. Maybe we thought it was to prove we were stronger than the other. Can you imagine a king being bested by a mere woman?"

Gray dropped to the sand, stuck her toes in the water. Gentle waves wrapped around her lower body. She motioned for Alex to sit with her.

"This is my beach. No others come here, except Neeren. It's where your father and I first met. It's where I feel closest to him." She smiled conspiratorially. "There wasn't a day that went by that I didn't want to smack the self-assured smile off his face. It drove me nuts, but I could never take the king out of the man. I loved him even more because of it."

Alex traced a figure eight in the water as waves turned her violet dress dark plum. She waited for Gray to continue.

"Neeren is the same. He was raised to be a king. Was raised to know he was more powerful than any of the others. The women here worship him. He treats them well, has never harmed a living Parthen female, but he's different from them. Neeren has never been told no. After Daylen's murder, I fell apart. Neeren has treated me like a porcelain doll since, and I'm ashamed to admit I've let him. He will treat you the same if you allow it. I tell you this because he needs you to stand up to him. He will be forever alone if you don't."

She grasped Alex's hand. "You must be stronger, my dear. You must not be burdened with the need to protect all Parthen like your brother. You must only protect yourself. That is what will save us all in the end."

Alex stood and walked into the water, up to her waist. The ends of her hair smoked as though breathing. "I want you to know that I had good parents. They loved me and treated me well, but they died too. All of this is so much. Maybe it isn't the same thing as what Neeren went through. What you went through. But it matters to me. You'd would've liked them."

Gray followed her into the water and hugged her, kissed the tears on her cheeks. "I may have forgotten for a while, but we are warriors. We are strongest together. Domhall reunited our strength. Perhaps it's atonement for his part. I don't know. One rarely knows what my father is thinking. Now, about that dragon of yours."

"Oh come on, can you guys let this rest. Collum isn't my dragon."

"Did you sleep with him?"

"Seriously?" Her cheeks exploded with heat. When her mother simply nodded, she said, "Okay. Yes. I slept with him. But I've slept with other guys."

Gray waved her hand in dismissal. "Beside the point. Did he blow smoke into your body? Did your fire embrace him? Brand him? Did he bite you?" She reached out to trace Alex's tattoo. The leaves and petals on her arms strained toward Alex.

"Oh, my God, I just realized that I've seen you before. I had a dream about you."

Gray smiled. "I wondered when you'd remember. Even with no knowledge, you reached me in your dream. You are so strong, my child. But quit changing the subject. Tell me about Collum."

Alex knew she was blushing again. Maybe she'd catch on fire and have to dunk herself in the ocean. "Yes, to all of it."

"Then you have been claimed. You two are now one."

"Honestly, this seems like a bit of a sham. The next morning, he brushed me off. So, whatever. No big deal."

Gray dismissed her complaint with a wave. "Nothing but nerves. Ignore it. I doubt the noble dragon told you this, but once he claimed you, he claimed his mate for life. He can be with no other now. He might not be ready to admit it. Might even fight it, but sorry to say, you two are stuck together."

"Excuse me?" Alex stumbled in the water before saying, "Not funny."

Her mom grasped her arm, steadied her. "I'm not kidding."

"Oh, God. This is an immortal thing, right? Shouldn't I have some say in it? You know, like the way people talk about feelings and futures before making a commitment."

"Goddess, darling," Gray admonished. "You do have a choice. You can choose to stay away from him. In which case, you might be able to move on to another guy. You certainly have that right, but I doubt it will work. I've met the Dragon King. For a dragon, it is much different though. You're it for him. Once a dragon claims, he can be with no other. Oh, he'll survive without you I suppose, but he'll never love another."

"No one said the love word, Mother."

Gray laughed. "I suspect that's precisely why he pushed you away. It's likely he wished to explore your relationship, your feelings for each other before, bringing any of this up. Collum Thronus is a leader of honor, likely the most honorable among us." She shrugged. "Besides, your fire wanted him too. That's a pretty clear indication the pressure isn't so bad. Anyway, I imagine he'll find his way here eventually. That dragon has never quit."

"What if I don't want him? What if I'm not ready?"

"There is a way to test that theory." Gray pulled Alex out of the water. They ambled back to the castle arm in arm. "You have the power to dreamwalk, my darling. Go to him in his dreams."

A night bird warbled in the distance. Sparks flickered at the ends of Alex's hair. She pushed her fingers through the knots that always seemed to be there. "I don't know how."

"I'll teach you. Every night we were separated, Daylen joined me in my dreams. I watched him guide Neeren through the process when he was little." Gray started up the hill. "Come on, it's the middle of the night. If we're going to make it happen, we better get started before it's too late. Your dragon is probably an early riser."

"Mother, stop." Alex tugged on her arm. "I don't think I want to do this."

"Nonsense. That is only fear talking. You miss him. I'm sure you want to offer him explanations. You can even simply peek in to make sure he is sleeping soundly if you want. He doesn't need to know you were there."

"I can do that? Isn't it a bit voyeuristic?"

"Voyeuristic? This is the Parthen gift. You control the dreams you walk in. Let me help you. I missed so much of your life. I missed your first laughs, your first steps, your first loves and heartbreaks. I want to help with this. Will you let me?"

"It would be . . . nice . . . to see Collum asleep." She beamed at her mother. "Let's hurry before I come to my senses and change my mind."

~ ~ ~

They ran across the beach like children, drunk on the high of finding each other and the act of mischief they were about to perform. Four-footed sentries roamed the glowing halls as they raced through the castle. All bowed on front paws as they passed. In minutes, the two of them swept into her room. As soon as Alex closed the door, Gray began her instructions.

"It's very simple, my darling. You merely need to fall asleep with a vision of Collum in your mind. Since this is your first attempt, you may need someone to ground you, so I will stay until you fall asleep. If he's awake you won't be able to reach him. You gain admittance to the mind through the dream state. It's much different than telepathy. First, you begin with meditation. Visualize being in the room with him. Then walk into that meditation. Dreams, for many immortals, feel the same as reality. A few experience disorientation afterward, but I doubt that will be the case for a creature as old and powerful as Collum Thronus."

Alex paid close attention to every word. "The first time Neeren contacted me, I'd fallen asleep on the airplane and woke up in a tropical garden. I remember everything feeling very fuzzy. I think he brought me here."

Gray nodded. "He wanted to bring you somewhere familiar the first time you met. It was easier to pick a location he felt safe in, rather than trying to guess one of yours. Because of his power and your blood connection, he was able to bring you to a place of his choosing. You won't be able to do that yet."

"So, how do I reach Collum?"

"First, get out of the wet dress you're wearing and put on some comfortable sleeping clothes. I'll bring a blanket off the bed while you do that."

Gray motioned to the thick, yellow leather loveseat, by the south window. "That spot is perfect. I'll ring for wine while you change. It will help calm your nerves and make it easier to get into a meditative space." She pushed her toward the closet. "Go, Alexedria, we haven't a ton of time. Tonight, we fight the rise of the sun."

Alex stripped out of her wet dress. The garment was destroyed. It had been a beautiful dress for a beautiful day but, as the day ended, she reached for something more her style. She exited the closet five minutes later wearing a soft peach cotton tank top and pyjama bottoms. Thankfully, Neeren added casual clothes to the mix of high end garments. The closet was a combination of gently worn tank tops, bad-ass jeans, and Grecian influenced dresses.

Gray nodded approvingly when she saw her. "I suspected you would be more comfortable in something like that. No one who cares about fine Greek silk would have wandered into the ocean in that dress like you did earlier. It is good. It's fitting for a warrior to care more about the health of her body and less about what goes on it."

"You're still in your wet dress. Do you want to wear something of mine?"

"Thank you, dear, but no. The material will dry soon enough and I'm not staying long anyway. I'll change when I return to my room."

The knock at the door signaled the arrival of their wine. Gray thanked the servant at the door with a smile and returned hoisting an open bottle and two crystal glasses. "We have success. It's the good stuff."

Alex burst out laughing. She suspected in another time her mother was hell to handle. She hoped she'd get a chance to see her that way.

Gray poured the deep red wine into two glasses, handed one to Alex and gracefully lowered herself to the loveseat, curling her feet underneath her. She could have been wearing the crown jewels, Alex thought, not a dripping white sheath.

Gray raised the glass. "A toast to us, to finding family, and a toast to the dragon. May he sleep well this night and welcome your walk."

As the liquid hit her mouth Alex's tongue melted. She held the sweet elixir in her mouth for as long as she could before swallowing. "Oh, my God. You weren't kidding. This is amazing."

"It better be. It's from Neeren's private stock. He must have warned the staff to have a bottle ready for us. You see what I mean? Neeren will make sure the staff takes care of your every want and need. He will expect it of them . . . and no one denies Neeren. Now have another drink and think of the dragon. Let yourself drift if you feel the need to. Picture a space where you felt safe with him. Let your eyes close when they are ready. The wine will help you fall asleep quickly. My dear girl, you must so be tired. In the last few days you've spanned half the world, and begun a new life."

Alex savored the wine while listening to her mother's quiet voice. Even if this didn't work, she knew she would remember this moment as one of the loveliest of her life.

Gray smiled. "Allow your breathing to deepen as you drink. Picture his face in your mind. Think of the best parts of him. The best moment with him. Tell yourself you are going to see him. Think of the destination. Can you see the space, Alex?"

Alex's eyes grew heavy. The wine she sipped was drugged. A fact her mother had left out, she thought, as her lids closed. She'd be mad at her if she weren't already drifting off. Then again maybe Gray didn't know. She'd be mad at Neeren instead. First, she had to go find Collum.

She was certain her mother kissed her cheek and said, "I love you," before leaving the room.

As Alex drifted further into the world of dreams, her last conscious thought was . . . the night had been long and beautiful here.

Chapter 29

When Alex opened her eyes, she found herself at the foot of the bed she'd left earlier that morning. It felt like a lifetime ago. She thought of how Collum had kissed her there, pressing his mouth against hers—pressing her back against the wall. The heat radiating off the stone fireplace reminded her of their fire.

As her eyes adjusted to the dark, she studied the large male form lying on the bed. A shiver ran through her as she realized he slept in the room where they'd been together. Moving around to the edge of the bed, she studied his sleeping figure. His black hair was tousled, his thick, muscled frame on full display. She took her time admiring his body. Tattoos covered his arms and parts of his chest with intricate displays of dragons and Celtic markings. A symbol comprised of three swirling circles, on his right shoulder, caught her eye and she reached out to gently stroke it. Dark hair was sprinkled across his chest and legs.

He was one muscle after the other. *Beautiful.* A fierceness emanated from him even in his sleep. Alex raised her eyes to trace his chiseled jaw and full lips. Their eyes met. The heat of his gaze slammed into her gut.

"Enjoying what you see?"

Startled, Alex jumped back. She thought she'd be in control.

He reached his hand out to her. "Come here. I want to taste you." A promise of earth and fire in his eyes.

Her stomach clenched as heat pooled between her legs. She felt wicked and wanton. Knowing he thought it was a dream, she moved closer to the bed. As she traced her fingers along his chest, flickers of fire jumped out to burn him.

Collum groaned and grabbed her hand. He stared in to her eyes as he pulled her fingers to his mouth and began suckling them like he'd done on the plane.

Her knees weakened. The flames on her flesh began to move. She wanted to take charge this time. But it was his dream. She felt flustered a moment. She didn't know the rules.

"Take your top off," Collum commanded. He sat up on the edge of the bed and pulled her to him. "I want to see your nipples harden as I lick your skin."

She helped him pull her top off. He was urgent, insistent, controlling. His hands roamed her body. Alex felt power course through her. She stared at rippling muscles the color of honey and climbed on the bed beside him.

He dipped his hand into her waistband and yanked her sweats off. Alex adjusted, lifting her ass so he could have better access. Collum pushed his fingers into her slick wetness and rubbed back and forth. Alex whimpered, nipped his chest. Fire grew.

"Don't stop, Collum."

"Ah, baby, I'm never going to stop."

He grabbed her hair with his free hand and pulled her face to his. Roughly, he kissed her lips.

She grabbed his shoulders, gripping him as he began to ravage her mouth. Sparks erupted between them as Alex moved to the rhythm of his finger. She pushed herself closer, demanded more.

Collum curved his finger inside her, growling into her mouth, "God, I want you. Let me taste you." He laid back and lifted her above his head. In one swift movement, he set her wetness to his mouth.

Alex nearly screamed as tremors raced through her. His powerful grasp held her in pace as he clamped on to her thighs and held her against his mouth. Forced his tongue into her, licking, biting, clawing. On the verge of coming, she held onto the headboard as she groaned out her desire. Her fire craved Collum as much as she did and began to wrap around the hands holding her thighs.

"Mine," he snarled, low in his throat. "You are fucking, mine."

An instant later he flipped them over so she lay beneath him. Grabbed her waist and pulled her to him. Flesh against flesh. Her flame reached for him. Roaring, he surged into her body. Deep onyx and silver wings exploded from his back. Fire poured out of his skin. Flames leapt to life in the fireplace and the golden walls of the room bled lava.

Alex erupted as the energy in the room brought on the most intense orgasm of her life. She thrust against Collum as he plunged deep and hard into her. Her flames wound their way up to his wings. Savored the silky texture. Pulsed against the straining veins. In her lover's face, she saw more beast than man.

He stared down at her with red eyes. Dragon eyes. Forced her legs around his waist and cocooned their bodies inside his wings before leaping from the bed in one ferocious burst of speed. He pushed Alex against the wall, tightened his wings, made them one. His hands still gripped her waist. He ground his cock in and out of her.

She bit his neck and shoulders, licked the sparks glistening on his skin. Felt the fires rising under her own. Her hair caught fire as Collum slammed her against the wall, using his wings to catch the brunt of the impact. He fucked her. Wild. A beast driven by desire for his woman.

Alex took it all, gripped him tighter, as she neared orgasm again. Her flesh sung in the power, reveled in the fire from her dragon. Savored the fact that his dragon nature had taken over. Lava pulsed through the veins in his wings.

He pushed her further, brought her to the edge of sanity. As they came together, the room erupted in flames around them.

Alex gripped his hair and lifted his head from her neck as they fell back to earth. "Collum, you need to stop the fire now. I don't know how."

Half crazed, otherworldly red eyes, smoldered under her gaze.

"I'll burn the world down for you. You're mine," the dragon snarled.

She stroked his cheek, let herself sink into his wings. She petted him, murmuring, "I am yours, beast. Now, stop the fire."

Slowly the dragon shuddered and released a low breath. The flames gradually died out. He stepped back from her and let her body slide back to the floor before grabbing her hand and beginning to drag her back to the bed.

"Collum, wait. I need to talk to you."

His voice was raw, scorched. Gravel in his throat. "Later. I want more." He kept pulling her. The strength of the dragon evident in his grip on her hand.

"We don't have time. I have to go soon," Alex said as she pulled back.

He stopped then—measured her. The roomed cooled. Slowly, the dragon's aura left them. "This isn't my dream, is it?"

Alex shook her head. "It is, at least I think it is. But it's also real. I'm here with you. I'm new at all this. It's just that I can't stay."

"So, the witch was right." He retreated to the edge of the bed. "The Dreamwalker is your brother. You aren't mine."

"You found her already? Never mind it doesn't matter." She touched his shoulder. "Yes, Neeren is my brother. I have a family and I'm happy."

"I could force you to stay."

"No, you can't. You'll wake up soon and I have to go back."

"No." He sneered. "I could force you to stay."

"What do you mean, Collum?" At his blank look, she tried again. "Talk to me."

He shook his head, refused to make eye contact. "It doesn't matter. About what just happened. I wouldn't have let my dragon out if I thought this was real. If I hurt you, I'm sorry."

She sat beside him on the bed and took his hand. "Don't you dare say that. What we did was absolutely the most erotic thing I've ever experienced. Don't you dare regret it. Look, I don't know what this is between us, but I feel the power of it too. It's just that I need some time."

"Sure, but I still shouldn't have lost control that way. At least not without preparing you first."

"Oh God, stop that. You are so perfect I'm ready to jump you again just thinking about it. And if I recall, you reminded me very recently that we are immortal." She grabbed his chin and forced him to look in her eyes. "You didn't hurt me."

He threaded his fingers into her tangled hair. "You are so goddamn gorgeous."

Alex's heart melted and she kissed him lightly on the mouth. "So are you, you big brute." She leaned back. "Look, I want my family. I'm not going to leave them, but I want you too and I'm sorry I left the way I did. The elders will come for my brother and me. I'm going to fight them. I'm going to fight them with all the power I have. It turns out I have a lot of it. I'm releasing you from your oath. You don't have to protect me anymore. I won't let another person I care about be hurt. Please don't come when they find me."

His hands tightened in her tangles as he said through gritted teeth, "Sweetheart, you are fucking nuts if you think I'm not coming for you."

"I said I don't want you too."

"Yeah. Heard you. Don't give a shit. Still coming."

Alex jerked her head away from him and she climbed off the bed. "You are the most infuriating person I've ever met. Can't you respect what I want? I'm trying to be noble here."

"Again, don't give a shit, because I realized something too, little girl." He stood in front of her, naked and cut from fire and stone. He held her chin, forcing her to look into his eyes. "You and I belong to each other, and I'm not leaving it to some fucking cat to protect you."

As she stood speechless at his declaration, he kissed her. Long, hard, possessively. Ended it when she gripped his chest, full of frustration and wanting. Then before she could grab him back for more, he turned his back, climbed into bed and said, "Now, get the fuck out of my dream, sweetheart."

~ ~ ~

She opened her eyes back in her room at Neeren's castle, tangled in her cashmere blanket. He'd pushed her out of his dream. How the hell had he done it? Astounded, she looked to the sun slowly rising on the horizon. Had it even been a dream? She needed to find out more about this power.

She was exhausted. Her body ached from their lovemaking. She felt the ridges of a bite mark on her shoulder. Gray told her she'd retain control. But she hadn't—not for a second. Maybe her mother didn't know as much about dreamwalking as she thought? Or it was something else. How strong was Collum? God, he was fierce. She sighed. Maybe he was her dragon. She sunk into the loveseat. Closed her eyes as the sun burst above the sea. Content, she dreamed of fire.

Chapter 30

Collum woke with the smell of her lingering on his sheets. Some part of him recognized she'd been dreamwalking from the minute she appeared in the room. He hadn't cared. Dreamwalker or not, she was his. Controlling the dream had been an unconscious act, an extension of his natural ability to control the thoughts of those around him—of anyone really. He was one of only a handful with the power to do so. It was his most closely guarded secret. Immediate death met anyone who discovered it. Control of the dream had been instinctual. He prayed Alex's naivety of the immortal world would keep her from asking questions.

His hand wandered to his erection as he imagined her body next to his. He was stiff and ready. Thoughts of how they'd ravaged each other last night consumed him. He stroked himself as images of their lovemaking ran through his mind. Pictured himself thrusting against her while holding her in his wings. Pictured the flames that soared around them when they came. Remembered the fierce whimpers she'd made while she pulled him in closer. She was the most amazing woman he'd ever met and he couldn't fathom being without her.

He lay in the tangled sheets, fully intent on pleasuring himself, when he heard approaching cars coming up the road. The smell of rangers drifted in the window. So, he thought, three days to find him. He'd hoped for more time, but he could deal with a few rangers.

Collum stood and called on his inner dragon. The beast in him awoke instantly with the same memories of taking its woman. Collum relished the feel of the ancient nature taking over. The dragon tattoos across his chest, over his body had been his choice. He'd gotten them so no one would ever doubt who he was or where his loyalty lay. Guardian to the immortals he might be. Dragon was what he was. The beast waited only momentarily before turning to stalk its prey.

When his dragon took over, Collum retained awareness of all his acts. That awareness reminded him not to kill all the Elemental soldiers approaching his land until he had a chance to question them. He released his wings, leaped from the balcony and took flight to search for intruders. Located them about five kilometres down the road from his home. Having crossed onto his property, they were fair game. The beast flew directly to them.

Two black Mercedes peeled around the bend, churning up gravel and dust. He dove at them, spewing fire, ripping a giant fracture in the road. The cars swerved and screeched to a halt. He landed directly in front of the first car with his wings spread and his eyes spitting fire. Four young soldiers jumped out, clearly shaken but prepared to battle the creature in front of them. The dragon sneered. Again, they sent weaklings. Where were the great warriors of the Elementals he knew of? Before they could lift their hands, he spit a bolt of lightning and split the lead soldier in half.

"Why have you trespassed on my land?" the beast barked.

The three remaining soldiers recoiled.

One vomited.

The dragon sighed.

One man stepped forward, shakily decreeing, "Collum Thronus, King of the Dragons and Guardian of Immortals, by order of council members Taurin and Ealian Gondien we are here to bring you in for questioning in the matter of treason against the Elementals by the Taleisin family."

The dragon laughed a deep throated, dark laugh. "Quite

the mouthful. Do you boys know where you are?"

He looked each of them in the eyes before sucking in another breath and releasing a lightning bolt that split the soldier who'd spoken, in half. As the smell of burning flesh filled the air around them, he looked to the final two men.

They stood, white as chalk as the dragon smirked at them.

One finally found his voice. "You can't do that. You've committed murder and by doing so committed treason against the elders."

Collum shook his head at the young man's folly and allowed his beast to do what it wished. The beast roared, spread its wings and let loose a stream of blue fire at the third man who had dared to command it. Fire consumed his flesh in mere seconds. The man lay screaming on the ground, his skin on fire and melting against his bones. The beast offered no mercy. They'd come to his home and threatened him. They should have known that here his word was the only law.

The dragon turned to the young man who'd vomited earlier. His voice echoed with ancient magic. "Go back to your council. Tell them to stay away from dragon land. I was old before they were born and it's *my* word that lays judgement. If they come at me again, I'll kill them as quickly and as easily as I did these three. Do you understand me?"

The soldier nodded in acknowledgment. The beast watched, waiting with barely concealed impatience as its prey walked back to its car on shaking legs. As the car retreated, Collum returned to the man still writhing on the ground.

"You may come for revenge in the afterlife." He used the tip of his wing to pierce the man's heart. Bored, he took flight and quickly made his way back to the castle.

~ ~ ~

He landed in the courtyard, absorbed his wings into his body and let the beast rest. As he spun to head into the home, he noticed the little witch from the night before walking toward him with a cup of coffee.

"I thought you might like this after last night. So how was the killing and maiming?"

She'd caught him off guard again. "You're a strange bird, you know that?"

"I've been told. I prefer to think of it as being highly witty."

He reached out for the coffee and took a sip of the strong brew. "Glenn really does make the best coffee in England," he said while savoring the taste of the cinnamon on his tongue.

The old man had started putting cinnamon in the coffee about fifteen years ago. Collum had been hard pressed to find a decent brew outside of his home since. He made sure he returned home regularly, mostly to check in. Didn't want Glenn flying off half-cocked every time he missed a meeting. He'd almost lost him once—to his piece of shit father. Glenn had had the audacity to tell his father not to beat him. It'd taken Collum three months to nurse him back to health. He didn't know much about the man's private life, and frankly, he didn't care that much either.

"Glenny and I have been having a lovely visit while you were off hunting. He's the best. I hope you know how lucky you are to have a guy like him on your side."

"I do, Mar. I've known since the day I met him."

"Good. Just making sure you weren't a total loser. Now we should probably eat before the food gets cold. I suspect he'll get angry if his perfect, Eggs Glenny, gets cold before we eat."

As she turned on her heel, Collum marveled at how she managed to walk in five-inch stilettos before nine a.m.

Breakfast was waiting on the table when they reached the dining room. Large portions of steaming Eggs Glenny, filled their plates. The dish was a version of Eggs Benedict but with massive amounts of paprika and fresh cilantro mixed in the sauce. The taste was spicy and fresh at the same time. It was one more thing Collum couldn't get enough of.

He shoveled spoonfuls into his mouth. "I've been looking forward to this dish for weeks."

"Thank you," Glenn said. "I trust you took care of the mess on the drive. Or, do I need to send some of the young dragons to clean up?"

Collum hid his laughter under his breath. Glenn hated blood on the driveway. "Yes, ask some of the men to look after it for me. A good fire should do it."

"Very good. I'll see to it right away. You and Miss Del Voscovo enjoy your breakfast. Let me know when to have your bags packed."

The man exited the breakfast room as Mar waved and sung, "*Buenos Dias,* Glenny" from across the room.

They made plans while shoving eggs into their mouths and guzzling back the rich black coffee.

"Tell me again how you think we find her," Collum said.

"Well, good old Domhall left me a few cryptic hints. One of which was the notion of a portal. He found me about ten years ago, when I was sixteen and coming into my powers, asking about creating a spell to make a portal, based on the desire to locate a missing person. He wouldn't give me much more to go on and I never fully developed the spell, but in the end, I gave him all the work I had done. He paid me a bloody fortune."

She paused for a moment to sip more of the coffee. "Actually, it was that conversation that made me decide I wanted more power. Meeting Domhall let me see what I was really capable of."

"So, he's been planning this for ten years?"

"You know, for a big beast you catch on pretty quick."

"Yes, Mar, I've heard the big dumb dragon line before. You'd do well to remember that this dumb dragon was ravishing civilizations before you were a thought in your oldest ancestors' minds."

"I think I like you better when you're drunk," she pouted before carrying on. "Anyway, I couldn't finish the spell then, but knowing what I know now, and knowing that Domhall has figured it out, I'm certain I can as well."

"How are you certain he's figured it?"

"Oh Dragon, you need more coffee. How did Alex and her Parthen brother leave your courtyard? When you say a portal, I hope you'll let me slap your forehead for good measure."

He scowled at her and set his cup down. "The Parthen can't make portals."

"Nope, that's one thing the Parthen can't do, but apparently Domhall can. Give me a day or two and I'm fairly certain I can as well."

"We don't have a day or two."

"There is something else he told me at the airport that I didn't get around to telling you last night. He said something about loving to travel and he hoped I'd visit Athens one day to explore the history. I am willing to place bets that the Parthen King's Island is near Greece. I think if you get me close enough, I can create a portal to the island. It'll be weak, but we won't need much strength if we're close enough."

"Why do you need to be close? Can't you do it from here?"

"Okay, so you have to promise not to yell at me again. I mean we were both drinking last night so I didn't bring it up then and I didn't want to heap too much on your plate so I waited until now to tell you everything. I mean it's a fab castle, and I'd heard about Glenny's coffee . . . Honestly, every house I've been to has some poor sop in the kitchen trying to recreate this coffee, so I wanted to get a drink of it before you rushed . . ."

"Mar," Collum roared across the room with so much force a blast of fire followed it.

"*Dios Mio,* man, I thought I asked you not to yell at me," she yelled back while dodging the flame. "Okay, so, after talking about the history of the Greek culture, Domhall handed me a binder with all the papers I'd originally given him. Since we're in a hurry, I know I can't spend weeks on it, but I do believe if you give me a bit of time and get me to Greece, I can find your girlfriend."

Collum looked at her, exasperation tinged with respect. "Get your bags. We leave in fifteen minutes."

~ ~ ~

It ended up being late afternoon before the plane took off. First, there had been a young dragon who'd broken a wing when trying to fly. As king, he'd needed to make plans for the kid's recovery. Then they couldn't get his plane out of the hanger because the captain had pulled out parts for repair.

If it had been only him, he would have taken flight and been halfway to Greece by now. But he had the witch with him and he couldn't carry them both that far. They drove to the ferry to get off the island, followed by another hour to Heathrow terminal before settling themselves in for a five-hour, first class flight. If all went well, they'd be in Greece by ten p.m. that night. Depending on how long it took Mar to figure out the spell to open a portal, he was hopeful he'd reach Alex in as a little as thirty-six hours.

Chapter 31

Lachon surveyed his office from behind an antique teak desk. Law books lined the linen colored walls. Normally inspired by the knowledge that surrounded him, today those books felt like tombs. He knew in his bones that the daughter of Gray Taleisin was alive but he couldn't prove it. Rangers he'd sent to speak with the record keeper had disappeared. They'd last made contact prior to checking in at the Vancouver airport. The fools hadn't even made it to her island. All the feelers he sent out came back with the same message. Something had changed. A power had shifted but so far no one could get a hold on why. Then, two nights ago, reports came in from a spy in England that Collum Thronus had been seen with Domhall Taleisin and a young woman at the Heathrow Airport.

Lachon was no fool. He knew what that meant. He'd suspected it from the beginning if he was being honest.

Thronus with Domhall was a variable he didn't want to deal with. Thronus was old, older than old. If the dragons were now involved? If Thronus was somehow involved with the girl, it would change things. He didn't want a war with the dragons, but if the council was right about who her father had been then she was far too dangerous to live. Goddamn he was tired of all this bullshit. And he missed his friend.

Taurin and Ealian burst into his room brandishing a cell phone like a sword. Ealian was practically purple her passions ran so high and Taurin was whiter than normal. They dressed in faded gowns reminiscent of the sixteen hundreds. Their pale and dirty locks hung around their faces. Ealian's breasts attempted to break loose from the too small dress she wore.

He wondered again why he hadn't removed the brother and sister from the council long ago. Elders or not, something was wrong with them. Perhaps they shouldn't have lived so long.

Taurin wailed, "The dragon has killed my soldiers. This is an act of treason. You must send your people after him and kill him."

Lachon's heartbeat raced. "What are you talking about? Sit down for God's sake. You and Ealian rushing in here like tornados solves nothing."

"Nothing. Indeed, you seem to solve nothing, don't you Lachon?" Ealian seethed.

Her tattoo was dry, the colors of the wind faded but even those shook against her skin. It was a reminder to Lachon that Ealian, at least, was dangerous still.

"Why don't you tell me what you're talking about and we can find a solution that doesn't involve war with the dragons."

Taurin practically fell into the leather chair. Ealian slammed her body into the other seat, her small breasts battering against her skin. Taurin grabbed her hand. Lachon noticed again the strange relationship between the two. He wondered, not for the first time, if Taurin's choices had warped his sister's uncontrollable passion.

"I sent four of my men to Thronus's home in England to see what the bastard beast knows, since you didn't seem to be bothered to do so, and he killed three of them," Taurin screeched. "This is an aggression that cannot be allowed against us. You must hunt him down."

Disbelief froze Lachon's features. "You sent four armed idiots to a dragon's home and expected what exactly? And you did this without my knowledge. May I fucking remind you that I make the laws for our kind. Not you. Dammit.

The council means nothing if you act alone. You know that. And may I also remind you that our laws are not dragon laws. Thronus doesn't answer to any of us. He was long ago named The Guardian of all races. The beast is a law unto himself."

"He protects a child that is a danger to us, Lachon," Taurin whined.

"I know this. And I am working on it. But running off half-cocked won't help us." Lachon took a steadying breath. "What did your man report to you?"

Ealian composed herself enough to speak. "He said he was old before we were born and he would kill us as easily as he did our men."

Lachon slammed his fist onto the desk, disgusted with them like never before. "You've endangered us all. Surely you must know this isn't the way to handle things? My God, what's happened to the two of you? Never mind. Don't tell me. Just get out."

Their blank looks only fired his rage further. "Leave. I can't stand to look at you. I'm tired of this . . . of you both." He swept his hand at the office door. "Now go away so I can think."

As they blustered and argued he managed to push them out the door. They truly were idiots, but idiots were dangerous. None of that changed anything though.

Twenty-five years ago, the council agreed Gray Taleisin should be wed to keep her in check. She'd grown too wild and there were rumors of her finding a lover that could produce a child powerful enough to upset the balance in their world. It was that simple. He'd hated the decision. As expected, it had almost broken Domhall, but he'd agreed it was the right decision. Taurin and Ealian were tasked with finding a strong mate for the young woman.

They'd thought it was all under control until the partner they'd chosen claimed he'd been made a fool. He'd killed her. First, he'd killed the man she'd maintained was her true husband. It had been a shit show of the highest order.

If there was a child from that original union? If that's who was coming into power, and he suspected it was, then they were in deep, extraordinarily deep, shit.

He spent the afternoon trying to figure out how to outmaneuver the dragon and his old friend, Domhall, but there seemed to be no good plan. If Thronus protected the daughter, it meant the Elementals were at war with the Dragon kind as well as the Parthen.

Shortly after nine o'clock that night, his assistant knocked on his door. "This came for you and it's marked private." She handed him a black envelope.

Lachon rushed her out the door and told her to go home before he set himself behind his desk. He sliced through the envelope with an old ivory letter opener. Five words in bold lettering materialized on the paper. Five words he didn't understand. He suspected that he knew who could. Lachon called his assistant back before she reached the elevator.

"Call the pilot and tell him to prep the helicopter for a quick trip to Victoria as soon as he can. Preferably now."

He turned back to the desk as she scrambled to do his bidding and re-read the words he suspected were about to change everything.

The witch can bind their powers.

Chapter 32

After that night with Collum, Alex immersed herself in family. Her mother remained with her almost every waking moment. Neeren, almost every other. The days were full of laughter and Alex pushed Collum from her mind. Whatever they might be, could wait. She had a life with her mother to build. She spent lazy afternoons floating in the water while listening to Gray's stories. They talked of her past and how she had grown up.

Alex told Gray about her adopted family and about Aunt Quinn. Gray listened attentively and asked questions about her adopted mother and how she had been treated. Often her eyes glazed over with sadness when Alex told stories of Aunt Quinn's sardonic humor.

The first couple of days blended together. Time was held sacred as the three of them learned about each other. Neeren taught her about their people. About their history. Often the two of them would walk alone. He led her patiently through his castle time and again, introducing her to all the Parthen on the island. He treated her with respect, but also teased her like any brother would his little sister. Alex soaked it in, enjoying every moment of being a sibling.

He reminded her often that they were the only two of their kind in the world. Neeren showed her remote areas of the island so she could see all that was hers now as well. He was clear that they would share the kingdom.

She often watched him under her lashes. Not once did she witness a display of anger or impatience. He was always kind and generous, but slightly separate of the world. His humor was subtle. There were times Alex felt like he was the only person in on a private joke.

His entire existence was a secret. He wore it like a cloak. The secrets would have broken lesser men. In him it added a strength of character that understood the ebb and flow of life. She wondered, though, about his severe self-control. She thought of the fights she and Collum had. How passion simmered just below the surface at their every interaction. She welcomed the day when Neeren might truly feel free. She doubted he ever had.

On her fourth day with them, Neeren found her on their private beach. She watched him study her from the top of the cliff for a few minutes before heading down.

"You may not be able to turn into a cat," he said, "but you definitely enjoy the sun as we do. Remind me to take you out on the boat so you can lay on the bow to sunbathe."

Alex looked over her shoulder as he spoke. She'd become used to him appearing out of nowhere. "You have a boat?"

"*We* have a boat." He pulled out his cell phone and showed her a photo of a glistening yellow and sky-blue yacht moored in the ocean.

It was easily one of the biggest yachts she'd ever seen. Coming from Victoria, that was saying something. She guessed it rang in at one hundred and thirty meters in length with four decks.

"Neeren, it's gorgeous. Are you sure you aren't pulling my leg?"

He arched a brow questioningly. "Why would I pull your leg? Her name is the Palladium. We'll make a date with Mother and spend a day on her next week. I have a few items to deal with before I can leave for the whole day."

He sat beside her, giving no care to the damp sand on his perfectly tailored tan trousers.

They rested in comfortable silence for a while, both stared out to the sea.

"It's been almost a week since this started, Alex. Soon, we'll have to discuss more than boats and family stories. I'd rather go on the offensive with those who seek to harm us. To be honest with you, I am sick of hiding on my island."

"I know, I guess I wanted to enjoy this life for a while. I never had a brother before and everything has been so easy here."

He leaned back on his elbows and gazed at the gentle waves lapping against the shore.

"It is easy because we are hiding. I have hidden my whole life. They call me the Solitary King you know. They say I'm mysterious." He laughed darkly. "It's always been about protecting Mother. I couldn't care less if the Elementals know about me. I'd happily have gone to war before now but I had to lessen the chances of anyone finding out about her. I couldn't risk our enemies destroying her. She'd already lost too much."

He looked at Alex with heavy eyes. "I'm tired of it. When the elders come for her and you, they'll find me. I'm going to destroy them."

Alex leaned into him. Felt the rage simmering below the surface. The intensity of his hatred frightened her. He'd never let it slip before. "I want to help you. You need to show me how to fight the other elements. I couldn't even call up my fire the night you lost your shit on the beach."

He stood and pulled her up with him. "That night was different. I'm different. It won't be the same with others. Everything you need to stop your enemies is inside you. Don't let fear and inexperience control the outcome. We will begin now. Stand in the water."

"What do you mean, you're different?"

"Only that I'm your brother. You can't overpower me the same way you can others."

Alex waded into the water up to her knees, cringing slightly at its coolness.

"Are your feet cold?" he asked.

"Yes, a little."

"Your flame is in the water. The tip of the tattoo begins on your foot. Ask it to warm you."

Alex thought back to the time when Collum showed her how to control her flame with her intention. She felt for the flame inside her, visualized it coming to life on her foot. Slowly, the water around her started to foam.

On the shore, Neeren clapped his hands. "Well done. You see how easy it is?"

"Sure, but I'm not afraid right now and I have the time to think about what I'm doing."

He walked to her and held her hands. As he did so, the water around them began to shift and grow. Waves swarmed around them until they were surrounded by a seven-foot-tall wall of water.

"I am in charge now, Alex. The only way to stop me is to force me to let go."

"I tried that already and I couldn't do it."

"Focus. Breathe. Channel your energy. The water will cover us if you don't stop me. I can breathe under water. Can you?"

"You won't drown me."

As she said the words, the water churned faster, closing in on them. It pushed against her legs and arms, climbed up her chest. Even then, Alex didn't believe he'd follow through. The water climbed higher. It tightened against her throat. Forced itself over her lips and nose. She choked on the liquid as it filled her nostrils. Fear left her rigid, frantic. She struggled to get away, but his hands held her in place. She thrashed against him, felt herself dying, choking on the fluid in her lungs. Still he held her, all the while staring with a calculated look.

As the last of her breath left her body, she felt her soul depart and immediately slam back into her body. As she held her breath again, she realized she was still there, staring at her brother—alive.

With clarity, she finally understood what everyone had been telling her from the moment this started. She was immortal goddammit. How many times would she need to be reminded of that? Once she understood, she focused her energy, forced her flame onto him before she drowned again. She pictured the tattoo on her flesh, how it wound its way up her calves and across her rib cage, over her shoulders, and down to her arms and hands. She pushed the flames off her flesh and on to his, asking the fire to increase in potency.

He fought against the fire. She marveled as water turned to ice like a shield over his skin. She envisioned a fire raging. Blisters appeared on his flesh and the ice melted. As waves rushing through her gave way, Neeren released her hands and the water receded.

He grinned while looking at the burns on his hands. "You see, you have the strength. You've always had it. But do not take so long next time. The next immortal you fight won't be as easy on you as I was. And if they take your head, you're done."

She bent over, gulping air she apparently no longer needed before punching him in the gut. "You son of a bitch. Don't do that to me ever again." She took perverse pleasure hearing the air rush out of his mouth. It wasn't enough, but it helped.

Coughing, he replied, "You wanted to learn. I taught you. Why are you so angry?"

"Because, you jerk," she screamed. "I drowned."

Cocking his head to the side, he gave her a look that made her feel daft.

"That was the point. Perhaps you'll best me next time."

"Try again, buddy. I bested you this time. I totally owned you."

Laughing, he replied in his awkward way, "Totally," and then winked at her surprised look. "Keep practicing and do not get cocky. Domhall arrives soon. Once he does, preparations begin. I will carry no more shadows, Alex." He kissed the top of her forehead and walked away.

~ ~ ~

Alex watched him go. His muscled back held taught. She pictured the tight line of his mouth. Dread at the thought of war, mixed with compassion for her brother.

Four panthers padded silently behind as he ascended the cliff. He gave no indication of knowing they were there until he reached the top. Alex strained to hear what he said. She watched as the panthers transformed into the four most beautiful women she'd ever seen. Each of them long and muscled. Strong. Not girls—Women. From her spot on the beach Alex could see their piercing yellow eyes. They waited patiently for Neeren's command.

"His ladies," her mother said as she came up behind her. "He thinks I don't know but I'm not stupid. Everyone knows. Everyone on the Island knows. Half the Immortal world knows. They might not know who *he* is, but the tales of his lovers are legendary."

Her mother's candour surprised her. The woman was perfectly composed as always. Short ice-blond hair swung gently over her ears, a white silk dress floated against her skin. Alex considered her own outfit—cut off shorts and a tank covered in sand. Her hair was a rat's nest from salt water and ocean breeze, but she couldn't bring herself to try and comb through it. She was worlds apart from her mother . . . and Neeren too. Doubted she'd ever be as quiet and composed as the two of them were.

"I wondered how he dealt with all the pressure. He always seems so poised and, well, kind of mocking. He comes across as always in control, when really, it's because he's getting laid all the time."

Her mother grinned. "Neeren is a study in complication. He doesn't feel anything for them. But would never leave any of them wanting. He cares about everything and he cares about nothing."

Alex looked at the ledge. Neeren and the four women had disappeared. "Where did they go?"

"Who knows." Gray snorted. "It's someone new every time. They all vie for the Kings favor."

"My brother, the emotionally detached male slut. Does that about cover it?"

Gray's eyes sparkled. "I've never heard it put quite that way before. I should be shocked, but yes, that about covers it. Oh, it feels so good to laugh, even at Neeren. It is good to see him as simply a man, not a king. Or a boy that lost everything."

"Glad I could help," Alex quipped before sobering. "Seeing him with those women makes me miss Collum."

"The dragon is a masterful man," Gray said.

"Yes, but it's more. I miss his smell. I miss seeing annoyance written on his face. How can I miss someone so much when I hardly know him?"

Her mother smiled. "Because you know he's meant for you, my darling."

"All of this." Alex swept her arms out. "Is so much. It's overwhelming. I don't trust myself right now."

"It's okay," Gray said. "You have time."

"Do I? Neeren wants to prepare for war."

Her mother absently straightened the non-existent wrinkles on her dress. "I know. He's been waiting for years, ever since Domhall found us. He's held back for me, for you. He's not wrong. Much was taken, from all of us."

The vengeance in Gray's voice rocked the earth below them. "My husband was murdered for the crime of loving me. It's time we reclaimed our lives."

Alex gripped her mother's hand. Anger and grief constricting her chest.

A bittersweet smiled transformed Gray's face. Wiped the agony from her features. "Once Domhall joins us, we'll make our plans. But not today. Today, we sit in the sun. We practice teaching your fire to overcome my earth. Are you ready?"

Chapter 33

The sound of tires on the gravel driveway alerted Quinn to her visitor. She calmly sorted her papers and waited for the doorbell chime. Before rising from her desk, she pulled her strawberry hair in to a loose knot, reached into the second drawer, and palmed her pistol. As the sound of the doorbell echoed through her home, she quietly tucked the gun against her back.

She adjusted her glasses and straightened her clothing as she slowly made her way to the door. Whoever was on the other side could wait. The hinge creaked as she cautiously opened the door. Her father waited on the front porch. His back was turned, his hands clasped behind his back. She cleared her throat. He turned toward her abruptly, awkwardly. Seemingly startled.

As they made eye contact, he said simply, "Hello, daughter."

Her pulse raced. Her ulcer reared its ugly head. She blinked once, then calmly closed the door in his face before wandering into the kitchen to pour a cup of chamomile tea.

Domhall, red-faced, joined her in the kitchen a minute later. He sat at the table. "Don't be like that, Quinny. I know it's been a while, but we need to talk."

Quinn gritted her teeth at the sound of her childhood nickname. She stirred one scoop of raw sugar into her teacup and stared out the window, looked over the ocean below and ignored him. She refused to give him the satisfaction of throwing perfectly good tea in his face.

He fumbled with his iPod. "C'mon, kiddo. Can we put our issues aside for a moment? I've come a long way to speak with you," he blustered. "Look at me for goodness sake."

She cracked her knuckles and pushed up the sleeves of her sweater. The sounds of K'Naan's *Hurt Me Tomorrow,* pumped out of the headphones hanging around his neck. Her composure dipped. She hated his goddamn music collection. She picked up her chipped teacup and walked out of the kitchen.

She heard him swear under his breath before pushing the chair back from the table and scrambling to follow her.

"Child, stop this nonsense. I have to speak to you of Alexedria."

She almost faltered. But, dammit, she refused to ask how he knew about Alex. *I won't be sucked into his game this time.* Not again. She settled in a tan recliner in the sunroom. The walls were lined with built-in books shelves, filled with the works of the greats (and the not so greats). It's where she went when she needed to decompress. From this room, she'd seen pods of killer whale's swim directly below.

Her skin crawled when her father entered the room. He hadn't changed much over the years. She pitied the people that still believed in him. She knew better.

"I have nothing to say to you. My niece is none of your concern."

"Your niece is my granddaughter and there are things you need to know."

"Mother told me everything before she died. I've handled it all accordingly. You have no part of this. Your time is long over." Her facade slipped momentarily as the sound of his music interrupted the silence. "Turn off that music."

Domhall fumbled with his iPod. The song ended abruptly. The silence was deafening.

"Your mother's death was very hard on me. I needed time alone."

"Her death was hard on all of us. Not that it matters. You were never much of a father to me. We both know it. I stopped relying on you a long time ago. Say whatever it is you think you need to say and then get out."

"Very well. It's probably best to do it this way anyway." He leaned forward in the chair. "Alexedria is no longer with Collum Thronus. She left him three days ago to join . . . her brother . . . and your sister."

Quinn stared at the pink slippers on her feet. They were Alex's. She'd started wearing them after Alex left, as a source of comfort, to remind herself that Alex was safe.

She stood, removed her glasses, placed them on the bamboo coffee table. When she finally turned, hatred lay on her flesh like a badge of honor. She reached in to her back pocket, raised her gun, and fired.

~ ~ ~

Quinn aimed straight for his head. A mortal wouldn't have stood a chance. At the last second Domhall raised his hand to deflect the bullet. It grazed his temple before embedding in the bookshelf behind him.

"What the hell," he shouted. "That was a point—fucking—blank shot."

"It's no more than you deserve, asshole." She dropped the gun, exhausted, and sank in to her chair. "I can't believe you'd come into this home, my home, with such a shitty lie. Do you know how much it broke me when Gray was killed? Sometimes I think you've turned into a monster."

He shuffled his feet and shoved his fingers through his hair. "I know you'll never forgive me, kiddo. Nor do I think you should. But I'm not lying to you. Not in this. Gray is alive. Truth is, I hid her."

Quinn searched the water below, looking for whales, for anything that would take her away.

Behind her, his breathing was heavy. He continued with

the tale. "I took her to a safe house and nursed her back to health. Once she could speak, she told me her secrets. The man the dragon killed was her true husband. They'd been desperately in love for over a hundred years."

His breath rattled on a long sigh. She steadied herself for what would come after that sigh.

"Alexedria was not the only child."

Her heart ached, her throat ached. Every muscle, even her skin. For all his playing the angels and working the game, he hadn't even considered her. The one daughter he'd never loved quite enough. He hadn't cared what all this would do to her. Neither of her parents had. Yet she'd had been the one who'd bent and rebuilt, over and over. They'd left it to her to pick up the pieces without giving her the courtesy of explaining why.

The waves crashed against the shore. Quinn thought of how her life was like those waves. Always churning, hiding pathetic stories underneath the depths.

"I hate you. Do you know that? I hate you. Your games. The elder's politics. You've destroyed lives. How could you not know about a husband before? How could you let them force her into that marriage? You could've stopped so many deaths."

"I thought I was protecting her. She was too strong, too fast." He hung his head. "I didn't want her to turn out like me. But you can't blame me for everything. I am not omnipotent, Quinn. Your sister was very good at covering her tracks."

"Don't remind me. She learned from the best." She finally looked him in the eye. "Before you continue you need to assure me that Alex is safe, because at this point I don't care about the rest of you."

"She is safe and in the arms of her mother."

"Oh, the mother that abandoned her for the last twenty-five years? The mother that always played her own agenda? That one?"

"Don't judge. There's so much more to the tale than this."

The bullet embedded in her copy of Tom Sawyer glared at her. "I'm listening, but don't think for a moment this will change how I feel about you."

"I understand. If you change your mind, I hope you'll allow me the chance to be your father again. But please let me finish. It's a complicated story that alters all our futures." When she would have interrupted, he plunged ahead saying, "Gray's husband was a Parthen. And not just any Parthen. He was their king. Your sister, their queen."

Rage simmered below the surface of her purple eyes. Wind whipped the trees outside her home. "Dreamwalkers."

"Yes, Dreamwalkers. So, you see, the elders had every right to be concerned about her impetuousness."

"You gave her to a monster."

"We did. But I didn't know. It's no excuse. I trusted the wrong people. Was blinded by wanting to keep my daughter safe. Instead, I let the machinations of others destroy her, destroy our family. I'm trying to right that wrong. Your niece could be the greatest threat our enemies have ever known."

He talked over her when she would have stopped him. Her reflection glowed in his eyes.

"Your sister told me of another, of a son, the new king, with all the same powers. I played a risky game but if the elders learned of the boy, it meant both their deaths. We killed his father. I couldn't rip his mother from him as well. But Alex would know no different. The only choice I had was to hide her. After all, no one knew about her lineage."

"Why are you telling me all this now? I mean why not keep me in the dark?"

"Because I've kept everyone in the dark for too long and I need one person, at least, to know the truth."

"I don't understand. It seems like I'm the only one left who doesn't know the truth."

"I'm ashamed to say, that assumption is incorrect. I need you, Quinn. You are the best of us."

Once more he paused. Quinn waited.

"After your sister told me her story, I realized she'd never be a part of our family again. She'd given her heart and soul to the Parthen. I believed then, as I believe now, I had only one choice."

He choked on his final words. She relished in the sound of the agony in his voice.

"In a final act of betrayal, I erased your sister's memories. I let her escape me. She raced back to her son with no knowledge she'd ever told me about him. I let her believe her daughter died. Ten years ago, when the child started exhibiting signs of abilities, I contacted Gray. Began to build a relationship again. Met her son."

Quinn focused on the cold tea in her cup. Chamomile, she thought, meant to soothe her. He'd kept them all alive, but in doing so, ripped their family apart.

"And now that Alex has grown up and come into her power, you can't keep the charade up any more."

"That's right. I knew once Alex gained her power, her brother would find her. So, I found him first, made sure all the pieces were in place to protect my family."

"And now you need me."

"And now I need you. There will be a battle. I gave us an extra twenty-five years, but our enemies will figure it out soon. I can't keep the secret any longer. The boy, your nephew, grows stronger every day. I believe his need for revenge does too. I need you to find out things I can't. My insanity has driven me from many rooms. You have access. You have people who will listen to you, people who are not without their own power. If we play all our cards right, we might be able to stop a war and destroy those elders who destroyed us."

"Who were they? Who chose the dragon for her husband?"

"Taurin and Ealian Gondien."

"And my nephew's name?"

"His name is Neeren. He is exceptional."

She tasted the name in her mouth. "You think, Neeren is out for blood?"

"I do. He is a king with immense power, whose father was slain and sister stolen. He has the power to destroy them. Now that Alex is safely with him, he'll take revenge. I'm certain of it.

Domhall paused. "Quinn, please don't tell your sister or the boy that I deceived them." He clarified, "He may not understand why I did what I did. I don't wish to hurt him. You should meet him. He is your blood after all."

"You trust him with Alex?"

"I trust that he loves her. Beyond that, is anyone's guess. Gray would never challenge him. I don't know if Alex is strong enough to stop him yet. In time, she could be. But she'll feel for him, want to stand by his side. Thronus has fallen for Alex, so in the end, if it came down to it, I'm sure he would put down Neeren. In truth, he may be the only one strong enough to do so."

"Put him down? What are you talking about? I thought you were going to protect him."

"We're going to help him keep his head and his throne. We're not going to help him destroy our people."

The weight of his confession sat heavy on her chest. She retreated into the kitchen to boil more hot water. The conversation was almost enough to drive her to drink. Trying to decipher Domhall's mind was like trying to diffuse a ticking time bomb.

Everything in her home was ordered. Everything had its place. The space was open and clean, a typical west coast home. She found herself on the large deck off the kitchen, listening to the crash of the surf, hoping it would bring troubled emotions under control. The wind whipped her hair free of the elastic. She welcomed the breeze. Let it sooth her. Caress her. Care for her.

She weighed the options for a time. Finally accepted she'd do what he asked. Couldn't leave Alex to Domhall's machinations. She'd grown to love that kid as though she were her own daughter.

She pushed up the sleeve of her top and looked at the almost invisible, flesh toned lines of her tattoo, thought back to her life growing up. She always felt like a muted version of her baby sister. So, she studied—everything. Excelled behind the scenes. She shoved her sleeve down as Domhall came up behind her on the deck.

"Will you help me protect them?" he asked.

She nodded. "What do you want me to do?"

"I need our family's records. Everything. And I need the records of the council members, Taurin and Ealian. We must know their strengths and weaknesses. You're the only one that can do this."

"If they find out, they'll kill me, and it's a sure bet they're keeping tabs on me right now."

"I understand it's a lot to ask. I need you. You are the only one that can do it. I'll protect you as much as I can. As soon as you acquire the records, we'll leave this place, and you'll be with Alex again."

"What about Lachon? Where does he fit in this?"

"I have plans for Lachon The Law."

"You realize that Taurin and Ealian have probably altered all of their own records by now."

Domhall smirked. "My dear girl, as if you would let that happen on your watch."

~ ~ ~

The next morning Quinn woke up with a pounding headache. They'd made plans throughout the night. Devised a way to steal the records without the council knowing. Domhall had finally left her home around four in the morning with instructions to meet him at the airport in thirty-six hours, where he'd collect her and the information they needed. Then he'd take her to see Alex. She still wasn't sure she could trust him. He was, after all, a little bit insane.

She desperately wanted to talk to Collum Thronus to learn what he'd been told from her mother. What a fucking mess this all was. And it all started with the goddamn council. If they'd left it all alone, her family would be together. Alex would've never been hidden. Maybe her parents would've made it. Maybe she'd have met her nephew. Maybe she wouldn't have lived her entire life hating the elders, and her father, for signing her sister's death warrant.

Quinn dressed in Levi's that fit her like a glove. Felt like butter against her skin. She disliked the new brands. She threw on a honey colored cashmere sweater that molded to her soft curves and accentuated her hips. Then, on bare feet, she headed to the kitchen for coffee and Tylenol.

A windstorm raged inside her. An ordered and gentle life was what she'd always needed most. Yet now, once again, thanks to her family, she'd been thrown into chaos. She'd have to leave her home, who knew for how long. The thought made her physically ache. Her head pounded. She poured her coffee and threw back three extra strength Tylenol, hoping to ease the pain. As she waited at the table, she rubbed her fingers against the indent where Alex had dropped a concrete paper weight their first month together.

When she heard the car in her driveway, she rose from the table, fluffed her hair, pinched her cheeks, licked her lips, and once again grabbed her gun. She wouldn't miss this time if she had to fire.

Chapter 34

Through lace curtains, she watched Lachon drive up the curved driveway. He'd been here once before, invited to a housewarming party after she first purchased the place. Back when they had been friends. She'd never said anything outright damming to him after Gray died, but never made an attempt to talk to him again either. They hadn't even spoken at her mother's funeral.

When the knock on the door came, she took her time answering. He'd often told her, "Patience is a virtue." Today she'd see if he believed his own advice.

She cracked the door open. Smiled respectfully, as one should when they greeted a member of the council. It was a practiced smile that did not reach her eyes. It was the same smile she gave whenever they'd come in contact at the Hall of Records over the past years. One that said she had nothing to say to him, could barely stand his presence.

"Good morning, Councilor Findel. This is unexpected. What can I do for you?" Quinn asked as she leaned a hip against the door jam.

"Please, call me Lachon. After all we've known and worked with each other for so many years."

She shook her head and simply replied, "Thank you for the kind offer but we must always remember protocol. Now, what can I help you with, Councilor?"

"It's important. May I come in?"

"Of course." Quinn stepped back. "I put on a pot of tea. Can I offer you something?"

"Yes. Thank you. I hope I didn't wake you?"

"Not at all, I'm an early riser." She shut the door and gestured for Lachon to follow her to the kitchen. Motioned for him to take a seat at the table while she poured them tea. She bent over to find the sugar in the cupboard. Purposely squirmed her hips as she did so. She stirred the sugar in the cup then licked the spoon. Offered him cream, which he politely declined.

Quinn set a cup in from of him and sat in the chair across the table.

"Your toes must be cold," he said.

She smiled serenely, flipped her hair over her shoulders. "You'd think so, wouldn't you? I had in floor heating installed a few years back so the floors are always quite warm. I have no need for slippers." She wiggled her toes. "Now, Councilor, please tell me what I can do for you?"

"I want to know why you called the Dragon King last week."

She took a sip of her tea and licked her lips, "He's . . . an old friend."

"The Guardian of the immortals is a strange companion for you. I'd never heard of this friendship before."

"Yes, well." She giggled. "Our relationship is personal and none of your concern."

"I doubt that." Lachon gulped the tea. "Would you like to try again?"

Quinn gave up trying to be sexy. She'd told Domhall it wouldn't work. She wasn't exactly known for being a sexpot.

"We had a contract that needed to be settled. I called him to finalize the contract. That's all." She kept her face composed and answered as close to the truth as possible so that Lachon couldn't accuse her of lying.

"I see and may I ask what this contract was?"

"It was the settling of a gift my mother left for him in her Will."

Lachon nodded. "Your mother died some years ago, why not give him the gift years ago?"

"I found the request when I was going through her things."

The morning sun streamed in through the kitchen windows. Lachon turned his profile to the sun before he asked his next question.

"And can you tell me where Thronus is now?"

Quinn quipped, "I can tell you that I don't know where Thronus is now."

"I see. And can you tell me if he liked his gift."

"I don't know the answer to that," she said, stumbling over the question.

"How could you not? What was his reaction when he saw his gift?"

The game ended then.

"It is the greatest gift he's ever been given," she whispered.

"He protects her?" Lachon asked.

Knowing what must be done, Quinn accepted her fate. "Of course, he protects her. He is her sworn protector."

Lachon stood. Kindness lay in his voice. "Quinn, I'm truly sorry to do this. What's happened to your family is tragic, but I must find the girl. You place us all in danger by helping her."

Quinn studied Lachon—a man she had always admired. The Law of their people. The closest thing her father had ever had to a friend. She stood.

"You know nothing, Lachon." She reached behind her sweater, pulled out the gun and fired point blank into his heart.

His head jerked back and, he fell to his knees. For a moment, Quinn thought she'd have to fire again. He was so large that even on his knees they came almost face-to-face.

She placed the gun on the table, stroked his jaw as his eyes began to close. His hands held his chest. Confusion clearly written on the lines of his face when he realized there was no blood.

"Don't worry, Lachon, it's only a tranquilizer. There's enough dosage in here to take down an elephant for three days. We estimate it'll be enough to keep you sleeping for two. Maybe you've figured it out by now and maybe you haven't. Father feels you have the right to know. Though I disagree with him, I am following his lead. So, listen up before you pass out. I have things that need to be done."

She cradled his chin in her hand and looked him in the eyes. "A son was born." She watched his eyes flare as he held on to reality for a few moments more. "Domhall may trust you, but I'll reserve judgment for now."

Dropping his chin, she dusted off her hands and picked up her gun. "Now, I have a nephew to meet and a niece to save. And if it wasn't clear already, I resign as record keeper. No matter what, I am a Taleisin first and I'll do everything I can to protect my family."

She left him on his knees in the kitchen, gathered pillows and a blanket from her bedroom to make sure he was comfortable while he slept on the floor. She chose her softest pillow and her favorite blanket. She changed out of her top and put on a T-shirt and zip up sweater she'd picked up from MEC the summer before. Added a good pair of breathable socks. Grabbed the bag of clothing left by the bed earlier the night before. Then picked up the untraceable cell phone Domhall left with her and dialed the number.

When he answered, she spoke quickly. "It's done. I'm leaving the house in seven minutes."

With all her gear in tow, she headed back into the kitchen. The mighty Law of the People lay on her floor. For a brief instant, she understood the obsession so many of her kind had with power. She'd taken down a giant because he hadn't for an instant thought she could. She placed the pillow under his head, brushed his auburn hair out of his eyes. Next, she laid her blanket over his massive body. Even in this forced sleep, she felt the power echoing off him.

He might have looked at her briefly with respect, as a warrior, but he was going to be out for blood when he woke up. She'd broken the law as sure as she'd brushed her teeth this morning. There was no going back. She took a moment to walk around her home and say a mental goodbye. In all likelihood, she'd never return. Not unless they could stop a war.

She stroked Lachon's hair one final time before leaving the house. Wasn't sure he could hear her, but decided it was worth a try.

"I'm sorry. But this was the only way. If you'd been on our side, maybe things would be different. Can't you see the other members of your council have turned dark? They don't follow your law. You'd be smarter to worry about them than about us. The drugs will wear off in two days." And since she knew it was likely the next time she saw him would be in battle, she kissed him on the mouth before she left and said, "Until we meet again, Law."

Chapter 35

Four hours and a ferry ride later, Quinn pulled up to the Office of the Records, in the heart of Vancouver's Gastown. The drive had been excruciating. She was certain someone had been following her most of the way to the ferry. Then she'd had to wait an entire hour for the next boat, which was stifling and claustrophobic. All the other passengers kept staring at her, like they could tell who she was and what she'd done.

She'd seen a few werewolves at one end of the bow, but they kept to themselves. Wolves were notoriously aloof with other immortals. Most of the crossing was spent in her car, counting down the minutes. Once docked, she'd peeled off the deck as quickly as possible and made it from the docks to the office in under forty minutes. She was sure there'd be at least one speeding ticket in her mailbox the next day.

She parked her Nissan Murano and hastily made her way through the crowds of hipsters lounging along the streets of Gastown. She'd never fit in this part of the city. Was as far from hipster as one could get. Quinn looked like she was in her late-thirties. When she'd found Alex, it'd been necessary to allow her body to age to fit the human timeline of being her aunt.

Elementals typically came into their immortality in their mid-twenties and then only aged one year for every hundred they lived. She'd allowed her aging to speed up a bit. Then discovered she enjoyed ageing. Liked sensible clothing that fit her well. Liked her skin and the laugh lines that appeared around her eyes. She stopped wearing makeup. Her style was uncomplicated and practical, the way she liked her life.

Her attempt to flirt with Lachon that morning had been ridiculous. Quinn didn't flirt. Didn't use her body to try and entice men. Her body wasn't her strength. Her mind was.

Her sister had been stunning beyond words. Lithe and delicate looking, with a fire that roared above the surface. There was no mistaking Gray's wildness. Alex, was even more tremendous. Her untamed beauty drew looks to her like moths to a flame. But it was her off-beat humor and intelligence that made her special.

She pushed through a group of twenty somethings on the sidewalk, her stomach re-coiling at what she'd done. The Law of the Elementals was currently asleep and vulnerable on a pillow in her kitchen. Most of their kind feared his name with good reason. Lachon never faltered in his vow to uphold the law of his people. She muttered a series of swear words under her breath at the front door of the office.

Inside the building, she walked quickly and without ceremony through the reception area. Most of the staff saw her sparingly. She traveled or worked from her home office at least three quarters of the month. After Alex came into her life it'd been necessary to keep her away from Vancouver.

No one commented on her brisk walk through the lobby. She wasn't known for small talk. She made sure the history of their race was intact. Had no need to be friends with her staff. She shut the door to her office, started up her computer, linked to the company network, and downloaded all the files on Taurin and Ealian. Then erased any personal documents that might mention Gray's pregnancy from both her computer and any external hard drives. She took all the photos from her desk and threw them in her briefcase along with her laptop. Once that was done she composed herself and headed to the archives room.

A few senior staff members greeted her warmly as she wandered through the office. At the door to the archive room, she hesitated a fraction of a second before swiping her electronic key to gain entry. There was no going back now. Hell, there was no going back after she'd shot Lachon Findel. The lock slid open. Quinn walked through the doors determined to change her family's destiny.

~ ~ ~

Inside the room, the air was cool and dry. The temperature strictly regulated. Most of the documents were sealed in plastic sheets. There were thousands of years of archived materials in here. The staff was careful not to let any of the papers become damaged. The sweeping changes Quinn herself instituted over two hundred years ago, were the reason most of their history remained intact. Everything in this room had been scanned and saved on triplicate hard drives so that even if the papers themselves were lost, the information would be safe.

Quinn deleted what she needed. Only a few Elementals on earth had access like she did. Domhall used to, until he went nuts. A couple of judges had more limited access. In the end, they'd all know the youngest keeper they'd ever had, betrayed them.

It took less than sixty seconds to locate the files needed. No one who knew this room like she did. She'd designed it after the previous archives room had failed to live up to her exacting specifications. She shoved the files into her briefcase and picked up the file on Lachon the Law as well. No matter what Domhall thought, she was damn well going to be prepared if she had to fight him. She exited the room, refused to look back. The archives were in her past now.

Three minutes later, waving a polite goodbye to the front receptionist, she entered the elevator. It had taken her less than an hour to destroy the very foundation of her life.

"Have a great night, Ms. Taleisin," said the young girl at reception.

Her name was Brie. Quinn had handpicked her to join the team. Brie was short, and round, with shining, intelligent eyes. Quinn broke a little inside. Her goddamn family was ruining everything. If it weren't for Alex, she'd let them rot.

Back on the street she pushed her way through a throng of hipsters nursing fifteen-dollar bottles of beer. On the dash of her Murano was tucked a perfectly printed out parking ticket.

"Are you kidding me? Goddamn." She looked around for the meter maid, kicked the tires of her car.

A couple young ladies smirked at her. She happily gave them the finger before ripping up the ticket, climbing into her car, and driving away from her life.

It took over an hour to reach the airport. Traffic was always shitty on the number One Highway. That afternoon it crawled at a standstill. She was sure building security was right behind her, or that Lachon had somehow freed himself and would reach her, but no one came.

When she finally reached the airport Domhall was waiting for her at stall four-thirty-four. Neither of them said anything. When she climbed out the car with bags in tow, he hugged her. For the first time in twenty-five years she gave herself a minute to let her dad hold her and make her feel safe.

He used his magic to get them through the airport and customs. Within minutes they were on his plane, headed to Greece and to her sister. Quinn held her breath until they were in the air.

"You did well, darling. Thank you."

"Go to hell. I didn't do it for you. The only one I care about in this is Alex. You and Gray can re-disappear for all I care." She laughed, loathing herself. "Do you even care that my entire future is over? For your golden daughter. I can't believe I did this. I left a man drugged in my kitchen. I betrayed all the people I work with, people I hired. Any chance I had at a normal life with my niece is gone thanks to you."

Domhall leaned back in his seat, scrolled through his iPod and put his headphones on before replying, "None of that matters. Destinies are at stake."

~ ~ ~

The plane landed on a private runway on Hydra Island eleven hours later. Quin hadn't slept. They drove through the villages on the island, both aware many eyes followed them. It seemed her nephew had been busy fortifying his corner of the world. They parked at the port. Domhall led her to a small speed boat, ready and waiting to take off.

"How did you arrange all this?" Quinn asked.

Several men and women slid back into the shadows, the minute they stepped on the boat deck.

"I'm a man of many talents child." Domhall grinned. "I have a few good people that help support our needs. Now sit back. This sucker has kick." He nodded to the driver of the boat. "Home Jeeves."

Ten minutes into the ride across the ocean, the hair on her skin tensed. The air around them calmed. The winds ceased and a ripple in the fabric of the earth opened, allowing them entry to Neeren's kingdom. As they passed the threshold, a large island appeared. The driver released the throttle, dropped their speed and easily made his way up to a shining silver dock lined with black panthers.

Domhall faced her, grinning like a teenager. "They brought out the welcoming party."

Quinn gripped her satchel, scanned the dock for Alex. A lone man stood at the front of the group. He acknowledged her with a slight smile before calmly turning to Domhall.

"Welcome, Grandfather. We have been expecting you."

"Hey, kid. I noticed the silent escort through Hydra. Assumed you'd be waiting."

"Well," he replied, "I cannot have you sneak on the island like the first time, can I?"

Chapter 36

Quinn climbed off the boat, openly studying this stranger that was her nephew. Domhall's voice interrupted her analysis.

"Neeren, may I present Quinn, your aunt. Quinn this is Neeren, King of the Parthen and your nephew."

She continued to stare at him. Found herself memorizing his face . . . just in case. She wanted to say something, but the words stuck somewhere in her chest. And then the young man, in front of his people, bowed to her before dropping to one knee.

"I have waited far too long to meet you. Mother has told me many stories about your youth. Thank you for protecting my sister for so many years. You forever have my loyalty and gratitude." He grasped her hand and kissed it before rising.

Quinn squeezed her eyes shut a moment. He meant it, she realized, even if it was too practiced, to feel completely genuine. He was a man who understood perception and diplomacy. Still, she was willing to give it a try if he was. It was why she'd come. To meet her blood, the boy she'd never known.

That boy stood before her as still and silent as a piece of marble. He held his lean muscles deceptively taught. Bare feet peeked out from beneath tan slacks. She released the breath she hadn't realized she held. Looked down at the hand still holding hers. Squeezed.

"Neeren, we have a lot of lost time to make up, don't we? I'm sorry this happened to us. I have to admit I'm still in a bit of shock, but I can't wait to know you now and to build the relationship we should have always had."

He reached out, trapped her in his arms for a bear hug that took her off her feet, and whispered in her ear, "Thank you for giving me the chance to be your nephew."

He put her down slowly, took her hand, raised his voice so the rest of the assembled group could hear. "Come. I think it is time we all joined Mother and Alex at the house. They've been waiting most impatiently."

Together they walked down the dock. A tribe of panthers followed. Quinn could see that Neeren was no fool. This was his kingdom and he would have his display of power mixed with his happy reunion.

It was in her nature to absorb all she saw and catalogue it for dissection later. She noticed animals watching them from the tree-line, with more along the edges of the cliffs above. The sun poured down on her as they climbed. Neeren easily matched his pace to hers. Seemed quite content to do so.

"We're almost there," he said. "Alex was very excited to hear you were coming. So was Mother. You'll find she has changed much from the woman you knew."

She recognized the subtle protective quality to his tone. "I suspect none of us are quite the same."

He nodded, a slightly ironic smile on his lips. "Touché."

Quinn decided the sizing up of each other was complete. It was time to be family. She linked her arm with his. "This is heaven."

He clasped her arm with his other hand. "Indeed."

As they reached the top of the cliff Quinn had her first good look at the estate. Every inch of his castle glistened in the light. And it was a castle, make no mistake. Hundreds of Parthen men and women stood waiting to greet them.

Alex stood in the centre of the group dressed in a violet silk sheath that clung to her curves and fell just below her knees. Her hair flew untamed, the ends burning in the sun.

Quinn could see the fully formed flame tattoo wound around her flesh. It had only been a week, yet her niece stood before her fully evolved and more beautiful than she could have imagined.

Alex broke free of the group and ran to her.

"See, didn't I tell you everything would be okay," Quinn said as she dashed away tears of joy.

"You did. Good thing I listened to you," Alex replied. "My mother is here. Come on, you have to see her."

Alex led her back to the group. Quinn searched for her warrior sister in the crowd. When Gray stepped forward she gaped at the vulnerable woman standing before her. Surely, this woman couldn't be Gray? Surely Neeren had been wrong? She couldn't have changed that much. This woman was cut from glass not born of earth. Her white hair held no light. Her shoulders held no strength. She was a delicate doll, not the fighter Quinn knew.

She offered her hand, "Hello, Quinn. Thank you for protecting Alexedria and for collecting the information for father to help us. You didn't have too. But I thank you for being there when I couldn't be."

Quinn stared at her for a minute longer then reached out and slapped her across the face. "Are you kidding me. That's the hello I get? Who the fuck do you think you are, and where is my sister?"

Her sister responded by hurling herself at Quinn. By swearing and hitting her. Quinn took it all. Held nothing back in response. Years of anger, frustration, and loss exploded out of her, directed at the only other person on the planet who could take it all and forgive—a sister.

Domhall restrained Alex. Neeren held his hand up to his people to stop any of them from interfering.

Quinn met her sister punch for punch, sob for sob. Until, slowly the anger that had been rotting in her gut turned to something else. Grief, confusion, curiosity. Gratitude that her sister lived. She wiped the tears off Gray's face. Held her tightly and stared into her eyes. The pain and loss was obvious for anyone to see.

"Don't you ever do that to me again."

"I swear. Never again," Gray replied.

Eventually, they used each other to get up, pushing each other to the ground while standing. They were covered in sand and grass.

"Look at what you did to my dress," Gray scolded as she shot her a mischievous look.

"Thank God. Since when did you start dressing like a dead doll anyway? Now take me to your closet so I can throw everything out."

They ignored everyone and made their way into the castle arm and arm, letting the rest follow at their own pace.

Chapter 37

Collum called ahead to ensure everything was ready when they reached Athens. His staff in Greece met them at the airport and delivered them straight to his home. Mar gave him a surprised look when they drove up to a modest, white washed apartment building on the edge of the city.

"I don't need to call attention to myself," Collum told her when she turned questioning eyes on him.

"Patience, *Mi Amigo*," Mar replied. "I've never been to Athens. Couldn't we be tourists for a teeny, tiny bit?"

"We aren't here for vacation. You told me to get you to Greece. I did. Now, you get me to Alex."

He pushed open the door to his home, showing her that what looked like an apartment building from the outside was instead, one massive house.

"I'm not an idiot either, Mar." He grinned at her accusatory look. "I don't share my living space with strangers. Dragons don't live with roommates."

Her lips twitched. "There's the archaic dragon we all know and love." She pushed through the doors into the wide-open entrance hall. Ancient artifacts lined the room. "Some of these pieces must be five hundred years old. Does the Greek government know you have a museum of ancient treasures in the middle of a suburb?"

"Of course, they do. Who do you think is better at protecting history? A two-thousand-year-old dragon or a twenty-five-year-old soldier, fresh out of basic training, suffering from quick finger trigger syndrome?"

"Riiiight, point taken, Beast of the Realm. Makes sense. Look, can you point me to the bathroom? I stink like airplane and I need to wash up. Also, I don't suppose you brought any of Glenny's coffee with you. I could use a cup."

Collum signaled the maid waiting in the wings. "Sorry, Glenn doesn't share his coffee. If you want to sample it again, you'll have to come back to England for a visit."

"Is that an invitation? I thought you didn't like my obnoxious witch ways."

"You were right it seems. You grow on people."

"Damn right, big boy."

Collum smirked, and turned to the young woman waiting. "Show the lady to a room in the East Wing."

~ ~ ~

Downstairs in his den, Collum paced. They'd been there an hour. The sun had set. He lit candles rather than turning on lights. Greece reminded him of ancient times. When he'd been less tame. When he'd taken whatever he wanted. Played with the Gods and Goddesses of the ancient world.

He was preparing to go over financials when Mar rushed into his den, covered in bubbles, hair dripping soap into her eyes. A towel wrapped haphazardly around her torso, barely covered her breasts.

"You might want to get a robe on before . . ."

"Oh, shut up," she interrupted. "I figured it out. I know how we can use the portal. Now, sit down and find someone to make me a Bloody Mary. If I'm not able to sleep my jet lag off, then I'm damn well going to drink through it."

"Catalina," he bellowed.

The girl ran in the room, nearly colliding with the witch dripping water on his marble floor.

"Get her a Bloody Mary and a robe," he shouted at the maid.

She took off out of the room at another run.

"Now, tell me what you know. And keep a tight goddamn grip on that towel."

"Yeah, I know, God forbid you see another woman's assets." She flopped her dripping wetness on to the cream leather love seat and pulled a throw from the back of it over her lap.

"Get on with it and tell me," he growled.

"It's her blood, Collum. More specifically, a Parthen's blood, but she'll do."

"Explain."

"I knew I was close all those years ago. Thought I had everything right to open the portal. I'd worked on it for two years, but in the end, I couldn't find the right spell and Domhall gave up on me. He paid me very well, took all my research and thanked me from the bottom of his top-forty music loving heart and left. It pissed me off that I never completed the task. But when I was upstairs lying in that gorgeous freakin' tub, I started thinking how nice it would be to have a family home. You know, somewhere your relatives could all come . . . and wham, my brain finally connected the dots. It's blood, the blood of the family. That's how you get a portal to Parthen. You have to be of their blood."

"Son of a bitch," he yelled. "Mar, I think I love you."

He picked her up, wet towel, wet blanket and all, and wrapped her in a huge bear hug as Catalina came rushing back into the room with the pitcher of Bloody Mary and two glasses. She dropped the drinks on the turquoise tiled floor.

"Get out, Catalina. Take the night off."

The girl tore out of there as fast as she could and both Collum and Mar broke into laughter.

"You know she's going to think we're having crazy kinky sex, right?"

He put her back down on the leather couch. "I'm two thousand, Mar. I'm too old for crazy, kinky sex."

"Please, you probably know more crazy shit than the rest of us put together. Now, enough with this joking around. Since she dropped my Bloody Mary, I'm taking whatever's in your glass back to my room. And you're going to fall asleep and call out to your lady. You need her to come to you in your dreams and you need to get some of her blood. Think you can do that?"

"I'm Dragon," he replied, power flowing from every pore in his body. "I can do anything."

~ ~ ~

He left Mar at the door to her room and walked the darkened halls to his wing of the house. Like his estate in England, every inch of this home had been designed with comfort and protection in mind. He traced the walls with his hands while he walked. They could try to keep him away, but those who underestimated him had been proven wrong time and again through the years, just as they'd be proven wrong this time. He knew he could reach Alex. Dragons could always find their mates.

Upon entering his room, he removed his clothing and all pretence of being tamed. Let his wings expand in the small space. Wings engorged with the fire blood of his ancestors.

The room looked out over a private garden. It was perfect for nights such as this. He walked to the window ledge, leaped into the night. Allowed the dragon in him free reign as he flew in to the darkening sky. His roar echoed in the night air. He used the ancient telepathy of his kind, harnessed the energy of the moon. Flew higher, reached deeper, every inch of his soul concentrating on reaching out to Alex.

Telepathy was a primal tool. One he wielded well. "Alexedria, come to me." Over and over he spoke the quiet command, sought her. Soared as near to the night stars as possible. The dragon in him flexed, pushed against his human flesh barrier. He allowed the beast more strength, fed his ancient nature with visions of his woman.

Her image surfaced. She lay in a pristine white room. He heard the ocean crashing below her. Smelled her. He pushed at the edges of her mind. Called to her. She twisted and turned. Moaned his name. He bared his teeth. The dragon soared.

As he flew, his finger nails thickened, twisted, turned to claws. His skin turned obsidian black. After a final sweep over the city, he headed back to his home and his bed, to await his woman.

He landed back on the upper patio, claws dug into the concrete ledge. He found his way in to his bed, still half beast, too exhausted to retract his wings. He left them instead spread wide in the room. She was coming. Let Alex, truly see him, he thought, before exhaustion carried him into a deep sleep.

Chapter 38

Alex stood at the foot of his bed and marveled at the creature before her. Confusion clouded her mind. She'd left her mother and Aunt Quinn arguing in Quinn's room hours before. It had been an insane day. Almost too much to manage. She'd given up hope of having a family years ago. Now they colored every corner of her world.

She remembered thinking, before falling asleep, how nice it would be, to be alone with Collum in his rock castle. To be cocooned with him for a while. She'd fallen asleep with his name on her lips. Dreamed of flying through the night sky with him. She'd missed him. Seeing his face made the ache in her gut settle. Perhaps that desire to see him had been enough to convince her sleeping mind to seek him out?

Did he normally sleep like this? Half dragon, half man. Breath caught in her throat at the sight of his wings. Their massive expanse shimmered silver black. He'd wrapped those wings around her the last time they'd been together. She tiptoed to the bed, reached out with aching fingers. Hoping if she touched them very lightly it wouldn't disturb him. Would they feel like silk or like steel? She stroked one finger along the edge of a wing and felt the soft velvety texture. Rested her whole hand gently along one of the veins rising from the wing. The vein pulsed under her caress.

She looked up to see Collum staring at her with eyes turned black.

"Keep touching them," he told her, his voice deep, guttural.

She stared into his eyes while stroking his wings. They trembled. A low growl escaped him.

"Do dragons purr, Collum?" she asked as she bent down to rub her face along the velvet of his right wing.

He lifted his left wing, stroked her legs, the tip reached up between her legs. "Do you, little kitten?" he replied.

Lust burned her throat. She climbed on the bed and lay against him.

"The dragon wants you tonight and I'm inclined to let him have you."

"You know that I am here don't you."

"I know."

"I don't know how it happened."

"Crawl inside my wings, Alex," he commanded her.

Desire was a fire raging in her gut. She pulled the silk nightie off, kept her eyes locked with his. He growled again and heat pooled in her uterus. Her tattoo pulsed against her skin. She waited, let him look his fill. God, it felt amazing having this man look at her like that. Like he would die without her.

"Fuck, Alex, I need to feel you."

She let her body slowly sink on to his. Soft female flesh met muscles carved from rock. Collum closed his wings around them, nuzzled her neck.

Alex sensed the wildness in him, soaked herself in it. She rocked her body within the confines of his wings. Gyrated against veins throbbing under velvet. She controlled her fire, wanted to feel the heat of his body without the fire taking over.

Collum licked and nipped at her neck and breasts. He rolled them over until he held himself above her, slowly scorched his way down her body.

She writhed beneath him, enclosed in the cocoon he'd created. His tongue and mouth found her core. He feasted on her, suckled her until she was nothing but the desire he'd built in her. Her voice sounded foreign to her as she begged for more.

When he lifted his head, she saw the world in his eyes, the slits deep and dark. His voice gutted her. This ancient being wanted her.

"Release you claws, kitten."

She thrashed below him. "I don't know how yet. I've tried but I can't transform to a cat form."

He used the tip of his wings to scratch the inside of her leg, drew blood. "Bullshit. I can taste the feline in you," he thundered as he raised up and thrust himself inside her body.

She came instantly. Little claws exploded from her body, tore at his back. Collum thrust into her over and over. She arched her back, met every thrust with strength of her own. Her hands locked into his hair and forced his mouth to her shoulder.

"Bite me," she begged him.

Her dragon did as he was told. His fangs descended, sunk into her flesh. He clamped down on her shoulder with his sharp teeth and growled into the flesh with each thrust. She came over and over with each suckling motion. Could feel her fire screaming in release to join with him. With a final thrust her dragon lifted his head and thundered his release into the night.

Alex slowly became aware of Collum licking the wound on her shoulder, crooning, "My fierce mate," into her skin.

She smiled into his sweat-dampened hair. "Yes, I'm yours, you big beast."

He pulled away from her, rested on his haunches, tipped her chin with his finger. "I'm coming for you soon. I'm done playing. You can't hide out with your brother forever, only coming to me in dreams. It isn't enough for either of us."

"I know that, but I'm not ready yet. It's not like I'm actually hiding. I want more time to find out how my family connects." She smiled radiantly. "Grandfather and Aunt Quinn came yesterday."

"Excuse me?" He dropped his hand. "I don't think I heard you correctly?"

"Oh God. Don't get all upset about it. I had no idea they were coming. They showed up yesterday. Neeren must have been in contact with Grandfather."

Collum climbed out of the bed and marched to the window. "So, let me get this straight. Everyone except me—the one person going nuts without you—is on your fucking island."

"They're my family, Collum."

"Right, and I'm just a good lay."

"That's not fair."

He sneered at her. "Really? Seems real convenient you want everyone near you except me. But you have no problem fucking me, do you princess?"

"You're a prick."

"Nope, just don't like being used."

"You started this. You came to my room first, remember."

"I was stupid. Should've never let goddamn Domhall near you."

"Wait a minute. I want my family to be near me. I want Domhall to be near me." She climbed out of the bed and threw her nightgown back on before adding, "He's not as crazy as you made him out to be you know."

"Yeah, figured that out on my own, sweetheart. Don't any of you realize that if they're all there now, the elders will soon follow? Don't you think the council will wonder why Quinn isn't keeping their precious records?"

"Even record keepers must get vacation time, Collum."

He turned back to her. "Don't be stupid, Alex."

"So, I'm a slut and stupid?"

"If the shoe fits."

"You're an ass sometimes. You don't know everything, you know. And I can make my own decisions thank you very much."

"Wrong again, sweetheart. I'm two thousand fucking years old. I do know everything and you can tell your shithead grandfather that too."

"You know what? I'm outta here. You're gonna feel like crap when you calm down and I hope you drown in it."

"Don't count on it, princess. And don't come back to me until you're ready to stop playing games. I'm too old for this shit." He turned away from her and stared out the window.

Alex was about to remind him that he should be old enough to know better than to react the way he was. Except she didn't get the chance. She blinked, or breathed, or something, and suddenly was back in her bed on Neeren's Island.

He'd done it again. He'd pushed her out of the dream. What the hell was going on?

Chapter 39

Collum threw on a pair of black silk shorts and stormed out of his room. His long strides chewed up the hallway. Moments later, he pounded on Mars' door.

"What?" she yelled while opening the door and pulling together the edges of a burgundy robe. "It's four in the morning and I'm not a morning person."

Ignoring the complaint, he pushed past her into the room. "I screwed up. Yelled at her to leave before I asked for some of her blood."

"Seriously? Why are guys so hot headed?" She sighed while shutting the door. She fished an elastic band out of her robe pocket and used it to pull her hair off her face.

"You compelled her to come to you once, do it again."

"It won't work. I said some shitty things then told her not to come back until she was ready to apologize . . . or something like that."

"For realz? I thought you knew women. You never tell a woman she has to apologize to you. You excel at fitting the stereotype of big, dumb beast, you know?"

"I don't need more attitude from you, Mar. What do you ladies want? I pour my heart out to the girl. I tell her she's mine and we belong together. I let her see my dragon and we claim each other and it still isn't enough."

"Ummm, I may not be up completely on dragon history, but remind me again of what's involved in a dragon claiming please."

"That's a bit personal."

"I don't want a play by play, thank you very much. Is there biting involved?"

He stopped pacing and stared at her. "Yes."

"Is there the ingestion of blood involved?"

"Yes."

"Well then, Slayer, I'd say you have your blood. It's in you." She jumped up from the bed. "Whoop, whoop. Let's go. No time to waste. We need to get a move on before it dissolves in your system. Let's hope you took enough."

"Fuck. She's gonna be livid."

"You can make it up to her after you see her. You could start by telling her you love her, instead of using your archaic, you're mine line."

He tried to interrupt her to defend himself but she covered his mouth with her hand.

"Honestly, I don't want to hear about it. You might know business and war and running the world, but I know women. Now, we have work to do. Go get dressed. I can barely stand looking at you—marble muscles."

Collum hadn't thought about what he was wearing (or not) before he ran out of his room. He never had cause to think about covering himself in his home.

"Right. Sorry about that."

"Hey, I'm not complaining too much. I mean, Alex is a lucky girl. But since she and I are going to be best friends, I probably shouldn't see her guy mostly naked."

"You're strange," he said over his shoulder as he left the room. "By the way you look gorgeous at four in the morning." He winked at her astounded look and blushing cheeks. "I know women darling, I just forget all that when I'm around Alex." He shrugged. "I'll meet you in ten minutes."

~ ~ ~

Eight minutes later Collum met her back in the den. Mar changed into leather leggings, a bustier and stilettos. Collum stood in his standard uniform of black jeans and T-shirt.

He helped her move all the furniture out of the way. Then stood in the center of the room. She slowly traced a circle with beeswax around the two of them while chanting what he assumed was a Wiccan incantation. After ten minutes of constant chanting, the beeswax circle began to glow. Next, she poured a sea salt and herb mixture on to the glowing circle. The glow rose to their waists and the floor beneath them began to fluctuate. She reached out to Collum and took his hands in hers. Energy electrified him as she held on with impossible strength.

"This is going to hurt," she warned, slicing his wrist open before he had a chance to react.

He barely noticed the knife. Watched as his blood poured directly in the center of the circle. He sensed the presence of others in the room as she chanted, calling out to her ancestors, asking for permission to break the fabric of place and time. He wondered if she realized those same ancestors stood beside her.

She was a site to behold. Her skin glistened. Her hair lay thick, curled up at the ends, sweating around her shoulders. Gone was the little flirting Italian girl. In her place stood a being of immense power. No wonder Domhall had sought her out.

The chanting lasted for minutes, for hours. They held hands. He waited. His blood soaked into the carpet. Time became irrelevant. Beneath his feet, the floor began the shimmer.

"Hold tight, Dragon. Here we go."

The visions in the room disappeared as the floor vanished beneath them. Hand in hand they crossed the threshold into Neeren's hidden kingdom, and Alex's bedroom.

Chapter 40

Lachon opened his eyes. The lids scratched like sawdust against his retina. It felt like he'd been chewing on cotton balls. He lay perfectly still, tried to recall how much he'd drunk the night before, tried to recall anything about the night really. He turned his head into the pillow and inhaled. His senses flared to life on a deep ragged breath, were assaulted with her smell. Images of strawberry blond hair and delicate curves and the flash of a gun flashed in to his mind. He bolted upright. Pain shot through his temple.

"Goddamn."

Cradling his head, he surveyed the surroundings. Apparently, she'd given him a pillow and blanket after drugging him. He extended his arms above his head. Stretched out his stiff back. Reached for his cell phone to call his men, only to discover it was no longer in his pocket. He vaguely recalled her saying something about shooting him up with enough tranquillizers to keep him down for two days. He gently rolled to his side and climbed to his feet to search for her landline. The pounding in his head was relentless. When he finally located the phone, he was unsurprised to find no dial tone. They weren't going to make this easy on him apparently.

He stumbled outside to his vehicle to see all the tires slashed.

"Goddamn," he bellowed, then gripped his head again. Disgusted with himself, he began the lengthy walk to a neighboring home.

At the end of the long driveway sat a bottle of water and a note with a message from Quinn.

"Good luck on your walk. There is a phone at the winery one mile away. Morjin and Hurveet are good people so don't be rude to them when you get there. P.S., there is Tylenol above the fridge if you need to go back and get a couple."

"Goddamn," he yelled to the wind again before turning back to the house, water bottle in hand, to get the bloody Tylenol.

~ ~ ~

Twenty minutes later, Lachon walked up the drive to Strawberry Creek Wines. A log house rested at the top of a hill covered in blooming vines. A larger home nestled further inside the property. Presumably that was the primary residence. He approached the house and knocked politely. An older Sikh woman opened the door.

He smiled. "Sorry to bother you ma'am. I stopped at my friend Quinn Taleisin's just down the road from here, but she isn't home. And I drove over a nail, or something, in her driveway. Can I borrow your phone to call for a pick up and AMA?"

The woman, (Morjin?), gave him a once over. "You're a friend of Quinn's? She's out of town."

"Yeah, guess I should've called first. I must've drove over a piece of metal or a nail in her yard. Anyway, my cell is out of power and now I'm stuck out here."

He pulled out his wallet and showed her his identification. "I'm a police officer. I'm off duty and wasn't expecting to need my phone today." In his world, he was the Law so it wasn't as though he were actually lying to them.

The woman's face relaxed as soon as she saw the badge. "Of course, sure, come in. My husband is in the kitchen making dinner. You can join us if you'd like."

Lachon thanked her again, but refused dinner. He made a quick call to his staff, told them to meet him at Quinn's place. Then assured Morjin and her equally kind husband that he didn't need a ride back. He was happy to walk. It gave him much needed exercise he promised them.

He made it back to Quinn's a few minutes before his men arrived and removed all the evidence of his night on her floor. A black, Rolls Royce helicopter, filled with four tires touched down in the center of the yard. He grimaced when it landed on Quinn's Tulips.

"What the hell are you wearing?" he asked when four men jumped out in full combat gear.

His first in command, Idris, answered for the group. "Quinn Taleisin hasn't been heard from for two days. Files have also been found missing from the archives. We thought it best to come prepared."

"Ah Christ," he groaned. "What's missing?"

"The deleted files are related to the Taleisin and Gondien families. It was a thorough job. Only the keeper would have that much access."

So, they were erasing any evidence of Gray's marriage and death. The only people left who knew the truth about what'd happened were himself, Domhall, Taurin and Ealian. He wondered, not for the first time, if he knew the whole truth. How much he'd been lied to. How much he'd been blind too. Her death was one of his greatest failings.

He shared none of his thoughts. He trusted Idris. In truth, he was the closest thing to a friend Lachon had had in years. But he needed facts before opening Pandora's box.

"Get the tires changed and have one of the men take my vehicle back across on the ferry. I need to be flown directly to my office. I have a few calls to make."

"Anything else you want to go over?" Idris prompted.

"I'll let you know when there's something more. For now, just get me in the air."

Idris nodded and turned to bark orders at his men over the noise of the helicopter blades.

~ ~ ~

Fifteen minutes later, they had the chopper unloaded and back in the air, with Lachon and Idris on it. Two men stayed behind to deal with his car. Lachon rested his head on the chopper seat and closed his eyes hoping to quiet the pain in his head.

In record time, they landed on the top of his building. It was a tinted glass, thirty stories tall structure, in the heart of downtown Vancouver. He lived on the top floor. His offices encompassed the four stories below that. The building reeked of power and wealth. Practically screamed one-percenter. Lachon made no apologies for it.

He jumped out of the machine before the blades finished whirling. "Keep this quiet for now, Idris, and instruct the other men to do so as well."

Idris cracked knuckles covered in tattoos. "They won't say a word."

Lachon barely waited for his reply before rushing off the roof and into his office. He settled himself behind his desk, took a moment to inhale the musky scent from his books and sighed deeply. Knowledge was power. Knowledge kept that power from careening out of control.

He rubbed his hands along the teak desk. A soothing motion to remind him where he was. Who he was. Turned to look out at the view of the city below him. He thought back to what Quinn had whispered in his ear. A son. How had they been so clueless? He sighed again. It didn't change anything.

Understandably, Domhall had been conflicted. But even he admitted his daughter was on the edge of losing control. Taurin and Ealian were less conflicted about it, of course. Gray had openly belittled their leadership.

Not for the first time, he wondered about the twins' relationship with the older dragon they'd presented as a mate. Now, he wondered if they'd known about Gray's real husband all along.

He twisted in his chair lost in thought. Domhall had been his best friend for over a thousand years. The death of his daughter had destroyed that friendship. It had scarred Domhall. It had changed them all.

He studied the traffic below him. He liked this world, this city. Liked the pace of the humans here. He'd lived through a lot of times and places, but Vancouver suited him. It was how the wild lived on the edge of sophistication. There was a beauty to it that he loved. It was a beauty he enjoyed being a part of.

Feeling heavier than he could ever remember feeling, Lachon picked up the phone and dialled a number he knew by heart.

Chapter 41

Collum gazed at the woman sleeping in the king-sized bed. Her hair spread across the pillows in a wave of fire. He lost his breath looking at her. He adored the freckles sprinkling the edge of her nose. Admired her long limbs and muscled physique. Even in her sleep, the woman in the bed exuded strength, ferocity, and a lack of give-a-fuck. He laughed when he saw that she'd worn a torn, twisted sister T-shirt to bed.

She's nobody's princess but her own.

He and Mar turned, ready to fight, as the door behind them opened quietly and Domhall walked into the room. Just as quietly, he closed the door behind him before greeting them with, "Well, it's about time you two arrived."

Collum pushed Mar behind him when Domhall quickly added, "Calm down, Collum, and wake up my granddaughter. Neeren will be here in a minute. His sensors will have picked up the intrusion by now and I'm sure Alex will want to dress before he crashes into her room with twenty soldiers."

Behind them, Alex stirred, unconsciously recognizing the disturbance in her room. She called out to Collum in her sleep.

Domhall snorted. "It's always you apparently."

Collum jumped to her bedside, rubbed the wayward hairs off her face. Her eyelids fluttered open. She reached for him and his heart exploded in his chest.

Behind them Mar coughed loudly. Collum scowled at her. Alex bolted awake, dropped her hand and scrambled into a sitting position.

"Collum? How did you get here?" She pulled the covers to her neck. "Domhall? Someone better tell me what's going on and who the hell the dominatrix is."

"Dominatrix?" Mar smirked. "I'll have you know I bought this outfit at Holt Renfrew. Love the nightgown by the way."

Collum snarled, "For fuck's sake, Mar, can you take it easy on her. She just woke up." He grimaced at Alex. An apologetic smile on his face. "Hi, babe, you should get dressed now. That idiot brother of yours will be banging on your door soon. Ignore the witch in the corner. She's not so bad, I promise."

Alex's punch landed square in the middle of his chest and knocked him off the bed.

"Are you serious? You appear out of nowhere, in my room, in the middle of the night, after telling me to stay away from you, and that's the intro I get."

"Actually, it's five-thirty in the morning," Mar quipped from the corner of the room. "Trust me, I've been up since four a.m. when the big guy there came rushing in to my room crying about how he'd screwed up and might have lost you, blah, blah, blah . . ."

"Shut up, Mar," Collum bellowed.

On cue the banging at the door started.

Domhall rubbed his hands together. "Oh, this is gonna be such a good day."

Neeren crashed through the door, half panther, half man and finally—finally, with a hair out of place.

Collum launched himself at the other man. Landed a punch squarely into Neeren's jaw. Smiled when he heard the crunching of fist on bone. Then growled when Neeren kicked him in the gut, knocking him into the couch by the window.

Domhall and Mar moved to the edge of the room. Alex shouted at him to stop beating up her brother while Mar settled into a corner to watch the show. Across the room, Domhall re-sealed the bedroom door, shutting out the guards that were running to help their king.

"He doesn't need your help," he yelled through the closed door. "It's a sibling argument thing."

Collum watched it all transpire from the corner of his eye. *Absurd*. This family was absurd. His punches landed like boulders on Neeren's face and chest. Neeren countered with kicks straight to his torso. Collum punched the man in the face. Smiled as blood spurted out his nose. Nearly laughed as Mar shouted across the room, "I hope you have good cleaning staff here. It's going to take extra strong cleaners to get the blood out of the rug. You and I should definitely grab a coffee with Baileys when we're done here."

He almost lost it when he heard Alex reply, "Sure, it's not like we'll have anything else to do." Instead, he pulled himself together and threw Neeren against the wall— smirked when the wall cracked.

"Hey, watch it," Mar complained. "I'm trying to have a conversation here."

Collum simply growled at her and landed four more solid blows directly to Neeren's face. Blows that dropped the man to his knees. He might have failed to beat Neeren the first time. It would never happen again.

Neeren raised his hands in surrender. "Enough. I'm not interested in getting knocked unconscious in my own home." He swiped the blood from his bleeding lip and nose. "You've made your point. I won't get between you and Alex again."

Collum flexed his fists, rasped out, "Tell your tribe out there to back the fuck off and leave us alone."

Mar stepped out of the shadows and pronounced, "Wow that was intense. Is anybody else as turned on as I am?"

Domhall burst out laughing. "Come on, kids. Let's go find some coffee and icepacks."

Mar reached for Domhall's hand and together they walked past the other three in the room. Collum glowered at her. Glowered at them both. They were bloody ridiculous.

Before they could open the door, Neeren pushed in front of them. "I do not think it would be a good idea for you to open this door before me."

Collum knew what was coming. He almost pitied the other man. Almost.

Mar shot back, "Watch it. Do you know how hard it is to get cat blood out of suede?"

Neeren's mouth dropped open. "Excuse me?"

"*Si, se excusa.* I've had a long night and I could use some coffee *amigo*, so unless you're opening the door to take us to the kitchen, get out of the way."

Collum laughed under his breath as Neeren sputtered helplessly and Mar pushed him aside to open the door to the group of waiting soldiers.

"Hi, boys, say can one of you handsome devils show me where the kitchen is." She pushed her breasts out a little higher. "I'm, like, super thirsty."

The well-trained unit, completely lost their cool and stumbled over themselves to lead her to the kitchen.

Collum burst into booming laughter.

Neeren and Domhall followed Mar and the soldiers. Neeren still sputtered. Domhall patted his back, saying, "It's okay, son. Happens to the best of us."

Collum assured them he and Alex would be along right away before shutting the door and turning to his woman.

~ ~ ~

"You came."

"I told you I would."

"How did you do it?"

"Well, Mar had a lot to do with that. She's actually more of a sorceress than a witch, and a damn fine one."

"She's off her rocker."

"Oh, babe, you have no idea. She's going to give your brother a run for his money while we're here."

"I think it might be good for him. The more I see here, the more I think he needs someone around to mess up his perfectly ordered world."

Collum picked her up and carried her to a lone couch left standing by the window. He pushed broken glass off the seat and deposited them both on the cushion. He fingered her T-shirt, ran his hands over her waist. "I'm sorry."

"How did you get here. Why now, Collum? I thought you told me to stay away from you. You were mean to me."

He pulled her on to his lap. "I was. I didn't mean a word of it. Unbelievably, I discovered I don't function well when I think of you choosing someone else over me."

"I wasn't choosing another person over you. I was asking for time to figure out who I am."

"I know who you are, Alex. You are fire and life, and you are mine."

"I'm my own person, Collum. You need to remember that. Not all of my decisions will automatically be the same as yours and you can't stomp off in a temper tantrum whenever I disagree with you."

"I know. This thing between us messes with my sanity."

She stroked his arm. "I'm not all that sane about it either."

He held her chin with his hand. "Alex, I gave up hope of ever finding my mate. But you're it. You're her. Can you get behind that with me?"

"Tell me you are sorry again. And that you'll never speak to me that way again."

"I'm sorry. Never again." His eyes burned into hers.

"You're such a romantic." She pulled him closer and pushed her hands up under his shirt. "I missed you."

He growled in the back of his throat as he matched her touch and slid his hand up under her shirt to rub her stomach. His thumb gently pressed at the soft flesh of her breast. His black eyes scored hers, telling her everything he didn't know how to say, before he bent down to softly kiss her lips a thousand times over. Tiny, gentle love kisses. He kissed the corners of her mouth. Kissed her nose and her chin. Each of her eyelids. He kissed the top of her head and her neck, and then he kissed her heartbeat.

"This is what I offer you, Alex. A very wise young woman told me I needed to be honest with you before it was too late. I offer you my soul. It is yours if you want it."

The way she stared at him, he almost didn't finish, but he knew if they hoped to make it, he'd have to be honest about every part of their lives.

"I also offer you this truth . . . When you came to me last night I used the power of the dragon to call you to me. When I claimed you, I bit you. Do you remember that?"

Her face heated. "Of course, I do. I asked you to."

"I also ingested some of your blood, Alex. For a dragon that is a ritual bonding." He took a deep breath. Steadied himself for the storm. "In the eyes of my kind, we are well and truly mated."

She pushed his hands off her body, "Pardon me?"

He steeled himself. "Taking your blood is also what allowed me to find you here. It is the blood of the Parthen that opens the portal to this island."

Chapter 42

Neeren, Mar, and Domhall stood before the breakfast bar piling fruit and eggs on their plates when they heard the screaming begin.

"I think he just told her how we found you." Mar chuckled as she sipped her coffee. "I've got to give it to you, Oh Kingly One," she said to Neeren. "This is decent coffee. Not as good as my Glenny's, but then no one's ever will be."

Neeren choked on his coffee. "Could you please refrain from calling me things like that. My name is Neeren."

"Right . . . gotcha, Norman."

His head snapped up but before he could say anything else, Domhall interrupted him.

"I think I'll go wake Quinn and Gray and make a pit stop to check on the lovebirds upstairs. You two behave please."

"Sure thing, Dominator —totally behaving."

Neeren studied her from above the rim of his mug.

Between bites of eggs she said, "So, you want to tell me what the rest of the plan is? I brought King Thronus here to his woman. Pretty sure there's more coming down the tubes."

"And how did you do that, may I ask? There are wards in place to keep interlopers like you and the dragon from reaching my island."

"Well, I guess your wards aren't as strong as you thought they were, hey?"

"So, you say. Why don't you fill me in and I'll decide if they were strong enough or not."

She shrugged. "I used your precious sister's blood. Collum drank from her and I used the blood in his system to activate the gate to the portal."

"He took her blood?"

"It's part of the whole mating cycle for dragons. It was only a couple drops. Chill out for Christ's sake."

He watched, fascinated as she shoved more food in her mouth. "Mating?"

She leaned back in her chair and put her boots up on his fifteen-thousand-dollar table.

"Yeah that's probably why they're arguing up there. From what I could tell through the paper-thin walls in castle dragoooon, she loved the biting part of it. Pretty sure it's the married-without-knowing-it part she has issue with."

"I'm going to slice that dragon's heart out."

"Could you pour me another coffee before you do that? I'm honestly so ratcheted up right now. I mean, you people are nuts. In the past four days, I've had hardly any sleep, been drunk twice, flown on three transcontinental flights, and performed stunning acts of sorcery. Give a girl a break already. Or on second thought, you could give me a massage. My shoulders are killing me."

Neeren looked closer at the little witch across the table. She was dressed head to toe in winter gray leather. It was butter soft and of obvious quality. Her top, if it could be called a top, barely covered her breasts. She had a tiny waist he could probably wrap his hands around and her hair flowed in rich mahogany waves down the flesh of her bare back. Thick full lashes covered mischievous hazel eyes.

He walked around the table, laid his hands on her shoulders and slowly began kneading the soft skin.

"That feels amazing. Don't stop."

"I won't stop until you tell me too," he purred at her.

His fingers pushed into the muscles finding an easy rhythm. Soon the woman's head rolled back and little sounds of pleasure escaped her lips. Neeren kept a steady pace, felt himself grow harder by the second listening to her mewling noises.

He moved his hands in larger circles, worked the skin up her spine. Reached further down her chest. "Does that feel good?"

"It's perfect," she groaned.

Emboldened, he pushed his hands lower and stroked the swell of her breasts.

She jumped up, smashing the top of her head into his chin. "Ow. What the fuck are you doing? I asked for a massage not a feel up."

He cracked his jaw. "You said you liked it. I thought that's what you wanted."

"Yeah, well next time ask *idiota*. You can't just grope a girl without asking first, you know."

"You were practically melting under my hands. What was I supposed to think?"

"How about listening to my words. A freaking massage is all I asked for. If I'd wanted more from you I would've said so. I'm not one of your little kitties you know." She sneered. "Yeah, I know all about you. Biggest male slut on the face of the earth. I'm not interested so back the F off."

"You are insane."

"And you're a chauvinist pig."

Domhall walked in the kitchen then with Quinn and Gray behind him. "A little decorum please. We can hear you two kids down the hall."

Neeren caught his mother's eye as she said, "What have you done now, Neeren?"

Chapter 43

Lachon and Taurin walked across the tarmac to the waiting aircraft. Ealian strolled ahead of them, almost at the stairs to the private vessel. She wore a sheer lace dress that did nothing to hide her bare breasts. Tiny, black panties barely covered her bottom. Sickened, Lachon watched Taurin and half the men in his employ ogle the woman.

"It is good you called us," Taurin said to him. "Ealian and I wondered when you planned to act against the Taleisin family. It is past time to put them all down, my old friend."

"I haven't said we are putting them down. Only that justice must be served for the crimes committed and the stealing of secured information."

"And yet, you bring twenty armed men."

"I always bring soldiers when I'm uncertain what I'm walking into."

Stewardesses, employed by Lachon for over fifty years, welcomed them as they boarded. They prepared to show the three elders to separate resting areas. Lachon was pleased to see Idris waiting patiently near the rear of the plane. Over the speaker, the captain informed the crew they'd lift off as soon as the runway cleared, and asked the passengers to secure themselves.

Lachon preferred to spend as little time as possible with the two siblings. He made his way to his private quarters after giving strict instructions to Idris to join him for a debriefing two hours before they landed. Lachon watched as, heads and hands together, the twins made for their room.

As he settled in his room, he thought about what was to come and the choices that had been made—by all of them. What would the past years have been like if they'd acted differently? What would happen now if the wrong choice was made? He kicked off his Italian leather boots and removed his navy-blue sweater to lay back on the king size bed. The passing clouds eventually soothed him. He remembered feeling happy once. Could he again?

The abrupt knock on the door broke through his self-reflective mood. He bade whomever it was to enter.

Ealian crossed the threshold on silent feet. "Lachon, we need to talk."

He lurched up wishing he'd have thought to ask who it was. Felt dirty as her eyes roamed over his bare chest. "I'm tired, Ealian. Can we talk later?"

She sat beside him on the bed without waiting for an invitation. Rested her palms on his flesh. "You wound me, Lachon. We have been so close forever." Her hands played with the auburn hair on his chest. "I need to know we're still strong. Can you promise me you won't forsake us?"

He grabbed her hands before she took it too far. Stopped her stroking of him. Her petting. Ealian's power of compulsion had always been strong. Lachon had seen it used for both selfless and selfish reasons.

"Lachon, why do you fight against me? We could be so good together."

"Ealian, that isn't what we are. You know that. The only way the council stays strong is if we don't cross lines we shouldn't."

She pouted. "How can you say that to me after all we have been through."

"It was one drunken night three hundred and fifteen years ago. Let it go already."

Lachon could see the gears turning in her mind. Judging the best course of action to get what she wanted. She softened her voice, crawled further up the bed and rubbed her body against his bare chest.

"Let me taste you, Lachon. I can make you feel amazing. You know that I can."

"Yes." He sighed. "I know that you can, but I don't want you that way."

She sat back like a hurt child. "Why? Everyone wants me."

He knew he must tread lightly to keep her under control. The last thing any of them needed was her losing control of her wind element while on an airplane.

"Ealian, you are passion and desire, everything every man could want, but I see you as my sister. We have been that way for too long for our relationship to be any different. Of course, you set my blood to boil but I cannot be with you the way you want. It would be wrong."

She smiled sweetly at him then. "One kiss, between brother and sister?"

"I do not wish to lead you on. To hurt you."

"Lachon, you wound me when you refuse me. Do you think yourself above me?"

"You know that isn't it."

As her eyes cleared, Lachon was reminded she was a danger still.

"Then what is it? I simply ask you for a kiss. A sign of affection for the bond we hold."

He touched the side of her face. Recognized the malice in her eyes. "Very well. How could I deny you? Of course, one kiss."

She climbed over him, sat on his waist and placed her mouth against his. Knowing what she craved, he wrapped one hand in her hair to hold her against him.

She ground her body into his as she whimpered into his mouth. "Take me, Lachon."

"No. It is only this."

She heaved against him then. Forced her tongue inside his mouth. Lachon fought her with his tongue. She reached down, grasped his cock through his pants, rubbed him through the fabric, began to rub herself against his leg. He grabbed her hand and wrenched his mouth free of the kiss. Reminding himself to be gentle, he lifted her and settled her beside him.

He schooled his voice, removing all emotion. "Enough, Ealian. No more games."

Tears clouded her eyes as she looked away from him. "I want more from you. Why do you not give me more?"

"I'm not having this conversation again. I've told you why countless times over the years."

"But you have no one else. Be with me."

"Stop now. I love you as a sister, nothing more. It will never be more."

She stood. Anger clearly written on her features. "You are flesh and blood like the rest of us. Your heart fills with sin like the rest of us. Remember that you did not stop until after I held your cock in my hand. You would do well to climb off your high horse."

Lachon leaned back against the headboard and rested his arms behind his neck. Refused to give her the satisfaction of appearing concerned by her words. "Are you threatening me?"

She sneered. "Do not forget to respect me. And what I am capable of."

"I will always respect you, dearest." He sat up and grasped her hands. "I've always known what you are capable of. It is why I aligned myself with you long ago."

She smiled at him. Her face softened. "You've sinned as much as I have."

"That remains to be seen, my dear."

"You would tell me if you knew more about what was going on than I did, wouldn't you, Lachon?"

He stood then. Pulled her body against his. Began his own game. He rubbed his hands along her arms with a touch that was both comforting and a reminder of his strength. "Of course, I would. Just as I know you would do the same for me."

Her eyes drifted off again. Lost the focus of moments before. "I should go check on Taurin. He's probably wondering where I am."

"Yes." He grimaced. "Taurin needs you."

She smiled sweetly at him. Replied, "I'm all he has you know," before blowing a kiss and walking out the door of his room.

Idris poked his head in seconds later. "You okay, man?"

Since the day Idris began working for him, Lachon thanked whatever force sent the man to Vancouver from South Africa. He'd been tempted on more than one occasion to fire him for crossing the line, or disappearing without notice, but could never bring himself to do it. Idris was something of a super soldier. Not only that, he had Lachon's back. And Lachon needed that badly the past few years.

He and Idris were as different as night and day. Idris hardly spoke. When he did, it was usually to remind Lachon of how stupid he was. Still, without fail, he followed command. Intricate tattoos covered the man's dark skin. Lachon had no idea what they meant. He'd never asked. Over the years, they'd become strange companions. Not quite friends, but maybe something stronger.

"God, that woman gives me the creeps," Lachon said the minute Idris shut the door.

"Yeah, she gives everyone the creeps. Thankfully, she ignores the rest of us and fixates on you and her freak of a brother."

He cautioned, "They are still council members. Only, ever say that around me."

Idris pulled a bottle of whiskey from behind his back and handed it to him. "Here. Thought you'd need this in case you need to wash the taste of something vile out of your mouth."

Lachon arched a brow. "Seriously . . ."

"Yeah, I know, I'm watchin' it . . . and your back." He winked, exiting the room without another word and shutting the door behind him.

Lachon took a long pull of whiskey from the bottle before going into the bathroom to brush his teeth.

Chapter 44

Alex studied her extended family while shoveling food in her mouth. The entire clan, including the weird witch, had settled around the large, glass dining table. Neeren's staff served them a breakfast of fruit and pastries.

Neeren refused to speak to Collum after hearing that under dragon law, Collum and Alex were considered mates. Collum rubbed it in by touching Alex every time her brother glanced their way.

She swatted his hand away from her hair as Neeren grimaced . . . again. He wore a permanent grimace that morning. Honestly, she was still trying to understand it herself. She knew there was a different set of rules in the immortal world than the human one. But even though logically she knew she wasn't, she still considered herself, a human. Twenty-six years of living as a normal young woman weren't going to disappear. She'd told Collum as much when they finally calmed down enough to talk.

She'd agreed to dating, seeing where this thing between them went. She might be falling hard for him, could barely concentrate when he wasn't around, but she wasn't considering herself married yet. For that she'd need some time. And they'd both need to survive whatever came next.

Her grandfather was a source of confusion as well. He sat at the head of the table. For all intents and purposes, appeared to control the world. But she'd had first-hand experience with his erratic behavior. Still, somehow, he'd played them all. Pulled all the strings necessary to get them in one room. He caught her eye and smiled, almost as though he knew what she was thinking.

His voice carried across the table to the assembled group. "A plane carrying the remaining council members has landed in Athens."

Silence descended over them as they looked at him with varying degrees of dismay and acceptance.

"Neeren," he said. "I think it best if you extend an invitation to visit your kingdom."

The table broke out into a frenzy of activity as Neeren stood. His trademark smirk fell from his face and he released a long, slow breath. Alex wondered if he'd held that breath his entire life.

Neeren nodded crisply and replied, "I'll see to it," before leaving the room.

Alex grabbed Collum's hand. "I thought we'd have more time."

He squeezed her hand and turned to Domhall with a scathing tone. "Was this always the plan? To bring them here and eliminate them?"

"What did you expect? That we'd hide with the Parthen forever? It's the only way my family can be truly free. You know that."

"So, you lied to everyone. How many more lies, Dom?"

"Who is lying, Collum? Who has always been lying?"

"Don't go somewhere you can't back down from, Dom."

The two men glowered at each other before Domhall broke eye contact.

"Are you going to let Neeren kill them all?" Collum asked. "You know I can't condone that. If you invite them on to your land it becomes murder. I have to judge that."

"They tried to kill my daughter. They destroyed my family. What would you have me do?"

Collum pounded his fists on the table and roared back, "Find another way, Domhall."

"There is no other way. Don't you think I've thought of this? We can't involve the entire race. You were all I needed, the last puzzle piece really. Jesus, don't you see that I'm trying to stop the bloodshed."

Alex studied the group, turned to her Aunt Quinn. "Did you know his plan?"

"I did. Trust me when I say I'm telling you the truth. I have no love for my father, but I love you with all my heart. I will do anything to protect you and the rest of this messed up family."

"Grandfather?"

When he finally looked at her, the pain in his eyes was easy for Alex to see.

"They would have found us eventually, you know that. Taurin and Ealian have darkness in them." He sighed before looking at Collum again. "And the first thing they would have done is gone for your lover's heart. I need you to understand. I cannot live with this any longer. The stain on my heart . . . knowing what I was party to. I've barely survived. I'm prepared to answer for my choices. Justice must be served."

"What about the justice I'll be called to serve when this all comes out?" Collum asked.

"Leave it to someone else," Domhall replied.

The air in the room tightened. Alex saw the change in Collum. It scared her.

"You know, there is no one else," Collum growled.

"Do I?" was her grandfather's reply.

"My role in this begins and ends with Alex," Collum said, anger ringing in his voice. "You put her in danger with this foolishness. They're coming for her, you idiot."

Neeren walked back into the dining room as the two men stared each other down. "I have sent ambassadors to meet them at their hotel. I've extended the invitation to discuss our situation tomorrow morning."

Collum questioned, "Did you know your grandfather called them? And what happens tonight? Do you sneak into their minds and eliminate them?"

"Of course, I knew. This has always been the only outcome. You know that as much as I do," Neeren said. "In answer to your last question. If you must know, I can't reach them. I've tried but they are protected by wards similar to the kind that hid Alex all these years."

Alex watched everything in a kind of trance. But she grinned when her brother turned his attention to the witch slurping her coffee in the corner.

"I suspect you had a hand in that," he said.

The witch licked pastry sugar off her fingers, raised her eyes, and gave a little shrug. "Go figure witches, hey? Always getting involved where they shouldn't. Keeping people from committing acts of murder and mayhem."

Alex choked on her coffee as laughter bubbled up. It felt good to laugh. If she managed to stay alive over the next few days she planned to do it more often.

Domhall replied, "Those wards are there for a reason. I wouldn't let Mar pull them down even if she could. Look at me all of you. I have my family under one roof. Alive and well. With new friends to keep things interesting." He winked at Mar, nodded slightly to Collum. "Tomorrow is a new beginning for us. Raise your glasses in a toast to the future. Whatever it may look like."

Fire pulsed against Alex's heart. The purr of the Parthen built under her skin. She raised her glass in salute.

Chapter 45

After the toast, Collum dragged Alex from the room to watch the sunrise across the ocean. Hand in hand they walked along the path to reach the water. Silhouettes peeked out from behind sand dunes and palm trees. Followed them like silent sentinels. When they reached the water's edge, he pulled her close and rested his mouth against her neck. Her hair burned against his. Low flames danced under their skin.

Alex sighed into his shirt. "Everything will be okay. I promise. I won't be as easy to get rid of as they think. I'm tougher than you give me credit for."

He lifted his head from her. Surprised at what she'd said. "I've never met anyone tougher than you. I knew it the first time I met you when you tore a strip off me for kissing you. Not many people would do that. Trust me lover, you earned my respect that first morning."

"But you're always talking about how you have to protect me. I'm just a child compared to you."

"Don't rub it in. I already feel like I'm robbing the cradle." He guided her down on the sand beside him, scratched his fingers along her back. "Seriously, Alex, once you learn how to control your abilities, you'll be one of the most powerful creatures on earth. I know you can protect yourself, but I'm old. No matter how tough you are, I'm always going to protect you."

She lowered her brows, wariness entering her voice. "Because of the promise you made my grandmother?"

"No dumb-ass." Collum hooked his thumb under her chin and lifted her face to look at his eyes. "Because I've fallen in love with you. Did you think this is out of a debt to your grandmother? Jesus, Alex, give me a little more credit."

He wound one hand in her tangles. The silk of her hair, wrapped around his fingers like she'd wrapped herself around his soul. "I've never reacted to anyone the way I do with you. It's all you and your neo-liberal, shit kickin', environmental lovin' heart, babe."

"You're a big suck you know that?"

"You ain't seen nothing," he replied as he pulled a fuzzy blue teddy bear out of his jacket pocket and handed it to her.

"What is this?"

Heat crawled along his neck to his ears. "I picked it up in the airport that first day. I figure since it almost cost you your life, I should give it to you."

"You bought this in Vancouver?"

"Yep. You see, babe, you've been distracting me since day one."

Alex bit her lips and flopped back on the sand. She pulled Collum down with her.

"I hope you don't mind sand in all your cracks and crevices," she crooned flirtatiously.

As sinister grin curled his lips up as he pulled his T-shirt off and threw it in the ocean. He could wait for his human raised warrior to tell him she loved him back. He'd learned patience a long time ago. And he wasn't afraid of proving to her, as many times as she needed, that he wasn't going anywhere.

Chapter 46

The sun beat down on Collum like fire. Alex's skin glowed with it. Behind them, past the edge of the cliff, the ocean churned, the only indication of Neeren's agitation.

Collum stood next to Alex, on the edge of control, ready to become the dragon he was if necessary. Behind them stood the rest of the family and a dozen of Neeren's most trusted soldiers.

They met half a mile away from the house, on a ledge that looked out over the Parthen kingdom. The Mediterranean breeze wafted over them. The earth stood sure and solid beneath their feet.

To the side, a breathtaking buffet had been laid out as befitting a king and his guests. Tables were draped with sky blue cloths and covered with platters of salads and lobster. Champagne rested in silver buckets filled with ice. Chilled trays of crisp strawberries, covered in thick cream were laid out on a side table. Ten seats fitted with thick yellow and blue cushions were pulled out from the table. It was a setting for reconciliation, not for war.

All day, Alex and Collum had made love against the ocean. Claiming each other with fire as the sun fell and the moon rose. They'd spoken no further of love or mating. Words had felt inadequate. Instead they simply let their bodies claim each other. It had been enough for both. Now, they stood together, hands entwined, fire pouring through their veins.

Collum noticed their adversaries first. Parthen security

forces led them from the dock to the group waiting at the top of the ridge.

Lachon the Law and the head of his security force, Idris, led the visitors. He was a member of the wolverine race and had been with Lachon for over two hundred years.

Collum and the man, made eye contact. A barely imperceptible nod passed between the two.

The twins, Taurin and Ealian Gondien followed them. Both were dressed in old velvet robes that swamped their frail bodies. Their glassy eyes landed squarely on Alex. More Elemental forces followed and stood with the elders. They all waited to see what would happen next.

Neeren, Collum, Alex, and Domhall walked to meet the members of the council. Lachon, Ealian, and Taurin met them. Collum noted the caution written on their faces. Idris held back slightly behind the group. He and Collum made eye contact, nodded.

Once they all stood in front of each other, Neeren and Alex stepped forward.

Neeren spoke first. "Welcome to our Island."

Lachon stepped forward, extended his hand. "Thank you for the invitation. I'm afraid you have us at a disadvantage. You appear to know who we are. We cannot say the same."

Alex shook the extended hand and replied, "Yes, that was necessary. My name is Alexedria Simine, this is my brother, Neeren Simine, King of the Parthen. You had our father murdered."

Taurin and Ealian gasped and backed away. "Two children. Did you know? How did this happen?"

Lachon raised both his hands to stop them from speaking. Idris intercepted them, became a brick wall behind their backs.

"So." Lachon smiled, nodding his head at Domhall. "There were two?"

"There were," Domhall replied.

"And how do you fit in to this, King Thronus?" Lachon asked.

Collum had quietly watched the beginning part of the play. Let the game pieces move as they would. He stepped forward with deceptive calm. His body coiled and ready to strike.

"I'm the female's protector." He placed his hand on Alex's shoulder. "And her mate. She's under the protection of the dragons now."

Behind them, Ealian screeched, "This is treason. You are the guardian of all immortals. You cannot pick a side."

Collum growled at her. Took a step forward. "I do not answer to you. You forget who I am."

Around them, winds whipped up leaves and sand. Behind them the ocean surged. The soil groaned beneath their feet.

Lachon spoke. "Forgive her, King Thronus. Taurin, please calm your sister, the day is only beginning." His next words were directed to Alex. "My apologies. We were unaware of your mother's," he paused before saying, "other life."

Standing at her side, Collum made sure she felt the heat of him in her bones.

"Are you sure?" Alex pointed to Taurin and Ealian. "Perhaps some of you were threatened by it? Perhaps some of you wanted her dead?"

Lachon glanced at Taurin and Ealian. "Touché, but I'm afraid you have no proof."

From the shadows, a queen appeared. The wind whipped hair the color of ice against her face. Her dark plum eyes flashed with an inner light.

"I am your proof."

Lachon swore under his breath.

Domhall announced her. "I believe you all remember my daughter, Gray."

Idris grabbed Ealian's hand.

Taurin bowed to Gray and said, "So you're alive. How very interesting that is. And how strange that we didn't see it coming."

Neeren stepped closer to his mother. "We have prepared a meal so that a discussion of restitution may begin."

"You are a dreamwalker, as is your sister," Ealian cried. "We will not eat with you—you are killers."

"Kettle. Black," Alex said.

Ealian wrenched her arm free of Idris. "The only restitution to be had is your death."

Collum growled low in his throat and spoke directly to Lachon. "Control her or your days of battling will be over."

Lachon stepped in front of the woman. "Ealian, I'd rather not die before lunch. I believe your brother agrees with me. Now, I'm sure we can all act civil for a bit longer." He nodded to Neeren. "We will, of course, accept your hospitality and join you for lunch."

Neeren smiled as Ealian fumed. He turned his back on them to clasp his mother's hand. As they crossed the meadow, the rest of the group followed. From the shadows, Quinn and Mar emerged to join them.

Collum maneuvered himself and Alex to the rear of the group so he could listen to the multitude of conversations. He knew she wanted to be upfront with her brother but needed her with him and it was easier to keep an eye on your prey when they couldn't see you watching.

Lachon sidled up to Quinn as the group made their way across the meadow. "Feeling guilty about anything?"

"Nothing at all. What about you? Like sentencing my sister and her unborn child to death perhaps?"

"Quinn," he began, "You know I did not know."

"Oh, Lachon, that is a poor excuse. Are you really such a weak man? I don't forgive you. I don't care about you." She gave the man a scathing look before she and Mar walked on.

As Lachon watched her go, his shoulders appeared heavy with weight. Domhall caught up with him. "Been Quinned have you?"

"What?"

"Oh nothing. It's just no one can knock a person down a peg or two quite like my glorious daughter."

"She does have a way of making me feel like a piece of shit. How are you, Domhall?"

"I miss my wife. You?"

"I'm confused. Why are we here?"

"That's up to you, buddy."

Collum listened with interest. Perhaps Domhall had given them a chance at redemption after all.

As they neared their seats, silence descended. Blood pounded under Collum's skin. It was a table set for a beautiful death.

~ ~ ~

Collum gestured for Taurin and Ealian to take their seats across from Neeren and Gray. He and Alex sat to their right across from Lachon and Idris. Domhall sat on the other side with Quinn and Mar.

Lachon spoke first. "It seems your family is becoming larger, Domhall. What is it you think to request from us?"

Alex said, "You really only need to direct your questions to my brother, mother, and myself." She sneered at the man across the table as servants poured them wine. "After all, it is our lives that were destroyed."

Lachon nodded. "As you wish. What is it you hope to accomplish today?"

"Well, I'm a bit new at all this, so I guess I'd like to know why?"

"That is the question of all questions, isn't it?" Lachon turned to Taurin and Ealian. "Would either of you like to handle that?"

Ealian swallowed her wine and levelled a scathing look on the trio. She looked directly at Gray. "You were reckless. You endangered us all. Look what you've done."

"I fell in love."

"With an abomination."

Neeren replied, "My father was not an abomination. My people are not abominations."

"You're dreamwalkers," Ealian snarled. "We know what your kind can do. Has done."

The wind whipped around them. The Parthen servants struggled to keep the meal from getting covered by flying debris.

Lachon spoke to Gray. "We did the right thing." He motioned to all four of the elders. "We all agreed it was the only sensible choice to keep you from damaging yourself. We chose what we thought was a suitable mate. You should have been happy with the dragon."

"He was a monster," Gray replied.

"And how were we to know this?" Lachon said. "If you'd been forthcoming perhaps things would have been different."

"Some of you knew, Lachon. Besides if I'd been more forthcoming, you would have killed my son."

Collum spoke up then and addressed the group. "All of the dragon kind knew of my father's penchant for hurting women, for causing pain. I'm curious as to how you missed this vital information. Was there no vetting of a suitable mate?"

Answering quietly, Lachon said, "I take responsibility for this. I understood he was vetted. I should have checked myself." He said the last bit while looking at Taurin.

Alex interjected, "I still don't understand why you hate our kind so much. What's the big deal if we dreamwalk? All of you immortals seemed to have different powers. Why are we so horrible to you?"

Taurin answered. "Because you can kill us in our sleep you idiot. If you enter our dream you can kill us. Did you honestly think we'd allow that to happen? And it isn't only the elders. No Elemental will ever accept your kind."

The table fell silent, struck by the malice in Taurin's voice. Collum prepared to rip the man's throat out.

Neeren spoke before he could raise his voice. "The King of the Parthen was murdered. Someone must pay for that."

Ealian laughed. "A dragon killed your father." She pointed to Collum. "Talk to his people, not ours." She stood and Taurin stood with her. "And whatever this is supposed to be today, changes nothing. You've only made things worse."

Domhall uncurled his long legs and pushed his chair back from the table. As he stood he spoke for the first time. His words echoed across the field. "Time teaches many things to us. As will what happens here today."

The rest of the table stood, lunch forgotten.

The ends of Alex's hair caught fire, the ocean behind them churned, the earth beneath their feet rolled and the wind tossed all the players around the meadow like puzzle pieces.

Chapter 47

The world erupted in chaos. Alex watched as Ealian launched a windstorm at Gray. Taurin pulled the earth apart beneath Neeren's feet. Ealian threw a cyclone into the gaping hole. As Neeren disappeared into the chasm, Ealian threw a second cyclone at Gray.

Alex ran. Flung herself between the storm and her mother's body. An instant before she would have reached her, Collum swept her up. Wings exploded from his back as he catapulted them both in to the air.

Gray dove to the left a moment before the cyclone hit her. She hurled a wall of wind that knocked Ealian and Taurin back a few feet.

Above the carnage, Alex begged for Collum to let her go. "We have to reach Neeren. Please, Collum, before that evil creature closes the earth. You can't let him be swallowed whole. I need to protect my mother."

He refused her. "My job is to protect you and only you. Neeren and Gray can take care of themselves."

Her hands were pinned by her sides so Alex kicked him in the groin and bit his hands. She used the tools she had. Concentrated on finding the claws beneath her skin. They burst out and she twisted her hands and shoved the claws into the flesh of his legs. It was hardly a scratch but it was enough to make him loosen his hold for a fraction of a second.

Alex kicked out of his grip. As she fell toward the earth, Collum reached with one claw and grabbed at her foot. She smashed the lone claw with her boot and launched herself into the air.

She hit the ground running, stumbling slightly on the sandy soil as she raced to the centre of the fight. She felt the current from Collum's wings directly behind her. His heavy breathing vibrating like a scorching recrimination over her sensitive flesh. He could be pissed off all he liked, she wasn't running from this fight.

As Alex raced back toward her mother and the twins. Dodging Collum's grasp, she threw fire bolt, after fire bolt, to keep her way clear. Her mother held her own. The twins fought to reach her through the wall of wind she created. Wind fought against Wind and kept Taurin at bay. Gray was strong. Alex knew she'd hold on.

She saw Domhall valiantly attempting to keep the earth from closing in on the hole where Neeren had been thrown. Her grandfather didn't control earth though and soon even his vast powers wouldn't be able to stop it.

Alex propelled herself forward while looking over her shoulder. Collum's dragon was taking over. Her lover was more beast than man and was almost on top of her.

"Please, Collum. He's my brother. You have to save him."

"Goddamn it, Alex."

"You have to do this. You must. You're the only one who can." She spun around. Stopped dead in her tracks to stare at him. Held her ground. "If you force me out of this we will never make it."

He growled and dropped in front of her like a freight train. "You will not be hurt."

"I swear to you. I will not be hurt."

"Not a scratch Alex. Say it."

"Not a scratch. I swear. Now hurry."

Her beast swore a final time. The sound carried across the island. He shifted away from her and flew directly over where Neeren had fallen. He propelled himself higher, gaining more speed and momentum as he went.

As he arched, he shifted fully into his dragon form. Glistening obsidian scales covered his body. He was gorgeous, massive, ancient. His paws the size of a half-ton truck. Razor sharp talons glinted in the sun. Alex almost wept at his beauty.

He growled to Domhall below him. "Keep that goddamn break open."

He dove straight down, soaring into the chasm with the speed and force of a bullet train.

As soon as Collum disappeared, Alex raced through the battle to her mother's side. She hurled a wave of fire to reinforce the wall of wind.

On the sidelines, Lachon shouted, "Idris."

"Yes, Law."

"Take out the Gondien soldiers."

His lips curled back. "It's about time you made the right choice," he said before turning to join the battle.

Lachon rushed to Domhall, placing his hands on the earth. "I have this old man. There's enough power in me to keep this open a bit longer. Go help your daughter and granddaughter so we can rectify the mistake made all those years ago. They cannot beat the twins alone."

~ ~ ~

Terror surrounded Alex. She and her mother fought side by side against the two council members while behind them the earth quaked. Alex knew the twins shared their elements, making it almost impossible to defend against them, let alone beat them.

Domhall had explained their strengths the night before after scouring through their files. But she wasn't leaving her mother to stand against them alone. She couldn't spare a moment of thought for Collum or Neeren. She had to focus all her energy on staying alive.

Ealian screeched at them that they couldn't be alive, that she wouldn't let them live, that Alex was an abomination. Taurin remained utterly silent. Every move was calculated and swift. He fought like the devil, forcing the world beneath their feet apart time and again. The siblings fought like one being. She and Gray were utterly outmatched.

Ealian howled. The sound of a storm raged in her voice. She used her wind to throw them in the air over and over. "You're supposed to be dead. It's all we wanted. Your death was my gift to the dragon. Why couldn't you just die like your husband."

The wind became a hurricane. The force threw Alex in the air as Taurin opened a giant rift in the earth behind them.

Ealian's laughter echoed in the wind. "He was so easy to kill. I let my dragon play with him for a while. I wish he hadn't cut his tongue out but one can't live on wishes and prayers, can they? Your lover wouldn't tell me who he was even after I told him I'd let you live." She turned demented eyes on Gray. "Can you imagine? He wasn't worth your time really."

At the words hurled their way, Gray faltered. The wind protecting them slowed. The earth rushed up to meet Alex and she landed with a thud. Grief twisted her mother's beautiful face. Out of the corner of her eye, Alex saw her grandfather running toward them with a ball of fire in each outstretched palm. She summoned the last of her strength, raised fire to her fingertips, and screamed to keep the twins focused on her.

She and Domhall threw their flames at the same time.

Ealian noticed too late. The flames slammed into her. The winds whipping around her body forced the fire into a frenzy. Ignited a blast so large her entire frame became engulfed in an instant.

Alex's second flame missed Taurin. The fire thrown by Domhall glanced off his arm. Taurin screamed his sister's name as her body disintegrated to ash. He threw up the earth, erecting a barrier between Domhall and himself. And using the last of his dead sister's wind element, blasted Gray across the field.

They were alone and Alex was as bereft of energy and power as any human.

The look in his half dead eyes as he spoke told her she wasn't long for this world. "You half-breed bitch. That was my life you just killed. I'm going to destroy you like I did that interfering cow, Kaylen."

The dim-witted brother she'd read about in the papers her aunt had brought them, disappeared. "You all thought she wasted away from the grief of losing her daughter. I'm surprised by your family, little girl. They truly thought *that* woman would waste away? It was poison you realize. She was threatening to tell certain things about my beautiful Ealian. Disgusting lies. She was jealous of Ealian's beauty and her power over men."

He stalked Alex, taunted her as she backed away.

"I got rid of her before she could cause more trouble. Except she'd already done it hadn't she. You live."

Alex choked back a cry of sorrow for a woman she'd never known. She heard her grandfather tearing at the earthen wall behind Taurin. He would break through soon, but it would be too late to stop what was going to happen.

Alex refocused her energy and concentrated on pulling her tattoo off her body. It was—had always been— ready to do her bidding. She might die today, but she was taking this bastard with her. As she felt the earth crumble beneath her feet, she unleashed the molten rope, and with precise control, wrapped it around Taurin's neck.

His screamed ricocheted off the cliffs to the ocean below. He clawed at the fire that held him, attempting to rip it from his neck.

As the soil beneath Alex's feet gave way and she sunk into the cold earth, she saw was a fully formed dragon burst out of the ground with Neeren in his claws. She screamed Collum's name, praying he heard her before the earth swallowed her whole.

Chapter 48

Collum saw her the exact moment Domhall burst through the earthen wall, the exact moment the rope around Taurin's neck gave way. He roared. Agony tore the fire from his chest. He dropped Neeren like a used doll. Every sound around him ceased to exist.

It took him five precious seconds to reach the gap in the earth. Each second was another death. He soared into the earth behind her. Her name ripped from his lungs.

Thunder echoed across the island. Torrents of rain poured down on the inhabitants. As the last waves of the sound faded, the dragon surged out of the earth with Alex wrapped around his neck.

He turned his ancient eyes on the sniveling creature running from the battle to the cliff edge. Terror trailed behind him like a river.

The dragon gently laid Alex next to Domhall. He draped his wing over her body, breathing deeply into her hair. Her scent drove warmth into his favored skin. After assuring himself that Domhall and her mother would care for her, he flew after a dead man.

With the ease of an owl picking off field mice, the beast swept him up and flew over the edge of the cliff to the ocean. Then with utter silence and precision, he plunged the man headfirst into the waist deep water below.

Taurin choked and sputtered. "You, stupid animal. It was your father that started all this." He laughed, utterly deranged. "Do you think this absolves you?"

The dragon towered over the inferior being. He was lethal, destructive, every inch a killer.

"You will drown now." His voice was black. It resonated with death.

When the dragon spoke, the history of the world rumbled in his speech. "You will swim as far as you can and you will drown yourself." Razor-sharp claws lay like death in the sand in front of them. "You will remain locked beneath the ocean for one hundred years. Do you understand."

Of course, there was no choice. No question. No one could withstand the dragon's command.

"I understand," Taurin whispered.

"When one hundred years are up, I will come for you and rip your head from your body. This is my judgement for the murder of Kaylen Taleisin and the attempted murders of Gray Taleisin and Alexedria Simine."

Tears poured down the other man's face as he struggled to ignore the shadow of Collum's voice. Yet no being stood a chance against the power of a beast who controlled the rise and fall of the mind. A beast who had done so for longer than any being could fathom. It was over before it began.

As Collum knew it would be. As it always was.

On grieving legs, Taurin walked into the ocean, to his living grave.

His will followed, the dragon turned from the site of his enemy collapsing into the waiting waves.

~ ~ ~

He noticed Domhall standing at the edge of the cliff watching him. As the rage left his body, he let the dragon fade. Collum kept his wings though, and flew to the man.

"It's done."

Domhall nodded. "It had to be you. It's why Kaylen chose you to protect our granddaughter. God knows she deserved better than me. And you were her best friend. Thank you."

"Why didn't you tell me everything long ago?" he asked of the man who was once his greatest friend. His partner. It was a secret they'd both take to the grave.

"I was ashamed. I'm losing my mind, Coll." Domhall shrugged. "Besides, you boys are always so focused on balance. You'd have tried to fix things long before it was the time to do so."

"You could join us again, you know."

Dom smiled sadly. "No, I stopped being a guardian the moment I agreed to send Gray to your father. We both know I was corrupted."

Collum nodded slowly. As much as he wanted the man to be whole again, they both knew he wasn't.

"Check into the witch. She has potential."

"She's too wild to be a guardian, Dom."

"Hmmm, well some of us think you guardians could use a little stirring up."

Collum laughed. The sound rumbled across the cliff. The dragon inside him eased. "Maybe you're right."

"You need to get Alex to agree to the binding. It's the only way Lachon will agree," Domhall said. "It's how we keep the balance. You know that."

"You'll handle Neeren?"

"My grandson's power will be bound before the week is over."

"Very well. I'll talk to her. But she's only to be bound against the Elementals. No others. I have hope for her. I think she is strong enough to be a guardian one day."

Domhall closed his eyes and took a long breath before reaching out a hand to his lifelong friend. "Thank you for avenging Kaylen's death. I am in your debt."

Collum clasped the other man's hands in his. Said, "There is no debt between us. You make sure you call me when you're ready to come back," before launching himself in the air to find his woman.

Chapter 49

Collum flew back to Alex and plucked her out of the dwindling battle. Silently, he took them to the beach where they'd made love the night before. He ignored her protests, sat her gently at the edge of the water. He absorbed his wings back into his body before quietly washing the dirt and soot from her face.

"We have to go back, Collum. They need us."

He ignored her protests as each cleansing swipe of water showed him more wounds. "No. You almost died back there. You promised not a scratch. I see a scratch."

"Did you kill Taurin? Oh God. He murdered my grandmother."

"He will never hurt anyone else."

He sat back on his haunches and stared at her. There was nothing more important than her.

"Your family is capable of protecting themselves. We're staying right here until my heart attack is over and then we're flying directly back to My. Goddamned. House. Where we will stay until you get over your shit and admit you love me."

Tears began to fall from her eyes.

Immediately contrite, he said, "Are you hurt? Why are you crying?"

"I love you."

"What?"

"I'm crying because I love you."

"Oh, well aren't you supposed to be happy when you fall in love?" He stood up, still full of fire from the battle. "Don't think that gets you out of coming home with me."

"Quit telling me what to do and be happy I said it."

"I'm happy."

He stopped his pacing as she broke out in laughter. "Something tells me this love thing isn't going to be easy between us."

Collum flopped beside her on the sand. "You know it won't be." He plucked dirt and flowers out of her hair.

He prepared himself for her anger. "I need to ask something of you, princess."

She stroked his shoulders. "What is it?"

"You must let the witch bind your dreamwalker power over the Elementals."

She leaned back from him and removed his hand from her hair. "That's never going to happen. That's what this war was about."

"No, this *fight* was about balance and keeping you alive. This was no war. The only way to keep a war from happening is to ensure you hold no power over the Elementals. It was promised to Lachon the Law."

"Grandfather won't let this happen."

"He engineered this, Alex. And as much as I hate to admit it, he's right. He spent twenty-five years trying to find a way to save your life. Finding a witch powerful enough to perform the binding spell. You and your brother hold too much power. Power you aren't ready to manage. You must be willing, or a war you may not be able to stop, will happen. Hell, a war may still happen."

She dug her feet in the sand. "Why does no one feel it necessary to bind your powers? It seems to me you are more powerful than all of us?"

"I am The Guardian, Alex."

"Yes, I know that. You've said it enough times."

"But you don't get it. Only a few do." He sighed. "I cannot forsake my calling. It is my sworn duty to maintain the balance in the world. The final choices will always be black and white. I make those choices."

"There are gray areas. There is free will."

"No. There must be balance in everything. I keep that balance. The decision of The Guardian is the last decision, regardless of free will."

"And the right to my power falls under that category?"

"Your power disrupts the balance, Alex." He was stoic, a rock. "These are not gray areas."

"You would do this to me, for balance?"

He nodded. "I would."

"And my free will? What about that?"

"That is mine in this instance."

"How many times has my free will been yours, Collum?

"This is a discussion we cannot have, sweetheart."

"But you love me."

"I do love you. I must also protect you and sometimes that means my will must be followed."

Alex sighed, realizing the whole dreamwalking thing didn't even matter to her that much. But she needed Collum to be her champion not just her protector. "You can let her bind me, Collum. But after, you need to leave."

"I'm taking you with me, princess."

"No, not this time." She placed her hand on his lips when he would have argued. "I love you. I do. But I've only been immortal for a week. You've been for thousands of years. I don't understand any of this, not even who I am."

"I know who you are."

"Do you? You keep expecting me to blindly accept all this immortality stuff. You need to recognize that I grew up human. All my choices will be affected by my humanity. I don't think like you. I need to question everything, understand it all."

"You will."

"Maybe. I doubt it."

You're special. It's your humanity that makes you that way to me."

"Maybe. But I think I need you to go home for a little while."

"Because of my request?"

"Because of everything. I ache for you. I love you. But I need time."

He held her face in his hands and kissed her eyelids. "We're destined."

Tears streamed down her face. She kissed his lips before taking a step back. "I like cheap Tuesday at the theatre and gummy bears. I'll expect you to pick me up in two weeks. After you study up on what it means to be human." She turned to leave.

As Alex walked away from him, emptiness hollowed out his gut. His dragon stirred in protest, everything in him demanding that he stop her. That's when Collum realized balance wasn't worth losing her. Maybe that's what Domhall had been trying to tell him all this time.

He reached her in two long strides, clasping her shoulder to gently turn her around. The heat from her skin burrowed beneath his own, shattering two thousand years of armor. He bent a knee so he could look directly into her beautiful eyes. Brought up his other hand to brush the back of his fingers across her damp cheek.

"I forgot, Alex. I forgot what it meant to put love before duty, before balance. I forgot what living looked like. I won't lose you. You come first, from this day forward. If that means you need time, then I give it to you freely. But know this, sweetheart, I will never, for a moment stop fighting for you. You belong with me."

Her eyes widened, and he could read every conflicted emotion swirling in her violet gaze. *Love. Stubborn defiance. Hesitation.*

Satisfied she got his meaning, Collum straightened and kissed her cheeks, her eyes, her lips. He held her until his dragon calmed—until he tasted the answer on her mouth. "Two weeks, babe. Then I'm coming for you."

He released her and stepped back. "Be ready."

Magic Born,
Book Two in The Guardian series

Maria Del Voscova is a powerful Witch with a past. Her friends Alex and Collum are busy navigating new love, and guardian business. She doesn't want to burden them with her messed-up history. But we don't always get what we want. Sometimes, we don't always know *what* we want. Though Mar absolutely knows she doesn't want Neeren, King of the Parthen. She alone sees the darkness in him and it reminds her too much of the past. She knows better than to fall for his stoic, tortured-soul façade.

She's training to be a Guardian, a shadow, tasked with keeping the balance between good and evil in the world. It's what she wants: to be better than her family was.

The past has a way of catching up to Mar and the future has a morbid sense of humor. On her first mission, she's kidnapped by the very vampires she's been running from her entire life. Thankfully the guardians look after their own, and as it turns out, so does Neeren.

Mar finds herself caught in the middle of a battle between light and the darkness. She must choose between her family, the guardians, and a man who just might be the most dangerous of them all.

Available June 2018

CPSIA information can be obtained
at www.ICGtesting.com
Printed in the USA
LVOW03s0527011217
558261LV00002B/3/P